Praise for J. Lee and *The Hubley Case*

"A terrific debut."—Kyle Mills, *New York Times* #1 bestselling author

"*The Hubley Case* is intricately plotted and the action never lets up! A great read that fans of Kyle Mills and Michael Connelly won't want to miss."—Ward Larsen, *USA Today* bestselling author of *Assassin's Run*

"Move over Lee Child and Jack Reacher. J. Lee and his main character, Ben Siebert, take the reader on a page-turning ride that keeps you guessing to the end...I give this well-written book a whole-hearted five thumbs up."—Pamela S. Wight, author of *Twin Desires* and *The Right Wrong Man*

"*The Hubley Case* will blow you away and J. Lee is a must-read new talent."—Mike Lawson, author of the award-winning DeMarco Series

"Has the pace and the stakes of a Brad Thor or David Baldacci novel. Dynamic characters, vivid settings and intrigue that keeps you guessing until the end make this one a must read. J. Lee has burst onto the scene with a brand of storytelling that is hard to put down. I look forward to more like *The Hubley Case.*"—Steve Brigman, author of *The Orphan Train* and *The Old Wire Road*

"*The Hubley Case* is everything you want in a thriller. Killer opening, breakneck pace, smartly-drawn characters, startling reversals and, best of all, a truly satisfying ending. You'll be left hoping J. Lee is busy working on the follow-up. I know I am."—Drew Yanno, best-selling author of In the *Matter of Michael Vogel* and *The Smart One*

"With *The Hubley Case*, author J. Lee has spun a yarn of intrigue that captures readers from the opening pages and brings them on a wild ride. A smart, fast-paced thriller."—Alfred C. Martino, author of *Pinned*, *Over The End Line* and *Perfected By Girls*

THE HUBLEY CASE

J. Lee

Moonshine Cove Publishing, LLC
Abbeville, South Carolina U.S.A.

Copyright © 2018 by J. Lee

ISBN: 978-1-945181-42-9
Library of Congress PCN: 2017953999

Book cover design by BTS Designs.

SDW

To Kristen:

> A gentle soul,
>
> A special woman,
>
> A fantastic critic,
>
> A phenomenal mother,
>
> A perfect wife.

Acknowledgments

The process of writing a novel and getting it published has been anything but solitary or easy for me. To that end, there are a number of people I'd like to thank, in no particular order, for both their assistance and tolerance:

Mom and Dad, who have always encouraged me to pursue my dreams and given me the love and support to do so.

Rob Lee, for being my role model and teaching me the value of hard work and accountability. You truly are *Mondoman*.

Steve Boswell, for his faith in my writing and steadfast encouragement. Your handwritten note from many years ago still hangs above my desk today.

Dave Olverson, for his feedback, and sixteen years of challenging and inspiring me.

Andy Lane, for taking time to literally stop curing cancer and providing me with valuable editorial feedback.

My "test market": Kristen Lee, Dave & Julia Pohlman, Steve and Karen Boswell, Rob Lee and Andy Lane. Thanks for reading.

Kyle Mills and Mike Lawson, for their guidance and willingness to help a newbie to the business.

Ward Larsen, for his great support.

Pam Wight, for her generous time, effort and encouragement.

Drew Yanno, for his sage advice and the time he spent to offer it.

Alfred Martino, Steve Brigman and Caroline Taylor, for their support.

Kurt Keady, for his assistance with the agent-seeking process.

Mike Hearn, for his insight on the website.

James Abt, for his vision and execution of the marketing strategy, and for putting up with an author who was at times most certainly overbearing.

Ken Lizotte, my literary agent, for taking a chance on a new name in a new genre.

Gene Robinson and the Moonshine Cove team, for their help in making my dream come true and patience in bearing with a challenging first-time novelist.

And last but certainly not least, my beautiful, gentle and loving bride, Kristen, for hours of superb editing, endless encouragement, insightful feedback, enduring reliability, and sacrificial love that still captivates me to this day. Thanks for everything, Prin.

THE HUBLEY CASE

1

"Eu o vejo. Dez horas."
I see him. Ten o'clock.
"Apanhei-o."
Got him.

The Sao Paulo International Airport in Brazil was both less ornate and less expensive than its namesake city, a conclusion any visitor couldn't help but make despite the fact that the five-terminal complex technically resided in Guarulhos, not Sao Paulo. An impenetrable glass wall divided the international and domestic gates, and on both sides of it were dark and matte floor colors, chosen to conceal filth rather than woo tourists. Duty-free shops lined the terminal, offering items at less than half of what you'd pay downtown. Though still steep by U.S. standards, you could get a candy bar for R$6.00, just under three bucks.

It was not, however, any less crowded.

After a visit to one of the wealthiest cities in the southern hemisphere, you'd think Sao Paulo set the worldwide standard for congestion — with eleven million people and a density four times New York City's — but you'd be wrong.

With twenty million people flying in and out of GRU every year, chaos surrounded long lines for food, shopping, and security. Which was why, when his partner said he'd located the subject, a slight smile crept across his usually stoic face as he shifted his weight and focused.

The man in question was both avoiding the airport congestion and taking advantage of its financial perks, sitting quietly at the far end of a small café, sipping a cappuccino with crushed peanuts and a cinnamon stick while reading *USA Today*. After surveying the surrounding area, noting travelers, security officers, cameras, exits, emergency doors, access points and walking traffic flows, he checked the first page of the red folder he was holding. You could never be too sure. Thirty-eight years old, six feet tall, two hundred fifteen pounds, short, light-brown hair, almost blonde, large hazel eyes, and a dark birthmark just below his left ear.

It was definitely him.

Mr. Peter Hubley was a father of two young boys — Timothy and Samuel, ages three and one. He'd been married for just over four years to Sally Gordon Hubley, a former third-grade schoolteacher turned stay-at-home mom, and he played chess with an uncle once a week. The black briefcase resting on the floor next to him was of little significance other than to confirm that Mr. Hubley was returning to the USA after a week of international business.

According to the red folder, Peter Hubley was on United Airlines Flight UA30, an eleven o'clock departure, landing in Newark at 5:55 the next morning. A car had been arranged to take him to Newark Liberty International Airport Marriott, and he had a dinner reservation just outside New York City that evening at six. The next morning, he was scheduled on United Airlines Flight UA1030, departing at nine, landing in Chicago at 10:34 — a grand total of seven days away from home.

The subject's criminal background was nonexistent. His record was spotless and his intentions clear. He was an innocuous finance executive working hard for his family of four, quietly sipping his beverage, waiting to board his flight in twenty-five minutes. Two people sat next to him and he smiled as they took their seats. He seemed focused on his newspaper, his left foot resting on his right knee, the briefcase almost touching his right leg — as if protecting his company-issued laptop and the past week's worth of meeting notes.

While his partner watched Peter Hubley, Jose Luiz Lettnin walked away from the kiosk towards the bathroom. Once inside, he ripped the trusted red folder into shreds, disposing of its small pieces in the toilet before flushing them away forever. After a very brief moment of silence, he withdrew the Tylenol bottle, swallowed the pills, and splashed water on his face. Time now his enemy, he exited the bathroom and walked quickly, Floriano Felipe catching his stride so that they approached the café abreast. His partner's nodding head confirmed that they were in this together. *No going back.*

When they reached their destination, they didn't hesitate.

With planned synchronization, each withdrew his commercial Beretta M9 handgun and rapidly fired the fifty-meter range pistol from less than five feet away. Seconds later, both fifteen-bullet magazines were empty, and Peter Hubley's maimed corpse was sprawled across the floor, cappuccino dripping down what was left of his forehead.

2

The name on his passport read Matthew J. Baker. The same could be said for his plane ticket to Atlanta, the driver's license in his pocket, and all the hotel receipts from his two-week vacation in Brazil. Matthew J. Baker had a social security number, home address, and place of work. And if people really wanted to dig, they'd find two registered vehicles, emergency contacts and last year's property tax bill, all in perfect order. As far as airport security was concerned — both the local Brazilian authorities and TSA in the United States — Matthew J. Baker was very real.

His trip had been meticulously planned to ensure a suspicion-free return, layered with concrete evidence and verifiable alibis accounting for each and every day of it. Two hotel maintenance workers could testify if called upon that he'd spent the vast majority of those two weeks chasing beautiful local women and drinking an excessive number of mojitos and caipirinhas, Brazil's national cocktail. Hotel security cameras could corroborate said testimony, and signed receipts for three meals a day could verify he'd been grounded at the Rio de Janeiro hotel the entire time. What the workers didn't know was that he'd been overly friendly with them so that they'd remember his being there every day, and that those drinks were virgin.

All to irrefutably prove it was pure coincidence that Matthew J. Baker witnessed Peter Hubley's death and certainly had nothing to do with it.

He'd been instructed by Mr. Riddle to arrive in Brazil a week early for just that reason. Rio de Janeiro was chosen not for its popular tourist attractions or beautiful women — as he'd indicate if ever asked — but because it was both believable as a destination and an hour by plane from each of Hubley's stops during the finance executive's business trip. No chance of sneaking out unnoticed.

It all seemed overkill to him — the paperwork and the alibis and the cameras and such — but Mr. Riddle was a very thorough man who spared no expense and paid strict attention to detail. He wanted to ensure that there would not be a problem.

And there never was.

When Floriano Felipe Pereira and Jose Luiz Lettnin opened fire on Hubley, he ran his hand over his hairless head and gasped for the cameras. The past two weeks had been about acting — from inebriation to women-chasing — and it was merely an extension of that acting that would make it appear he was just as shocked as those around him to witness the heinous crime.

The Brazilians did their job, rapidly firing their weapons empty before the airport police even had time to react. He hovered against a wall a few hundred feet from his 10:55 Delta flight departure gate, watching the scene unfold as travelers screamed and scurried in all directions. Pure chaos enveloped GRU's international terminal in a matter of seconds as smoke emitted from the barrels of the two Berettas he'd provided the Brazilians.

When the police finally figured out what happened — long after Hubley's body only vaguely resembled a human being's — the two men did as instructed and lay down for apprehension. The police officers screamed Portuguese and pointed their weapons forcefully; and the two killers quietly obeyed and remained stoic. A few onlookers captured the start of the arrest with cell phone cameras, but most simply stared in awe and fear at what they'd just witnessed.

The man known to authorities as Matthew J. Baker pretended to do the same — but was secretly waiting for what he saw next:

Both killers' bodies started twitching, subtly at first — hardly recognizable if you didn't know to look for it — but very soon after transforming into noticeable spasms. The police officers were unprepared and didn't react well, actually stepping away as both men's necks and heads began to visibly shake. They regrouped and applied handcuffs, but that was completely irrelevant.

The spasms would lead to full body convulsions in a matter of minutes, the stimuli of being jerked up from the ground and forcefully walked towards a private interrogation room intensifying the effects along the way. Eventually, the backbone would continually arch against itself, and the killers would experience lactic acidosis and the onset of hypothermia. The neural pathways regulating the body's breathing would soon be paralyzed if the convulsions didn't beat them to it.

Either way, within a few minutes, Floriano Felipe Pereira and Jose Luiz Lettnin would be as dead as Peter Hubley.

3

"I'm not gonna blow smoke up your skirt, kid; the facts of this case really stink up the joint."

FBI Special Agent Nikki Benton couldn't figure out what displeased her most about that statement. Three immediate options came to mind: the sexist cliché from her boss of only six months, the degrading term of "kid" used in his first sentence, or the overall point he was making.

"Six days ago, an American businessman gets publicly massacred in an international airport — one of the world's busiest at that," Special Agent in Charge Marcus Redmond continued. " The two gunmen who somehow got weapons past security die nine minutes later, then the ambulance taking their bodies to the morgue gets hijacked. No interviews, no autopsy, no statements. Nothing." Redmond paced behind his oversized oak desk, the vein in his creased forehead bulging with frustration.

"Did we get an ID on the shooters?"

"From the fingerprints," he replied, rattling off two Brazilian names from the file he was holding that meant nothing to her. "Both men have ties to the PCC but no known connection to the victim."

She debated whether to ask or not, but her face apparently made the decision for her while also exposing her ignorance.

"Don't be shy, kid. This office doesn't deal with other countries' problems all that often. Even I had to look it up," he replied, smugly implying that it must be some real esoteric piece of information.

"What is —"

"The PCC, formally known as the Primeiro Comando da Capital, is Brazil's largest criminal organization. Its primary target is Sao Paulo's military police force, and it is extensive. Some fifteen thousand members according to the Brazil feds, but a lot of its members are already in prison as we speak and it appears to be strictly domestic. No known ties to the USA," he read.

Until now.

17

SAC Redmond plopped the file on the desk in front of her, tugged on the lapels of his undersized suit jacket, and paced towards the oversized terrarium in the corner of his office.

That terrarium was home to Spot, Redmond's ill-named Galapagos Tortoise and the Chicago Field Office's unofficial mascot. Redmond loved that reptile. Some coworkers joked he was more affectionate with it than his wife. As he squatted down to see Spot face-to-face and began whispering, Nikki was reminded of why. The poor thing was an endangered species and here Redmond was, housing it in a custom-made five thousand-gallon terrarium with a small pool of water and man-made mud hole. She didn't know what would happen to Spot when he grew to over five hundred pounds, as his breed was known to do, and she didn't dare ask. A small part of her thought it was adorable, the larger part cringed at the odor that Spot and his home emitted.

The office smelled like *tortoise ass.*

"What do we have on the victim?" she asked.

"Peter Hubley, an executive at InvestSecure on Clark Street, lives in Chicago, father of two, coming back from a week of meetings in Brazil. No criminal record, no questionable history, no flagged friends or acquaintances. Nothing at all that would make you think he had this coming. His personnel file is on the seat next to you."

He said it all without looking away from Spot. She dropped one file and picked up another, twice as thick, and began browsing its pages.

"What happened to the shooters?" she asked while reading.

SAC Redmond sighed as he conveyed the events, finally turning to face her.

"As they're getting arrested, they start shaking and convulsing. Starts off minor, like tremors or fear … they *did* just kill a man in cold blood and were headed to prison for the rest of their lives, right? But the shakes get worse, a *lot* worse. And on the way to the airport interrogation room, they keel over and die. Snap, on the spot. I'm getting airport security footage, but you can just watch it yourself on YouTube in the meantime. Plenty of people saw them croak and thought it'd make a nice home video. What's this world coming to?"

"Asphyxiation?"

"That's my guess, but with no autopsy or bodies, we'll never know for sure."

"Yeah, about that … "

"That's where it gets even better. The morgue they were being transported to is twenty-two kilometers from the airport. At some point in the fifteen-minute trek," he continued, disbelief in his voice, "the ambulance got hijacked en route, and both paramedics were shot dead on scene. Autopsy confirmed that a bullet to the head from point-blank range was the cause of death, and the Brazil police are still trying to get more intel on the hijacking. But it'll probably lead to a dead end."

"Why is that?"

"Look, kid, Brazil's more corrupt than Washington. *And,* you don't have any jurisdiction to investigate there. So you've got to start with Hubley. I need you to read his file, cover to cover. Do some serious investigative research. Figure out what we don't know. Talk to his boss, talk to his wife, ask questions, look for the secrets, anything at all that could explain why he'd be the target of two Mafia hoods over five thousand miles away."

The corruption comment was an ironic reference for an FBI employee who was three reports away from its National Director, but the rest of what Redmond said seemed logical enough.

After a moment's pause, he continued.

"Listen, I know I sprung this on you," Redmond said in a softer, more sympathetic voice as he took a seat at his desk. Rubbing his graying mustache and fixed on her in a way that made her wish he was still looking at Spot, he said, "I also know that in Phoenix you didn't see many murder cases and that, like I said, the facts in this one really stink up the joint. It's not ideal and I get that."

She straightened up in her seat, trying to exude confidence while waiting for him to come to his point.

"I need to know if you feel comfortable taking this on. I can reassign it, give it to someone else with more experience if you —"

"No, I'm on it."

"Because we can't afford to —"

"*Sir, I'm on it.*"

"Good," he replied, nodding. "Just stick to Hubley. Do the groundwork and look for what we're missing because right now, this doesn't add up. Find out what he was doing in Brazil, specifically what his agenda was, if he traveled there often, stuff like that. Get a list of all U.S. citizens flying to Brazil within a few weeks before and after his death and follow up on anyone suspicious. See if Hubley knew any of them. Maybe we'll get lucky and find a link that leads to a motive. Dismissed."

And just like that, after ten minutes of information dump, the meeting was over. Nikki got up to leave, two thick files in her arms and an even thicker one in her head, but turned when she got to the door to ask the question.

"Sir, why are we investigating this?"

"Pardon," Redmond replied, already checking his e-mail.

"Well, it's like you said … we don't have jurisdiction in Brazil, there's an FBI Brasilia office that does, we know the shooters are Brazilian, and both the initial crime and follow up ambulance hijacking occurred there … why is the FBI's Chicago Field Office looking into this?"

He looked at her through a narrow line of sight just above his reading glasses and below his forehead, either impressed that she knew this assignment didn't make sense as explained or upset that she'd questioned it. With limited face time the past six months, she couldn't be sure which.

"This morning I got a call from Thompson's office," he said, alluding to FBI Executive Director Charles Thompson, Redmond's boss and the head of the Criminal, Cyber, Response and Services Branch. "Interpol Brasilia contacted Interpol Washington and asked for our help in learning more about Hubley. The only reason we're the lucky field office is because Hubley happened to be from Chicago."

"Did they say anything else? There's still —"

"You know as much as I do, kid. Just do your job and I'll funnel any information that comes my way."

Great, she almost said out loud while exiting Redmond's office.

4

After a long, muggy summer, Chicago's crisp fall air felt good in Ben Siebert's lungs. The wind blew from the east and the mid-October lake effect chilled his face, prompting readjustment of his trench coat collar. He inhaled deeply, staring straight ahead.

Watching and waiting.

He'd been told Barry Lee Richard would stick out like a nun in a whorehouse. It wasn't a simile he cared for, but it certainly got the point across. Standing outside Dunkin Donuts near a streetlight, hands entrenched in his coat pockets, each holding a weapon — a gun in the right and a knife in the left — all there was left to do was watch and wait. The Marines taught him the value of patience, and it was a trait of particular value in his current line of work.

At just before nine o'clock, Barry Lee Richard emerged from his lavish office complex, wearing a mock turtle neck, tan sport coat and pair of charcoal business slacks. He was thin, well groomed, and imposing, but it was his height that justified the distasteful vestal reference. Standing a solid 6'8", Barry Lee looked like a giant among dwarves as he casually strolled past a junior high bus stop en route to his domestic battery trial.

To Barry Lee Richard, it was just another day.

Barry Lee's wife decided not to pursue legal action against her pig of a husband for reasons her own lawyer, the judge, and even her husband's attorney, Tim Knoble, failed to understand. Even the most devout or petrified wives didn't stand for six trips to the emergency room. And considering she'd been to the Intensive Care Unit three times in the last four years, it was downright perplexing that she'd never so much as filed a complaint.

After the final "incident," a bit of common sense finally prevailed from within Cook Country General, which was itself confusing to Ben with all the M.D.'s, PhD's and other "D's" walking the halls of Chicago's largest hospital. *You can learn every*

muscle, bone, vein and artery in the human body … yet it still takes
you six visits to the ER to figure out a woman is being abused?

Trip number six involved a broomstick handle, a badly blackened-face and permanently damaged right eye, and the hospital reported the incident to the Chicago Police Department. The CPD assigned the case to a mid-level officer who after one visit with the wife came to same conclusion any teenager would. Both the lieutenant and his female supervisor tried to get the victim to see the logic in pressing charges, elucidating that her life was destined to end far too prematurely if she didn't do something and do it fast. No dice. Not only did the wife refuse to press charges, but the mere suggestion of it enraged her, and she asked both officers to leave.

When the victim doesn't want to acknowledge abuse, there's not a whole lot the system can do. At least the cops tried. Ben had to give them that much, despite his continually reaffirmed skepticism of the profession on the whole. They questioned Barry Lee Richard the following week — not a very effective approach without an arrest warrant — but at least they let him know they were onto him. They then forced a hearing under a noise violation, responding to a complaint they got Barry Lee's neighbor to call in. Finally, corrupt police practices put to good use. The goal, a long shot but better than nothing, was to simply get Barry Lee's wife in front a judge, let her face and history speak for itself, and hopefully appeal to the judge's sentimental side to get the poor woman away from Barry Lee.

The phone tap Ben installed in Bill Knoble's office revealed the shady attorney telling his sister what a scumbag his client was, and his shock that Barry Lee's wife wasn't pressing formal charges. In addition to a blatant violation of the attorney-client privilege, Mr. Knoble's comments demonstrated how nasty Barry Lee Richard was, and precisely why Ben's services were necessary. It certainly didn't absolve Mr. Knoble of his regrettable decision to take on Barry Lee Richard as a client, but he'd deal with that later.

For now, this son of a bitch needed to be stopped.

Ben tailed Barry Lee Richard at a safe distance of two city blocks for a quarter-mile. When Barry Lee walked into the Daley Civic Center courthouse, Ben entered another Dunkin Donuts across the street and pulled out his phone. Surveillance already established by the hidden camera in Courtroom 4512C, he toggled between the live stream of the trial and his latest app, one that helped him find the closest Dunkin Donuts relative to his GPS position.

The forced trial went as expected. A concerned-looking judge reviewed the history and saw the wife's face as a "witness," but lacked the authority to do anything about it without her pressing charges. The Assistant District Attorney made a valiant effort to argue the obvious without saying it — that this woman would end up in the hospital or morgue if they didn't do something. But his plea was falling on powerless ears and he knew it.

Bill Knoble said little and focused primarily on preventing his client's mouth from getting him into trouble. He didn't have to try very hard, though. Barry Lee Richard was smart, and he knew the forced trial didn't have a prayer. It was a formality. In eight hours his wife would be home doing whatever he wanted, however he wanted. There would be no recourse.

Ben checked the other camera and saw that even the stenographer sensed the room's ubiquitous futility. The noise violation the cops charged Barry Lee with remained a simple misdemeanor and within thirty minutes the courtroom was empty, justice far from rendered. Barry Lee had to pay a $500 fine because the judge didn't like him, and just like that, the wife-beating, multi-million-dollar stockbroker left the court with less than a slap on the wrist.

Barry Lee was already on with his day, openly happy about the trial's outcome. It went perfectly as it always did and always would. Ben watched him exit the courthouse and pull out a pack of cigarettes from his tan sport coat, his confident smile telling Ben he would never stop.

There was no redemption.

————

Barry Lee Richard turned the corner at Dearborn to head west on Washington Street, parading cockily with money on his mind and a smile on his face. Another silly trial behind him and a calendar free until lunch with a six-figure-commission client, he had two hours to drink some draft beer at Stocks & Blondes Bar on Wells Street in honor of yet another legal victory. Why *not* walk the streets of Chicago before it got too cold?

The world was his oyster.

As he crossed Clark Street, he thought he heard his name but ignored it and kept walking. But when he passed Delmonico Gourmet Foods and heard it again — louder than before — he turned to see a man in green dress slacks and a black trench coat emerge from the adjacent alley. The man, clean-shaven with light brown hair, about 6'2" and one hundred ninety pounds, approached him slowly, both hands in his coat pockets. Barry Lee didn't recognize the face, but he'd forgotten a client or two before, so he decided to play it safe.

"I'm sorry, are you talking to me?"

"Who else would I be talking to?"

The man let the awkward silence linger longer than Barry Lee liked.

"I'm sorry, but I'm drawing a blank. What's your name?"

"Me? Oh, my name doesn't matter. What matters is I'm the one guy you never want to meet. But here I am." The man halted, now a matter of feet from him. The fact that Barry Lee was six inches taller didn't seem to matter.

"What the —"

Before Barry Lee could finish his sentence, the man lunged directly into him, making hard contact. Barry Lee felt the cold end of a small circular object that could only be one thing protruding from the man's right pocket. Then he felt the gun press into his stomach. Stymied and scared, Barry Lee offered no response and stopped moving.

"You try to run and I'll shoot you in both legs before you get five feet. Then I'll grab you by the hair and drag you to a place you'll learn lessons you'll never forget. I'll beat you so senseless you'll know how your wife feels. And then I'll go to work on you."

"What do you w —"

"I want you to shut your pathetic, lying face and do *exactly* as I say. You let out one scream … you make one sudden movement … *you even look at me wrong* … I'll give you something to scream about. I dare you to call my bluff."

The man's eyes had somehow grown darker — ominous. He moved the gun into Barry Lee's chest with impressive force and removed his left hand from his coat pocket, locking it around Barry Lee's neck and pulling him in closer. Barry Lee could see the tension in the man's cheeks, the anger in his eyes. His entire face displayed an unspeakable intensity that literally sent chills up and down Barry Lee's spine. This was, without question, the scariest person he'd ever seen.

"Get in the car," the man ordered in a low, dominating voice.

The man jerked him to the right until he saw a black Ford Taurus parked on Washington Street, facing east, blinkers on and engine running. The driver had gotten out of the car and opened the back door — he couldn't have been more than twenty-five years old; white, blue jeans, blonde hair.

"I think there's been a mist —"

"You'd better start listening to me," the man whispered as he pushed the gun harder into Barry Lee's sternum. "I could snap your head clean off with my own two hands and leave your body for the vultures. I beg you to make me prove it. My word is my livelihood."

5

The phone call Ben Siebert wasn't expecting came Wednesday at 1:28 p.m..

It'd been a week since Peter Hubley was murdered in Sao Paulo, and he'd just finished erecting the nutcracker collection Anna and he had started as newlyweds eighteen years ago. Joe Leksa, his quasi-adopted son and part-time employee of sorts, was at community college getting his generals out of the way, so Ben was home alone in the four-bedroom house. Hearing the chimes ring outside after each gust of wind, it was a good day to be indoors in Chicago's west suburbs.

He still put the nutcrackers up in October every year because his pre-Thanksgiving timing used to summon Anna's playful smile of disapproval. He loved that smile, that sly little smirk that said his OCD in the matter of nutcracker displays was one of the things she secretly adored about him. He'd just finished lugging all fifty-eight unique dolls up from the basement when the dreaded phone started to ring.

"Ben, how are you?" a soft-spoken voice asked.

Nick Gordon was Sally Hubley's brother and the late Peter Hubley's brother-in-law. Ben had known Nick long enough to know that Nick and Sally were close as far as siblings went, and that Nick's masculine instincts had no doubt kicked in immediately after he learned of Peter's death. Men are wired from birth to protect and provide, or so said their Marine training at The Basic School. And when Peter Hubley's life was taken, Ben knew Nick would feel implored to step in on his sister's behalf.

"How are you holding up, Nick?" he ignored the futile lead-in question.

"Still in a bit of shock, but okay. Wish I could say the same for my sister."

"I'm so sorry about —"

"My sister's on her own with two little kids and nobody knows why."

The whole experience had no doubt been traumatizing for Sally Hubley. And Nick was appreciative of Ben's condolences, but Ben knew that wasn't why he'd called. They were cut from the same cloth. When you need something from a Marine Corps brother, you don't mince words.

"Sally needs your help, Ben. *I* need your help."

"What can I do?"

"What she's going through — with all the media crap — she needs someone she can talk to. I do my best, but she needs someone who *knows* how she feels, what she's going through. I know it might be tough … talking to her. I know it could rehash some nasty shit for you, and I'm sorry about that. But she specifically asked for you, man. She hasn't taken a phone call or answered the door all week, but she made it a point to ask for you. Believe me, I wouldn't be calling if it wasn't necessary."

It wasn't his first choice, and he had no idea what he'd say to Sally or how he'd say it, but both were of little consequence. Nick Gordon showed him what a true friend was nine years ago, and he'd been one ever since. He was there for him in a way no one else was. Had it not been for Nick, Ben was quite certain both he and Joe would be dead.

"Tell her I'll be there at three."

6

Sally Hubley lived in Chicago's Lakeview neighborhood, thirty miles northeast of Ben's house. Eastbound I-290 and northbound I-90 were relatively empty and Ben was walking up to her front door sooner than he'd expected. Chicago well into its fall season, he walked over a yellow-brick-road of fallen leaves and broken sticks covering the paver sidewalk that led up to her beautiful three-story home.

That's when the past began jettisoning itself back into his mind, and he knew it wouldn't stop anytime soon. The house reminded him of Nick and Lisa Gordon's home. The well-off neighborhood with its newly built cookie-cutter houses, just on the outskirts of the city. The tree-laden streets lined on both sides with NO PARKING signs. The large front-yard oak tree, three steps leading up to the front door and metal brass doorknocker all served as reminders of nine years earlier.

Sally opened the door and invited him in with a long embrace. He returned the hug and after almost ten seconds, she finally broke away and stepped back, giving him his first good look at her in almost two years.

A fair amount of her appearance remained the same. She still had long, flowing red hair that hung halfway between her shoulders and waist. She didn't appear heavier or skinnier than since he'd last seen her.

Her brown eyes, however, once full of spunk and life, were now swollen and puffy from crying. The straight, assured posture he remembered had been replaced with a slouch that conveyed indifference, and she was more underdressed than he'd ever seen her. Before then, he couldn't picture her in anything less formal than a skirt and blouse, much less a pair of black sweatpants and a sweatshirt. Oddly enough, that's what stood out more than anything.

"Thanks for coming," she whispered, not trying to force a smile.

"Sally... "

"Thank you, Ben. He's with Jesus now."

The comment reminded him of Sally's devout faith, reaffirmed as he stepped into her living room and noted the wall plaque displaying scripture. Her public display of faith was something that years ago he skeptically distained but had since come to admire. Sally Hubley was a God-fearing woman who wasn't afraid to show it, not a hypocrite who talked one way and walked another like he first assumed.

The living room was cozily decorated and inviting, a love seat and couch facing one another in front of a gas-burning fireplace that warmed the surrounding area. Well-placed lamps omitted just enough light to welcome people but not so much as to blind them. The entire room smelled like cinnamon.

A fresh pot of tea and two cups on saucers sat on the coffee table, spouting off steam. She motioned for him to take a seat on the couch next to her and started pouring the apple-cinnamon tea.

"How are you doing, Ben? With … everything?"

"I'm okay. Joe is too. He's taking classes at Harper College. Studying to become an architect. Smart kid; seems like he's got a knack for it."

"I'm so glad to hear it," she said with thoughtfulness so sincere he almost felt ashamed of himself. Here she was — a widow for only a week — taking time to care about him. Not many people in this world are so selfless.

"Your brother has a lot to do with that. You do, too."

"God is the ultimate healer. I'm glad Nick and I could be there for you, but your rehab was for His glory."

The word "rehab" hung aimlessly in his mind like the doldrums in the sky. It reminded him of what failure felt like. And of Anna's death and his many mistakes thereafter. For someone who'd tried to do things the right way before that phone call nine years ago, he sure bottomed out the two years after it.

He'd hated the phone ever since.

"I'm sorry," she said, noticing a change in his expression.

"Don't worry about it," he replied, affectionately patting her on the shoulder. "How are *you* doing, Sally? Is there anything I can do for you?"

He watched her reaction carefully. People mourning such an abrupt loss were subject to sensitivities the rest of the world simply didn't understand. Even the slightest act of generosity — an honest, good-willed intention — could set off a maelstrom of emotions with dire consequences.

He knew that all too well.

The first October after Anna's death, Nick asked if he wanted help putting up the nutcrackers. He held it together in the moment, but later that night he cried like a baby, punched through the sliding glass kitchen door and sucked on a bottle of scotch like a pacifier. In hindsight, the scariest part was that he honestly didn't recognize it as a problem at the time.

Sally offered no such reaction. No false assurances and no body language emerged suggesting he'd touched too sensitive a nerve. It was likely, based on her composure, that Sally's faith in God served her far better than his anger towards God served him. And that she really was managing her loss as well as could be expected. But he also knew from experience that you could never be certain.

"You asked me two questions," she said. "Can I answer the first one first?"

"Uh, sure Sally." He lightly chucked.

"I'm doing well. The ladies at church made me some nice comfort food, mac and cheese; my neighbor pitched in with some yard work, and Nick and Lisa have helped with the kids. It's Timothy and Samuel I worry about. They're the real victims here."

"They have a great support system."

"Yes, they do. It's just … it's sad. They won't know their father. Peter wasn't on board with having kids right away. Did you know that? But I was already thirty-one when we got married and … you know … the biological clock was ticking and all … "

He nodded, quietly waiting.

"It just makes me wonder sometimes … maybe if I hadn't pushed him for a family so soon, we wouldn't have had children, and he wouldn't have taken that new job, and he wouldn't have traveled so much … and … "

"Sally, this doesn't mean you should regret having kids. Or that you were wrong for wanting them, or that you're a bad person for wondering how things might've turned out if you hadn't. All it means is that you're sad the kids won't have their dad. Don't make this your fault. It's a tragedy — but you can't blame yourself."

"You did."

"And I don't want you to repeat my mistakes."

The regret from nine years ago of not going to the bank with Anna that Friday afternoon splintered through his mind like an axe through dry wood.

"I'm sorry," Sally said, wiping the corners of her eyes.

"No need to apologize. What about my second question?" he asked, steering away from the dangerous subject of blame.

If he'd known her answer, he never would've asked.

———

"Ben, Peter is gone and there's nothing I can do about it."

"I know. I'm so —"

"Timothy and Samuel have no father, and I have no husband. And you asked me if there was anything you could do."

"Yes?" he said, slowly. *Where was this going?*

"I want you to find who killed Peter and make sure they don't get away with it."

He stared back at the young widow, trying to get a read on her. Was this just a gut reaction for revenge, fueled by anger? Perhaps, but it had been a week — not by any means a long mourning period but usually well beyond the window of opportunity for vengeance. It also didn't fit her character. Was it a type of venting? Also a possibility but just as unlikely. Not only would it be a unique form of grieving, but Sally had shown premeditation by requesting him in advance.

That indicated something far different than bereavement.

"What exactly are you asking me to do?"

"It's nothing personal against the Brazil police. But I don't have a lot of confidence they'll get to the bottom of why my children's father is no longer with us. With the two men who did this ... dying ... I don't think they'll see it through to solve an American's death."

"Sally, with all due respect, you're not qualified or in the state of mind to make that determination. You're not an investigator. You have no idea what leads they have or what they're going to do. I can't just —"

"Don't you *dare* use that word with me, Ben Siebert." Her not-so-playful burst strength erupted from nowhere.

"What?"

"If you don't want to help, I understand. If you worry you'll be doing something wrong or against the Lord's will, I respect that.

But don't tell me you *can't* look into it. I don't know exactly what it is you've been doing since you resigned from the Marines, but Nick knows enough to realize you're fully capable of investigating Peter's death. And so do I. So please, don't use *can't* on this one. If you take a look and the Brazil police solve the crime anyway, what's the harm?"

"I don't know what it is you think I do but —"

"I don't want to know, Ben. The Lord uses people for all different means, and far be it for me to judge that. I know you're a good man. But you're my brother's best friend, and when Anna passed away and you left the Marines, he knew then and I know now you're far more connected and capable than you let on."

"Does Nick know you're asking me this?"

She put down her teacup and inched closer to him on the couch, placing her left hand, wedding ring and all, on his right quadriceps. Her determination was still there — but it was in a different form. In seconds it transformed into an effusive display of moist eyes and sincere words.

"No, and I don't want him to know."

"Why?"

"Because he'll want to know why I didn't ask him."

"Why didn't you?"

"Because I know enough to realize that you're the person to ask."

"Sally, I don't know what you're expecting me to do about all of this, but —"

"I'm not asking you to do anything to anyone. The Lord's revenge is greater than anything even you could exact on someone, and I wouldn't ask you to do that. I just want answers, closure. I'm asking for you to look into it, as much or as little as you feel comfortable. If that means you don't do a thing, like I said, I understand. But I can't remain idle, Ben. I can't sit here like a useless widow and single mother reading all the theories why my dead husband — *a loving father of two* — must have deserved this without asking for help from the one person I know can make a difference."

The paralyzing words silenced the room.

"Please just think about it," Sally ended the noiselessness. "My husband was a good man. I know he was a good man. And I can't honor or respect him without at least asking you to think about it."

Very few people surprised him. From the day he joined the Marine Corps, he was trained to be on guard and expect the unexpected. From terrorists to criminals to scum most citizens don't even know existed, he needed to remain a step ahead of them all.

And yet here Sally was, this beautiful, sweet Christian mother, knocking him off base. He couldn't find the right words to respond. The jumbled thoughts in his mind felt like a knotted string of Christmas lights. In fact, there was only one thing he knew to be certain.

Sally Hubley never wanted his shoulder to cry on.

7

"Your two o'clock is in your office, Mr. Knoble."

The surprise statement postponed his inevitable return to misery after the standard three-martini lunch. Eyeing his busty twenty-something blonde secretary with long legs and lips that could suck start a leaf blower, he momentarily regretted he hadn't been more intellectually selective during the hiring process.

"First of all, I'm the first person to enter my office. Always."

"But he said he —"

"Second, I don't have any appointments this afternoon."

He wanted to scream that he stopped Friday afternoon appointments years ago and that if she'd so much as checked the schedule like she was supposed to, she would've known that. But he thought better of it when she innocently slid her tongue across her full and glossy lips. He could find it in himself to forgive after all.

"Don't worry about it," he snarled at her before entering, hoping for an after-hours rendezvous with those lips sometime soon.

"Good afternoon," he announced once inside his spacious but decaying wood-floor office. The shades were drawn as always and a dim lamp barely illuminated the dusty room, but it was bright enough to make out a man just over six feet with a blonde crew cut. He stood by the bookshelf, eyeing fifteen-year-old pictures of former coworkers and clients, memories from better days. The man didn't look up when he answered.

"The plaque on your door says 'William T. Knoble, Attorney at Law,' but you haven't practiced any actual, ethical law in years. Have you, Bill?"

The blunt, lucid statement took him by surprise as he continued to size up the mystery man. He appeared well off, sporting a pair of pleated navy-blue slacks and a buttercream dress shirt, sleeves rolled up. He didn't see a coat. He was also a terrible judge of weight other than the go/no-go test for women, but the man looked relatively thin for what he guessed was about forty.

"Who's asking?"

"Take a seat, Bill. I won't be long."

"All right, listen. If you don't tell me who you are right now I'm gonna —"

"I'm the guy who made Barry Lee Richard disappear."

Sinking into his desk chair, he ran his balmy hand through the oily salt-and-pepper hair atop his undersized head. *Barry Lee Richard.* The son of a bitch investment banker who'd made his wife his own personal punching bag and got off with a $500 noise violation. That was a week ago today, and he hadn't seen Barry Lee since the trial. They were supposed to meet for celebratory drinks that afternoon, but Barry Lee never showed and he'd gleefully headed home. He'd tried to call his client twice since then but wasn't disappointed to get voicemail.

He figured the prick was probably beating up his wife again.

"What do you mean —"

"Relax, Bill. If I wanted to hurt you, I'd be done and gone already. I'm here on business and don't have a lot of time, so pay attention."

He could only nod, more than a little afraid as the clean-shaven man walked around to his side of the desk, towering over him in a particularly intimidating manner.

"I know you think Barry Lee was a pathetic waste of space, and I know you broke the attorney-client privilege telling your sister that."

"How do —"

"Save it. It's the only reason you're still alive."

What?

"I'll be honest. Your whole scumbag profession is just as bad as the scum you represent. Chasing one ambulance after another to get guilty men back on the streets is no way to make a buck, no matter how handsome that buck is. And I usually don't have a lot of patience for people whose idea of professional courtesy is to catch a lift ashore on the backs of hungry sharks sniffing for human blood."

He didn't shout but he didn't whisper. He also didn't blink for what seemed like forever, and his eyes grew darker, somehow.

"But then I look at you from another angle. A guy who used to have a respectable practice, then got greedy. You used to do it right. Then you made one bad decision and the slippery slope led to guys like Barry Lee Richard. But that doesn't matter, Bill. Today's your lucky day.

"Barry Lee was beyond help. But with you, there's still hope. You've got a human side. You donate more money to charities than you keep for yourself. You steer your nephews away from your shady lifestyle choices. You're ashamed of what you've become and you want a way out, but you can't find one. You can't start over and you feel trapped by your age and stupid decisions."

How did he know all of this?

"A man can't buy redemption with good deeds, Bill. Not when he represents clients like Barry Lee. The good might let you live with yourself, but it doesn't cancel out the bad. There *is* a way out, though. It's your last chance, and it's staring you in the face."

"What … what do you mean?"

"Here's the deal: you toss the garbage from your client list and you do it right now. The next Barry Lee that walks through your door gets his ass kicked out of it. You get yourself — and your practice — back to where it was years ago. Stick to the clients who actually need a lawyer, not a shyster. Do it right and do it clean; trust the law you pledged an oath to practice. No more filth, no more booze, no more sex with your secretaries. Agree to all of that, *right now*, and I let you live. Your call, Bill."

He could say nothing as tears began rolling down his face.

"*Say it,* Bill."

"O, o-okay."

"Bill, one day I might need a favor from an honest man. And I'll expect you to be that man. But until then, just know I'll be watching. You're a smart guy and you know what *last chance* means. Don't screw it up. Redemption begins today."

With that, the man turned and left the room, shutting the door just in time to prevent his secretary from hearing Bill cry the moment and years away.

8

A little over a year ago, when Joe had finally realized his future was in his own hands and enrolled in college, Ben gave him the Ford Taurus as a "working" gift. The deal was Joe had free use of the car but from time to time had to play chauffer when Ben needed a lift or simply wanted to go for a ride to clear his head. Today was the latter, so Joe merged onto the highway with no specific destination in mind, the external rhythm of the concrete expansion joints the only counter to the interior silence. Unfortunately, not even that was helping to clear Ben's head.

After meeting Tom Fedorak for breakfast in Chicago to explain Sally Hubley's request and get his most trusted friend's opinion, he had Joe pick him up just off Dearborn Street, and they drove by Senator Kevin Richardson's office en route to home. Usually that didn't mean much — half the people in Illinois don't even know who their senators are — but that day happened to be the one-year anniversary of the senator's son's drunk driving incident that left three innocent children and a single mother dead at the scene. And that meant protestors, a lot of protestors, both in front of the senator's office and on the adjacent streets. Members from the Drunk Driving Prevention Association, Students Against Drunk Driving and MADD, not to mention everyday folks who wanted to show support, all chanted in unison against the horrors of drunk driving, the voice of the dead crying out through the living.

But that wasn't the primary reason for the protests. As tragic as the accident was, it was hardly unique in a country where drunk driving kills some ten thousand people a year. What made Reece Richardson's case different — and what the public seemed to remember — was the senator's son getting a suspended license, rehab and probation for the crime. Illinois courts weren't legally allowed to sentence probation for drunk driving vehicular homicide cases without "extraordinary circumstances," and standard sentences across the state ranged from one to twenty-eight years in jail with a minimum 85% of the term served. Few felt it was fair the kid got off easy just because his father was a senator.

A lack of incontrovertible evidence prevented impeachment, and while Senator Richardson's political career was certainly finished come reelection time, that was over four years away and the public wanted his head now. The signs ranged from "HOW DARE YOU!" to "ILLINOIS POLITICS AT ITS WORST" to pictures of the children beneath the phrase "DADDY CAN'T BAIL THEM OUT!"

Ben had to admit he saw their point, but all it meant to him now was that he was momentarily distracted from thinking about Sally Hubley's request.

When Joe finally got through the crowds and was doing seventy on I-290W, the simple question returned. Why would Peter Hubley be a target if he was as squeaky clean as Sally presumed? He wanted to believe her, but experience had taught him to expect the worst of people, rather than assuming the best.

He'd hardly known Peter Hubley. He'd seen him a handful of times and they'd talked about the Bears. He didn't know what the man did for a living, other than that he was some sort of software expert turned investor. He didn't know his background or what he'd done for the first thirty-plus years of his life. Even Sally had only been married to him for a few years. Maybe Peter did have a secret or two. Maybe he did put up a front and live another life. Maybe somewhere, at some time, he pissed off the wrong guy and tried to run from it. Stranger things had happened, and without the facts or history, Ben had a hard time accepting Sally's innocent victim story at face value.

He took a long swig from the Aquafina bottle and savored the chill as ice-cold water snaked its way downward. Staring out the window at Chicago's Blue Line commuter train running parallel to the interstate, he tried to lose himself in thought so he could find the right answer. After ten minutes of considering the questions and pondering the unknowns, at the Manheim exit he cracked his aging knuckles and checked his watch.

"Joe?"

"Yes, Mr. Siebert?" Joe replied with the title that had grown both inappropriate and uncomfortable over the past nine years, yet remained because Ben lacked the courage to say so.

"When we get home I want you to book me a flight to Sao Paulo, Brazil. Direct flight, leaves tonight around nine-thirty. Later today I'll have a few more things for you."

9

Riddle could've looked on the bright side.

The hit on Hubley was perfect. The Brazilians' deaths and the public's response, textbook. The police were right where he wanted them, and it had all happened five thousand miles away. Meanwhile, he'd just turned on his private two-mile driveway leading to his twenty-three-acre gated estate. Encompassed by pristine rolling hills and North Carolina farmland, he relished the seventy-degree weather while inhaling fresh country air. Miles from another person, he acknowledged that most of the plan was unfolding as it should: precisely the way he wanted.

But he didn't get to where he was by accepting the glass as half-full. Rather, he'd demanded a pitcher overflowing with liquid success. After parking one of his four Lamborghinis, he removed his Ray Bans to walk around it and reflect on the luxury vehicle's greatest offering: exclusivity.

A mere eleven cars made per day, custom color every time, price tags from $400,000 to five million. This one was bright green and he relished that no robots were used to manufacture it — men were on the assembly line and women detailed the interior. Its signature branding – an uninterrupted curve from the front to the rear, inspired from an insect's contours – defined its mantra. *Only the very best can afford me.*

It wasn't concerned with losers who cared about its fourteen miles to the gallon or lousy trunk space. It catered to winners.

Energized, he called Terrance Smith to demand perfection.

"Good morning, Mr. Riddle," the voice answered after one ring.

"Terrance, do you know how Lamborghini got started some fifty years ago?"

"No, sir, I don't."

Of course not. That's why I own them and you don't.

"The founder, Lamborghini himself, originally built tractors and was having problems with his Ferrari's clutch. So he called to voice his concern and was told to stick to making tractors and let Ferrari stick to the cars. He could've listened, but what do you think he said?"

"I'm not sure."

"He said *screw you* and started what is now the premier car manufacturer in the world. Lamborghini didn't get where he was by listening to inferior minds."

"I understand, sir."

"Terrance, we have our own Lamborghini opportunity."

"Sir?"

"FBI Special Agent Nikki Benton's involvement was not part of the plan, and even with our contingencies, we need to take ownership of this situation. Let's not allow lesser minds to dictate how things get done."

"Her involvement is disappointing, Mr. Riddle. What would you like me to do?"

Those words never got old.

10

Terrance Smith reread Nikki Benton's classified personnel file and concluded his plan was going to work.

It was based on a push-pull strategy not even Dominick Riddle could replicate. The construction and dissemination of his created messages revolved around a specific target audience's desired perception. That target could be the general public, as it was for the Peter Hubley assignment. But that meant the *public* was the target audience, and the *public* was the perspective around which all decisions were based.

In this case, Special Agent Nikki Benton was the sole target.

Thus, all questions revolved solely around her. How should the information initially hit the market? Through what medium should it spread? What level of secrecy must it appear to have and what level must it actually have? How fast should it move through cyberspace? Were there any restrictions on its propagation? Were there any people whose knowledge of it would negatively affect Ms. Benton's perception? Should a reporter be bribed to write a favorable story, or should an anonymous tip be sent to the cops? Should an idea go viral via social media, or should it slow cook like stew meat in a crock-pot? Like a choose-your-own-adventure story, the answers would be all different depending on the target audience, so it was critical to begin and end with her.

This meant work. Just because the Peter Hubley job had performed so well didn't mean he could simply copy its playbook and get the same results. It required research, planning, and strategy focused around Ms. Benton, a far different approach than in Peter Hubley's case. It required expertise that only he possessed, a level of astuteness and execution and perfectionism you couldn't get anywhere else.

Which was why Dominick Riddle paid him five million per job.

His employer had already given him all the seemingly relevant information — mainly her personnel file and the Hubley case file — and he already had all the intelligence on Hubley. But he needed more on Ms. Benton, which Mr. Riddle didn't understand but respected. He needed it all, from her college transcripts to her wrecked engagement to her parents' death to her FBI personality tests and application. He needed to know what made her tick and why, what she'd believe and what she'd question. The devil was in the details and he lived next door.

It was certainly an art, which was why "Spin Artist" was how Mr. Riddle identified his specialty. But it was so much more than that. He was a *Strategic Marketer*, a visionary, a brilliant branding expert who controlled perception. He was the guy who turned dreams into truths and unlocked the tempting door of potential into the blissful room of reality. How a message was perceived and what that led to were very, very valuable — and it all started with him.

Very soon, Ms. Benton's investigation would take a sharp turn towards his desired destination.

11

It was past two a.m. on Friday night and Nikki Benton was slumped on the kitchen floor of her one-bedroom apartment, papers sprawled in all directions, gripping a yellow highlighter, seeking what didn't want to be found. She preferred tile to carpet to keep her alert albeit uncomfortable, but after four hours of reading, she began to wonder if the gym would've been a better use of her time.

After three exhausting days of research, it had been one dead end after another. She'd spent most of her time reading, but had also spoken with Peter Hubley's sweet widow only to hear what you'd expect. She'd sought the particulars and learned that Saturday morning was Peter's time with the kids, that he played in a racquetball league on Tuesday nights and that he didn't drink or smoke.

She'd reviewed the security tapes Redmond obtained from the Sao Paulo airport and found them equally disappointing. Both shooters wore lightweight black-and-yellow polo jackets with jeans. They arrived one hour before Hubley, carried no bags, and walked straight through security and the metal detectors. Aside from a joint trip to the bathroom, both men spent the entire time standing next to a duty-free shop. With no cameras in the lavatory, she could only guess that's where they got the guns. Right before they approached Hubley at the café, one of them went into another bathroom for two minutes, but there was nothing to learn from that either.

Beyond the brutal visual now stuck in her mind like a giant splinter, the tapes of the shooting offered nothing new. The surrounding people's reactions seemed genuine and nothing stuck out as suspicious. The footage of the shooters' apparent seizures and subsequent deaths had confirmed Redmond's theory that they wouldn't tell her anything YouTube hadn't already.

Frustrated, she'd then reached out to FBI Brasilia at the embassy, at which time she was promptly reminded of her jurisdiction and referred to Interpol Washington.

Interpol was a great concept. Designed to connect the world's police, it was headquartered in Lyon, France and had contributed to thousands of worldwide apprehensions. There were over one hundred ninety National Central Bureaus representing various countries that all shared information via I-24/7, Interpol's global communication network.

But most of the forty Interpol Brasilia employees were focused on Olympic safety, and Interpol didn't *send* agents anywhere. It merely acted as a facilitator, and as such she didn't get very far, even though Interpol Brasilia had asked Interpol Washington for help — ultimately leading to her Friday night on a tile floor. When she asked why the Brazil police initially requested Interpol's help, she got the bureaucratic runaround. That part still didn't make sense — something was missing. But without knowing who else to ask, she was forced back to Peter Hubley. Just like Redmond told her.

She called her old boss in Phoenix after that, who reminded her to "stick to the facts." When she lamented that's exactly what she'd been doing, he told her that's why they pay her the big bucks and that the answer was somewhere in those pages. The conversation served only to remind her of how much she missed him and his office. He was a good man with strong priorities, and leaving his cozy office and beautiful Phoenix weather to come to Redmond's windy city office with its thick tortoise-ass smell was something she'd lamented doing a number of times.

Wearing cotton elephant pajama pants, fuzzy socks and a faded "Can't Touch This" T-shirt from her MC Hammer days, she'd just poured her third cup of day-old coffee when her cell phone started to ring.

Two-forty in the morning. Some life you have.

Caller ID verified it was the office, one of the temps Redmond employed on the graveyard shift to help agents with grunt work they didn't have time to do.

"Benton here."

"Agent Benton, it's Craig. I'm sorry about the hour, but you told me to call anytime."

"No problem, Craig. What's up?" she asked, chiding herself for the part she played in making Craig's life as pathetic as hers.

"I checked the flight logs like you asked," he said, per Redmond's initial request. "And like we talked about, I didn't get much. There was no one with any serious criminal history or who knew Peter Hubley. But I reran the search again tonight and found something that doesn't fit. Check your e-mail."

12

Tom Fedorak obtained Peter Hubley's business itinerary and e-mailed it to Ben three hours before his flight. Usually better not to ask Tom how, the five-page document told Ben that Peter visited three cities: Sao Paulo, Curitiba, and Sete Lagoas.

Combined with the background Sally gave him about her late husband's job, it was clear Peter was in Brazil to evaluate three local businesses for possible acquisition. InvestSecure, his former employer, had a knack for gobbling up hi-tech international firms with undervalued price tags and quickly turning them profitable. The itinerary noted the companies with descriptions that fit the bill. A few phone calls verified their credibility and convinced Ben the firms probably had nothing to do with Peter's death.

Nevertheless, in the name of thoroughness he visited each city and firm. He took plenty of pictures and used his iPhone's voice-capture feature to document his findings, but by the final day of the six-day whirlwind trip, he was ready for his own bed in America.

And, had little to show for his efforts.

He'd spent only one day in Sao Paulo. It was the world's seventh largest city and felt like a bigger, busier version of New York. Very progressive and bustling with young people, it was engulfed by fast-paced culture and pretty women, which outnumbered the men six-to-one. He made a cursory visit to the first business on Hubley's itinerary and then headed to the airport, where he'd retraced Peter's steps. He sat down at the same café Peter sat prior to his death. He pictured the shooters: where they were standing, how they approached, and their short-lived walk from the café to their own demise. The security tape Tom gave him provided plenty of perspective, but the airport was back to normal and there was little to learn. He'd been to Sao Paulo several times, so he didn't stick around long before catching a flight to Belo Horizonte.

As he recalled from years earlier, Belo Horizonte was much smaller and less modern than Sao Paulo. That was reflected in the people more than anything. In BH — as locals referred to it — folks respected family customs and traditional male and female roles, including an old-fashioned courting process. They dressed differently, opting for less trendy, hand-made workpants and dresses, rather than the modern, foreign-branded jeans and low-cut tops seen in Sao Paulo. Progressive education was less important; men had blue-collar mining jobs and cared more about working hard than working on their appearance. Women were homemakers with conventional responsibilities, taught their skills by women from the generations before them. He'd been told "Date in Sao Paulo, marry in BH" were words to live by for young Brazilian men.

The capital of the state of Minas Gerais in southeastern Brazil, BH was the first of Brazil's planned communities. "Minas Gerais" meant "General Mines" and, true to its name, most of BH's revenue came from the mines and agricultural commodities. There was little English signage and hardly any tourism. There wasn't even a postcard stand at the airport.

Yet it was contemporary and lavish compared to Sete Lagoas.

Seventy kilometers north, Sete Lagoas was at first glance rustic and poor. The local shops were rundown and decrepit and the bustle of Sao Paulo seemed a world away. But while outdated, dirty and cheap were the three words that first came to mind, traditional, independent and conservative were better descriptors.

He'd re-traced Peter's steps: driving through the rural countryside to get to the second company on the itinerary, an electronics-manufacturing firm in the middle of nowhere. Trash covered both sides of the crumbling road in a way that was reminiscent of India, not Brazil. But unglamorous environments meant cheap real estate, and he passed Fiat, Mercedes-Benz and Caterpillar production facilities along the way.

His final stop was Curitiba, a college town if he'd ever seen one.

With a population of just under two million and several major universities within blocks of each other, it was a plethoric breeding ground for young people, commercial malls and bars. The streets were clean and the traffic lane lines freshly painted. The stores projected newness in all directions. A few years back Curitiba won the Global Sustainable City Award for its urban development, and Ben could see why. Aside from the native Portuguese he heard spoken, it reminded him of Gainesville, home to the University of Florida.

After a quick stop at the start up engineering firm that focused on locomotive control systems and scoreboard display design, Ben sat at the restaurant sipping orange juice — a popular lunch drink in Brazil — waiting for the only likely benefit of the entire trip to arrive.

The trip had mostly been a formality — going through the motions to try to learn something about the companies Peter visited, picking up what he could along the way. But success was unlikely even before he started and there weren't any surprises. He really only made those stops because he promised Sally.

But this last stop — he hoped to learn something here.

"Ben!" he heard his name called from across the outdoor patio.

He turned to see his old friend, all three hundred twenty pounds of him, painfully jogging towards him, a beaming smile on his face.

———

He first met Sidarta Perdigao fourteen years ago at a surprise party for a mutual friend in Houston. There were over a hundred people in attendance and two conspicuous misfits. Anna, ever the social bug, was mingling about while Ben guarded the punch when a man ten years his senior with short black hair and light-brown skin captured his attention by secretly spiking his drink with vodka withdrawn from his jacket pocket. Ben chuckled and nodded in approval, Sidarta offered him some, and a friendship was born.

He'd learned that the Brazilian-born Sidarta had lived in the USA and Germany as a budding executive for an off-road truck and engineering firm. He had a wife and two kids, and he was extremely learned and interesting. Ben was taken with how savvy and perceptive Sidarta was, using his gift of deduction learned in psychology classes at Princeton. At that particular time, he was investigating various vehicular options for some overseas Marine ops, so he took Sidarta's number and planned to stay in touch. But their friendship was officially sealed when Anna and Sidarta's wife approached the punchbowl together — having independently formed their own bond in the small world of surprise parties. The four of them hit it off immediately and had dinner a handful of times before Anna's passing and Sidarta's transfer back to Brazil.

Once Sidarta returned to his homeland, Ben gathered that he was very well connected. He developed a suspicion Sidarta was in tight with the local government and military, but he wasn't sure in what capacity. Sidarta just always seemed very knowledgeable and helped Ben navigate Brazil's red tape on a few occasions.

And now he hoped for his help again.

"How was your flight, amigo?" Sidarta practically shouted after a long embrace, grabbing a seat at the table.

"A walk in the park."

The ten-hour flight to Brazil had indeed felt like two. Between the mounds of reading and a little shut-eye in the darkened-cabin, Ben always relished long flights preceding busy trips.

"Good for you. I can't stand airplanes. Look at me … I practically need two tickets with those tiny seats. Airlines … they've gone from squeezing your pocketbook to squeezing your ass."

"You look like you've lost weight." Sidarta had put on at least thirty pounds since Ben last saw him.

"Sure, and you look younger."

"Younger than you, and that's all that matters."

"Touché, my friend."

"How's the new baby?"

"Always up, always crying, always a pain in my ass."

"Maybe if you took my advice and got yourself fixed, your Casanova-self wouldn't get any more bundle-of-joy surprises."

"Maybe if you pissed up a rope, you'd defy gravity."

Ben could only laugh.

"How are you, seriously?" Sidarta asked.

"Doing well. Keeping busy. You?"

"Ah, Brazilian government, the grind in my gears."

"That bad?"

"It's like they try to make it hard to do business with other countries. My partner in America has a fitting slogan: Brazil, the country of the future and always will be."

"Is he right?"

"You bet he is! Until the government realizes it can't tax other nations' profits away and expect more business, it'll be very hard to make money in Brazil."

"Maybe the government wants it that way."

"That's fine for now, but it's a global world and the Brazilian pie isn't big enough by itself to serve us all. But anyway, you didn't fly five thousand miles to talk about the government. What's on your mind?"

Just then the waiter came and Sidarta ordered for them in rambling Portuguese, assuring Ben he'd like the result. When the waiter walked away, he turned to Ben and waited silently for his answer.

"Actually, you're not far off. You've heard about the shooting at GRU?"

"Heard about it? I wish people would shut up about it. One American gets killed and you'd think the pope died."

"Well, he was married to a friend of mine. A friend who helped me through some tough times when Anna... " his voice trailed off. Even after nine years, he couldn't finish that sentence. "She asked me to look into it."

Sidarta didn't hide his shift in posture, facial tone or body language. Straightening up and suddenly serious, he leaned in and folded his hands.

"I'm not sure I can help, but what do you need?"

"The shooters belonging to the PCC...think that's true?"

Sidarta paused and appeared deep in thought, but with Sidarta you could never know. Silence engulfed the shaded outdoor table and it seemed folks around them grew quieter too.

"Possibly. But that's not the question you should be asking."

"What should I be asking?"

"Take a step back. Eight prison inmates founded the PCC in the early nineties. They were playing a soccer game and decided the Sao Paulo penitentiary system needed a new enemy, so they started a gang to give it one. Members call each other brothers and there's a thirty-dollar fee. They use the money to bail brothers out of jail and buy smalltime weapons. New members recite an oath, like college kids in a fraternity."

"Sidarta, they're almost fifteen thousand strong. They're in over twenty Brazilian states. It might've been grassroots at first, but they're the biggest organized crime outfit in the country now. That's saying something."

"Yes, they've grown. But that doesn't change the fact that they're low-tech. Half the brothers are in prison, and the ones that aren't are targeting police stations and city buses. Local targets, minimal security. Easy hits by any terrorist standards, very little planning required. No computer surveillance and certainly nothing like airport security working against them."

"You're saying you don't think it was the PCC?"

"I'm saying there's no way the PCC ran the operation. It might've been the workhorse, but it wasn't the brains. Think about how sophisticated that job was. How'd they get the guns through security? How'd they know which flight the American was taking? How'd they know he'd be alone?"

"Maybe they're getting smarter."

"Nobody jumps from where the PCC is to that in one job. You know this better than I. But, okay, let's say they're just getting smarter … "

Hearing it spoken aloud revealed its unlikelihood.

"Even if we make that assumption, there are still two unanswered questions no one's asking. The first is motive. The PCC is a domestic gang that focuses its vengeance on the military police. Why would it care about an American businessman? Even if there was a reason, there's no way the PCC would send two of its own to certain death just to kill him. All I've been reading about is how the American *must* have been connected to the PCC, but it's as if the entire world forgot what the PCC is.

"Killing the American would have the feds all over them, and not just the Brazilian feds that can be easily controlled with bribes. It would turn up the heat on everything they're doing. Believe me, the last thing the PCC wants is America's FBI up its ass. Yet no one seems to be saying that."

"It's tough to say that when there's proof the shooters were members."

"Why is no one questioning the PCC's motive? Everyone is focusing on the victim, looking for his faults. But the reality is that even if those faults existed, there's still not enough motive for the PCC. This will hurt them in the long run and they know it. They're not brilliant, but they're not stupid either."

"What's the second question?"

"Ah, it's more obvious and yet even more ignored, and it starts with what happened to the killers. Do you really think these two guys signed up for a job *knowing* they were going to die? Why would they do that? And why would the PCC take the risk to hijack an ambulance for their bodies?"

"You think they planned to get away with it?"

"That's the wrong question. I think we can safely assume they didn't both coincidentally die of natural causes five minutes after the shooting. Which means that someone had them do the grunt work, killed them both, then took the time and risk to recover their bodies. The question is, who would do that and, more importantly, why? Because whoever it is, it's the same person smart enough to plan it in the first place."

"Someone very well connected, plenty of resources."

"Not only that, but someone meticulous enough to cover up every loose end. Once the first shot was fired, it was out of his hands. The cops swarmed and every person with a camera started taking pictures. Whoever it was, he had it planned from the start. He wanted Hubley shot in a public place. He knew exactly when the shooters would croak and exactly where they'd be taken. A public massacre with no interrogations and no autopsies — just the way someone storyboarded it."

Ben nodded his head, revisiting the now-obvious questions. Sidarta was right. Even in America — where there might be prejudice against the Brazilian shooters — no one was talking about them. The news was focused exclusively on Peter Hubley, with everyone searching for his dark secrets.

Including him.

Six medium-rare sirloin steaks arrived, but Ben was no longer hungry. Frustrated for having not seen the loose ends, he was even more anxious to get back. He thanked Sidarta for his time, dropped R$100 on the table, and said he had to get going.

A surprised Sidarta put his fork down and whispered.

"I'll ask around, because it's you. But remember a saying we have in Brazil, my friend. *Quem morre de véspera é o peru.*"

"What's that?"

"It means he who dies the evening before is the turkey. Don't be foolish, Ben. Your friend has asked for your help, and I know you're a man who's there for his friends. But make no mistake, this is much bigger than the PCC. Watch your back."

———

As he climbed in the taxi, Ben could swear he saw him from across the street.

The same person he'd seen in BH the day before but chose to ignore. It was hard to be sure — his eyes weren't what they once were — and Sidarta had certainly put him on high alert. But he saw what he saw.

He was being followed.

13

At one p.m. in mid-October, Chicago's temperature was in the low fifties and a deeply overcast sky enshrouded the sun. Not even "Carol of The Bells" took Ben's mind off the fact he'd returned from Brazil yesterday with more questions than he'd left with.

He watched Sally Hubley walk from her house and pondered how much of his conversation with Sidarta need be revealed. He still didn't *know* anything — and aside from the fact a Brazilian man in his forties had followed him — had nothing concrete to share. He confirmed the tail wasn't on his return flight to Chicago. And the decision about what to tell Sally was a double-edged sword. He could reveal Sidarta's doubts, giving credence to her innocent victim theory but worrying her further, or he could leave her alone in the dark.

"Hi, Ben," she greeted him, brushing her long red hair aside as she climbed in the Taurus. Her eyes were still puffy and a forced smile played weakly across her face. "How was your trip to Brazil?"

"Not very informative."

"Did you learn anything?"

"I'm still processing things."

She didn't persist. Sally knew he'd tell her what he could when he was ready.

"I did tell you it wouldn't lead anywhere. There wasn't much chance it would."

She strapped on the seat belt, shrugged her shoulders and opened a new door.

"The FBI came to the house while you were gone."

"The FBI?"

"Special Agent Nikki Benton. Nice lady, but she didn't talk much. She was asking questions about Peter. Said she was doing some background checks."

"When did she come?"

"Monday morning."

A bit surprised, he turned onto the I-290E ramp towards Chicago.

"Did she say anything else?"

Like why Chicago's FBI field office was involved?

"I asked but she said she couldn't get into it. Just that it was standard practice whenever something happened to an American abroad."

An obvious lie. It was anything but standard for the FBI to meddle in affairs outside its jurisdiction.

"Is this Anna's wedding ring?" she asked, pointing to the chain and band hanging from the rearview mirror.

He nodded.

"Mind if I ask why you keep it visible?"

"I'm not sure. I put it there a long time ago."

The truth was he needed Anna to play a part in his life, no matter how small. He'd stopped wearing the band years ago because he didn't want anyone he dealt with to think of him as a married man with something to lose, but he'd always needed her and always would. The ring facilitated that need, along with her Sunday morning flowers and words he spoke alone but was sure she could hear.

"I can't even look at Peter's picture," Sally said. "Everything about him is buried in the basement."

That halted conversation for almost the entire forty-five-minute drive, which was okay by him. He did learn that the kids were okay, staying with Nick and Lisa Gordon, that Sally's Bible Study was a blessing to her, and that she was coping with but obviously still mourning her loss. When they arrived, he parked on the street in the two-hour spot.

"You haven't been here yet?"

"No, they called for me to come get his things, but you asked me to wait. So I told them I'd come when I had time. They offered to mail them but I said no."

"And they don't know we're coming?"

"No. Why?"

"Good."

"Ben, did you hear me? *Why?*"

"Because I want to see the office as it normally operates," he said, refraining from the second half of the answer.

Not when they're expecting the widow who just lost her husband on a trip they told him to take."

"Okay," she responded, her tone making it clear she knew there was more.

———

InvestSecure was a boutique private equity firm that specialized in the acquisitions of vertically integrated companies in the manufacturing and computer industries. It boasted a remarkable track record for turning unprofitable, highly indebted organizations into moneymakers — usually through significant organizational restructuring and cost cutting — then taking a healthy cut of the profits before selling it off for an even healthier return.

Its President, Chairman and CEO was Ryan Bodie III, a former stockbroker at the Mercantile Exchange in Chicago. Bodie founded the company twenty-two years ago without any venture capital start-up money or angel investments and to this day remained its sole owner, less a few shares offered to employees via an Employee Stock Ownership plan that summed to less than ten percent.

Despite numerous buyout offers and tempting Initial Public Offering opportunities, Bodie kept the company private throughout its entire history. From the not-so-public information Tom Fedorak provided, Ben estimated its fair market value at $450 million. It brokered domestic deals but specialized in international acquisitions ranging anywhere from $5M to $100M, and it employed 110 people, giving it a more-than-respectable $4M of revenue per employee. No apparent succession plan was in place for when the sixty-one-year-old Bodie retired, but there were three remaining Vice Presidents after Peter Hubley's death. Either way, its P&L and cash flow statements proved it was a very well-oiled machine that earned Mr. Bodie alone an estimated $16M before taxes each year.

It was headquartered on the third floor of an office complex close to O'Hare Airport, its fourth location over the years, convenient for those who flew internationally. Everything about InvestSecure — from the shared lobby's ornate fountain that looked like a waterfall with an aquarium backdrop to the pristine gold-colored elevators to the modern all-glass front doors leading into Reception — screamed success.

"May I help you?" the secretary at the front desk greeted Sally and Ben. Her nameplate said K. Hovey, and she was in her mid-fifties or so. Straight black hair hung to just below her neck and she removed a pair of black reading glasses before looking up from behind the desk.

"I'm Sally Hubley. I'm here to get my husband's personal effects."

"Oh, you poor thing," the secretary lamented, jumping out of her chair to give Sally a hug. "I'm so sorry for your loss." She was 5'6" and wore a black suit and black shoes without heels. Her affection surprised Ben; she struck him as more of a strict businesswoman.

"Thank you, Ms … ?"

"Oh, call me Karen."

"Thank you, Karen. The Lord will help me through this," Sally replied, a crack in her voice.

"You poor thing. I'm new here, only a few months, but I met your husband and he was quite the gentleman."

"He was a good man."

"I'm sure he was." Karen maintained heartfelt eye contact with Sally and made Ben feel a bit restless. It must've showed.

"And who are you?" Karen asked, turning to him.

"I'm a family friend."

"I asked Ben to come with me," Sally said.

"I see. Well, let me show you to his office. Unless, I mean … if you'd prefer me to just bring his things … "

"No, that's okay. We can go to his office."

"Very well," Karen said, extending her arm to both tell them to lead and showing the way.

Through another set of double doors was a long hallway with conference rooms and cubicles on either side. Glass windows lined its east side, letting in an abundance of natural light. Windowless, closed-door offices lined the other. Hanging ceiling tiles partially blocked open ductwork above them as they made their way down the carpeted hallway. Ben took mental notes as they walked, trying to determine if there was a reason to come back.

"So you've only been with the company for a few months?" he asked.

"That's right," Karen answered.

"Do you like it?" he replied, in the most sociable voice he could garner.

"Oh, yes. The people are friendly and I really like my boss."

"Mr. Bodie? He's the owner, right?"

"He is."

"He was also Peter's manager," Sally added.

Ben was hoping that would prompt Sally to ask one of the two questions he'd requested, but she remained silent until they reached the final office along the west wall. Upon entering, they were greeted by a desk with two cardboard boxes atop. No pictures, nothing on the whiteboard, no electronics of any kind.

"I went ahead and packed everything into a few boxes. Peter didn't have very many personal items. He was a hard worker. All business."

"He was," Sally answered, staring at the empty desk chair. "In the office, anyway. At home he was all play with our sons."

"Again, I'm so sorry."

"Do you have his computer?" Sally asked, Ben's first requested inquiry. "He had a few photos on it I'd like to get."

"Oh, you know, we actually gave it to the FBI."

"The FBI?" Ben inquired.

"Yes, they came by a few days ago and said it might be helpful, so Mr. Bodie gave it to the agent. He left his card. I'll be sure to make a copy so you can call him about the pictures. Take all the time you need, Mrs. Hubley," Karen replied before stepping out.

"Thank you. Call me Sally," she answered, fighting tears.

A few moments later, Sally seemed to shift into go mode. She grabbed one box and asked him to grab the other. When she exited the office, she didn't look back for one last glance or stand in the doorway making wishes she knew couldn't come true. Her strength surprised and impressed him.

As they passed Reception on the way out, Karen handed Sally a photocopied business card. It belonged to Marcus Redmond, Special Agent in Charge of Chicago's FBI Field Office. Sally nodded thanks and then asked the second of Ben's questions.

"Is Mr. Bodie here? I'd like to thank him for the opportunity he gave Peter."

"I'm sorry, he isn't in the office today," Karen answered. "May I have him call you when he returns?"

59

"Please do. And thank you again for your help."

They left InvestSecure for what Ben thought would be the final time with nothing more than a few pictures, some desk trinkets and a Bears banner. Once outside, the boxes in the trunk, Ben inhaled the crisp air and rotated his neck. The streets somewhat empty but soon to be jammed with gridlock, now was the time.

"I've got a few things to do. Let's hail you a cab to take you home."

"What —"

"I just have a few errands to run. I'll come by later with the boxes. Are you okay?"

"I'm fine."

He outstretched his right arm towards the sky and a minute later opened a Checker Taxi's back door for Sally before reaching into the front seat window with a $100 bill.

"Get her some safely and keep the change."

As the pale yellow Ford headed towards the interstate, he whispered to himself, "Time to go to work."

14

She watched him very closely from her car.

He wore white khaki pants with no jacket and brown dress shoes. He looked taller and stronger than in his picture, large biceps pushing tight against his green polo. His face looked younger than forty-one, in stark contrast to most Marines, who tend to age poorly because of the stress put on their bodies. Binoculars revealed his pointy ears and sharp blue eyes. And she noticed that he wore a SEIKO watch on his left wrist despite the fact he was left-handed. His movements were fluid and smooth, no jerkiness in his steps.

After driving Sally Hubley to InvestSecure in his registered Ford Taurus and spending twenty minutes in the third-floor office, he put two cardboard boxes in the trunk and hailed her a cab before entering Nancy's Pizza across the street. That was ten minutes ago. Little was said between the two of them, and her guess was he didn't want Peter Hubley's widow to see his next move.

A loaded Glock 22 and small bag of cheese popcorn next to her, FBI Special Agent Nikki Benton briefly considered approaching the Taurus but quickly thought better of it. Nancy's might've been buzzing with customers, but a man like Siebert would keep an eye on things. Advertisements covered the restaurant's windows, blocking her view inside. So she instead turned to his file yet again, committing details to memory and trying to put herself in Benjamin Siebert's shoes.

The more she read, the more she wanted to know.

He was a poster child for the unconventional; the superhero you openly disliked and the villain you secretly rooted for. Throughout his military career, he'd shied away from the spotlight only to be thrown into it. It didn't seem to matter what was expected or asked of him, he did what he felt was right, whether it was or not. He'd been privately honored and publicly reprimanded within the same month three times. He was everywhere and he was a ghost. There was no black and there was no white; this man was all gray.

Just as she finished reading his file again, the locked backseat car door swung open. In a flash, a man leapt inside behind her with incredible quickness, slamming the door shut. Before she could so much as turn around, she felt the barrel of a gun pressed into her seatback.

"You've got three seconds to hand me your gun and start the car."

———

"Where do you want me to go?" she asked after pulling out onto Higgins Road.

"Just drive," Ben Siebert directed.

She did as instructed, trying not to look in the rearview mirror but unable to comply entirely with Siebert's request. He scoffed at her twice, forcing her eyes back on the road. As she turned south on Cumberland, her hands weren't shaking but her mind was rattled. This was the first time she'd been held at gunpoint after ten years in the FBI, and she felt like a kid who'd defied her parents to see the scary movie and was now finding out why they said no.

Though her training at Quantico felt excessive at the time, it seemed insufficient now. All the lessons the instructors screamed at her — from how to size up a perpetrator's physical abilities to analyzing his intelligence to estimating his next move — without warning became useless. *Right when she needed them.* She knew enough from Siebert's file to know this was the wrong man to piss off. And though the file indicated it was unlikely Siebert would harm her, she sure as shit didn't want to litmus test that conclusion.

He kept the gun pressed into her seatback, hard enough that she was confident it'd formed an indentation on her skin. After driving for two miles, he told her to pull into a small forest preserve, shaded and concealed by a large cluster of oak trees, then stop the car and give him the keys. He then exited the vehicle and walked around its front to the passenger door, keeping the gun on her at all times through the windshield. When he reentered, he wasted no time.

"Who are you?" he said in a firm voice, aiming the gun at her forehead. She couldn't help but notice it was a fourth-generation Glock 27. The depressing irony that Siebert was holding the same gun the FBI standard issues agents uncontrollably crammed her mind.

"My name is Nikki Benton. I —"

"You're an FBI agent?"

"Yes, Special Agent. How did you —"

"Why did you go to Sally Hubley's house five days ago?"

"I was doing some background —"

"Don't lie to me."

"I'm not lying. I —"

"Why were you there?" His voice grew a notch louder.

"I was researching Peter Hubley. To look for the reason he —"

"But *why?*" What makes this the FBI's problem?"

"I don't know. I asked —"

Siebert used his free hand to slap the bag of cheese popcorn into the dash, kernels pouring all over the console and floor.

"Lie to me one more time and you're not going to like what happens."

Again her training deserted her when she needed it most. Tears welled up in her eyes and her heart responded with an aggressive arrhythmia that made her chest feel tight. She caught herself holding her breath, abandoning life's most basic act.

"I'm not lying to you. I *swear* I'm not lying. All I know is that Interpol Brasilia contacted Interpol Washington, and Interpol Washington contacted us. My boss told me to investigate Peter Hubley and try to find out why this happened."

"Does your boss always assume it's the dead guy's fault?"

"I wouldn't even know. This is my sixth month in the Chicago office. I've been pushing paper until now."

"It shows."

She didn't respond but wiped her eyes and looked at his. They were bright blue at first but appeared a bit darker now. He didn't grit his teeth or squint and, aside from his eyes, his face was stoic. She knew he was deciding right then if he should believe her.

"Why are you following me?" he demanded, grabbing his personnel file and holding it inches from her face.

"You flew to Brazil eight days after Hubley got shot," she whispered, a tremor in her voice. "Your itinerary had the exact same cities he'd visited right before —"

"They're big cities."

"And Brazil's a big place."

"I've been there before."

"Not for a long time."

"Not enough to go on," he replied, shaking his head. "Not unless you're desperate. Is your investigation really going that poorly? Wait a minute … did you have someone in Brazil tail me while I was down there?" he asked, readjusting his grip on the Glock to remind her it was there. As if she'd forget.

"Yes."

"You had no right to do that."

"Mr. Siebert, see it from my perspective. You're an ex-Marine and there's no record of what you've been doing since you resigned your commission eight years ago. As you already pointed out, my investigation's in the crapper. It was something to go on."

"Maybe there's no record because it's none of your business."

"Maybe it's not. But an ex-Marine officer with a secret life visiting the same cities the victim did a week after he was shot seemed reason enough to have you followed."

"You're really that hard up for leads? That you'd follow an American just because he visits cities thousands of people visit every day?"

"We had to start somewhere. You were the best option based on what we knew."

"Knew? You think for one second you know something because of some file?" He remained imperturbable. Cool and calm, like he'd never let anyone get to him. She couldn't help but be a bit impressed.

"I know more about you than you think."

"Okay, tell me."

"What?"

"Tell me about myself if you're such an expert."

"You want me to tell you about yourself?"

"Like your life depended on it."

She wondered how much of a stretch that was.

"Look, I don't —"

"No. You're the one who offered. Out with it."

"Okay." She collected herself, his eyes growing darker, more intimidating. "Benjamin Siebert. Forty-one years old, born to an accountant and a homemaker. Both parents deceased. Busted out of a small Oklahoma farming town at eighteen on a full-ride to Princeton. Off the charts brilliant, but what's even more impressive is that wrestling's what got you there. You wrestled all four years, All-Conference twice, and did it all while double majoring in Structural Engineering and Economics. The only reason you didn't have a 4.0 was because you told a history professor to shove his laser pointer up his ass after he insulted Vietnam vets."

"Go on."

"That's when you made a decision I don't understand. You were a stud athlete at the top of your class academically, after double majoring in two of the most prestigious programs at the most prestigious university in America. Debt free. You could've gone anywhere and done anything. Wall Street, private industry, engineering firms, whatever … they all must've been begging you to come their way. But instead of doing what your buddies did — living up your last work-free summer before the six-figure job started — you were at Officer Candidate School in Quantico, getting your ass chewed out every day to become an officer in the United States Marine Corps."

"Lots of people join the Marines."

"No ROTC involvement, no service academy pursuits, no indication of interest two weeks prior to graduation. None. Best I can tell, you didn't know what you wanted to do and decided last minute to abandon an almost certain wealthy future to shave your head, crawl around in a foxhole, and get yelled at for ten weeks."

"What's wrong with serving your country?"

"Nothing at all. I'm not saying it's wrong. But how many of your Princeton buddies joined you in that foxhole?"

"What's your point?"

"My point is that it was an odd decision for someone in your position. And that was the first of many times you went against the trend."

"Tell me," he said, keeping the gun on her.

"You made it through OCC and became a commissioned Second Lieutenant. After six months at The Basic School, you got your first assignment at twenty-two. You got married a year later and you and your wife, Anna, went where the Marines sent you. Alabama, Texas, Southern Illinois. Unlike most officers who split their eight-year contracts between four years active and four inactive, you elected to spend six active, the maximum allowed. You must've made an impression because you rose quickly. Made it to Major by the end of your eighth year. And when your contract was renewed, you were on the fast track to Lieutenant Colonel. The Marines saw the leadership in you."

Siebert remained quiet, neither humbled nor moved.

"But then tragedy struck. I don't need to —"

"*Keep going.*"

She focused on her breathing, commanding herself to maintain a steady flow of oxygen. Siebert's eyes had lightened a bit and he'd lowered the gun, but the seriousness on his face remained.

"Two years later, your wife got killed in a botched bank robbery. You blamed yourself and things went downhill. I can't find any examples of misconduct in the field but —"

"That's because there aren't any."

"If you say so."

"Brothers depend on you out there. I would never let them down."

"But you did start drinking and maybe got into drugs. You got arrested for public drunkenness and fighting and —"

"Let's put that in perspective: I was in a bar minding my own business when a guy belted his girlfriend so hard he knocked her to the ground. So I introduced myself."

"Broken nose and shattered jaw from one punch."

"I got lucky."

"I don't think you did. But either way, you don't have to defend yourself. I'm not attacking you."

"I'm not defending myself. I'm proving your files are dangerous."

"Dangerous? How so?"

"They don't tell the whole story. Wolf in sheep's clothing."

"That's a bit overdramatic."

"Is it? You think you know someone from reading some file that only has a few of the facts ... and you don't think that's dangerous?"

"Okay, you tell me. What happened after your wife passed?"

"She didn't pass. Life was ripped from her."

"Okay. What then?"

"I got depressed. I made some bad choices and couldn't stay in the Corps. The Marines were kind enough to give me a way out with honor. So I took it. Entered rehab, got cleaned up, been sober ever since. I'll bet some version of that's in your file."

"Sure is."

"But you know what's not?"

"What?"

"The files don't tell you that a bunch of silver spoon Princeton pansies *need* ten weeks of ass-chewing from someone who serves his country. They don't tell you that a man learns more about life in the field during those active years than his entire life before them. They don't tell you what motivates a man to get out of bed after the piss-ant burglar that murdered his wife walked free on a legal technicality."

Neither the bar fight's background nor the burglar's exoneration was in the file.

But looking into Siebert's blue eyes, she saw truth.

"Great book report on me and all, but you don't know me from Adam."

"You told me to tell you —"

"*Stop following me.* You don't need to put the pieces together. I'll solve the puzzle for you. I went to The Basic School with Nick Gordon, Sally Hubley's brother. We stayed friends and when Anna … well, Nick helped me through a tough time. He's the one who got me into rehab. I'm sure that's all in your file. What's not in your file is that during that time, I met Sally and Peter. Sally asked for my help after what happened. I drove her today as a friend. I was asked by the family. You weren't asked by anyone."

"That doesn't explain why you went to Brazil."

"That's none of your concern."

"My job — whether I like it or not — is to find out what I can about why Peter Hubley was murdered. I'm sure you can understand why doing that job would require me to look into an ex-Marine officer who knew the victim and went to Brazil a week after he was shot."

"Being at a dead end doesn't mean you drive down a one-way street."

"Mr. Siebert, I'm on your side. We both want the same thing. Why won't you work with me instead of against me?"

"The door swings both ways, *Nikki.* Let's recap. I'm minding my own business, helping a widow through a tough time. I catch you following me like I'm some sort of criminal and put you on the spot to find out why. I then learn you had me tailed for a week in another country and that you think you know me from reading personnel files. And now, now that the cat's out of the bag on your little covert operation, you want to know why I'm not anxious to be your partner?"

"It's your decision, Mr. Siebert, but you asked me not to lie, so I won't. I can't stop doing my job. I'll send more people to follow you if I have to. I'll stakeout your house. I'll get the background on your friend in Brazil and eventually I'll know why you went there. I'll do whatever it takes to do my job and do it well."

"Send all the people you want. But don't ever claim to know me again and be careful what you wish for. You don't have the first clue who I am or what I'm capable of."

15

The breakthrough came at 12:20 a.m. CST, well past the print deadline for Saturday-edition newspapers. But as in any industry, exceptions could be made. Printers could be stopped, paper trays and ink cartridges refilled, and electronic files updated with new material. The new layout could be transferred from computer to printing press, workers paid overtime, and distribution teams told it all comes with the job. The story could be on the front page the next morning.

In today's world, where tablets and phones told the news real-time on tiny screens that people could read on the morning commute, the sacrifice of starting over when a story called for it wasn't an option but a necessity. The online editions would of course remain current, but there was a subset of customers out there who wanted to feel the thin pages in their hands, who wanted to flip to page 12A for what the front page couldn't hold while sipping a warm cup of coffee. Those people expected a story like this in ink, no matter when it broke.

What began as hearsay had materialized into front-page news in a matter of hours. It'd been sixteen days since Peter Hubley was murdered at GRU airport in Brazil. And until that point, no one had any idea why. Speculators had offered their opinions of course, and several conspiracy theories about Hubley's double-life had emerged, but there was no substantiation until late Friday night.

It started with an identical blog post, made to about twenty sites by a blogger with the alias *brazilexpert101*. Due to a total lack of credibility, it was initially ignored. The Internet is both practical and dangerous for the same reason; anyone can post anything. Wikipedia was just one example, with countless inaccurate posts making it through the screening process. Because of that, the 9:41 p.m. CST blog post was dismissed as just another theory, written by someone who didn't even have the balls to reveal his real name.

The reporting community had the first laugh, but *brazilexpert101* had the last.

At 10:32 p.m., the corroboration began.

A Brazilian newspaper published an online article stating a police captain confirmed that Peter Hubley previously met with high-ranking members of the PCC, the largest organized crime outfit in Brazil. This was widely rumored since Hubley's death but never before confirmed by the police. The captain was unavailable for comment, but at least now there was a name. This certainly didn't prove the blogger's theory, but it got it closer than any other had.

Thirty-two minutes later, at 11:04 p.m., a YouTube post emerged and spread like soft butter on hot toast. It was relatively mundane as far as YouTube posts go — one man, fifty years old, Brazilian, goatee, black hat — staring into the camera, no reading papers or prompts. What distinguished it was the man himself. Pictures of such men weren't readily available; but in the Internet Age, they weren't scarce either.

In the video, he identified himself as the brother of one of the PCC founders and one of the gang's current leaders. Although his identity couldn't be confirmed, people's acceptance of what they see and verification of it are two different things. If it walks like a duck and quacks like a duck, people think, "duck." And despite the late hour, the video moved through cyberspace quickly, from YouTube to Facebook to Fotki. The man claimed that Peter Hubley had "used American influence on wrong people" and that he "deserved what he get." He went on to say, still in broken English, that if any American thought he could use the PCC as his dog, he'd receive the same fate as Hubley.

No details were offered, but that was unimportant. The video was instantly hyperlinked to the original blog posts and Brazilian newspaper article, and suddenly the blogger's story had traction. The final straw, though — the bow atop the package that American readers would tear into like it was Christmas morning — was the picture.

It surfaced at 11:34 p.m. and was grainy, black-and-white, and heavily under-pixilated. Just as with the blog post, the newspaper article and the YouTube video, this made it far from ideal journalism. But if a picture is worth a thousand words, its connection to a video is worth ten times that. And despite the lack of clarity or a time-date stamp, it showed something that garnered attention: a smiling Peter Hubley shaking hands with the PCC leader from the YouTube video.

Twenty minutes later, an off-duty police officer cornered outside a bar in Sao Paulo independently verified the police captain's quote from the newspaper article. Now there were two sources backing the blogger's story, both from the law.

So when the *Associated Press* picked up the story and ran it at 12:20 a.m., the sacrifice of stopping the printers, retransferring the layouts and working overtime to get it in Saturday's print edition was worth it. By the end of the weekend it'd be in every major periodical, and being last in the newspaper business meant being left out. After two weeks of fruitless searches, the public would finally get its answer.

It was Hubley's fault after all.

The only uncorroborated claim in the blog post was Mr. Hubley's alleged affair with an unidentified Brazilian woman. It speculated that if the woman was involved with someone in the PCC, the motive might've been personal as well as professional. It was the weakest allegation, lacking both the woman's name and any description of her beyond "stunning" — a portrayal that fits many Brazilian women. But it didn't matter.

The *Associated Press* referenced the blog and the affair it alleged, simply stating the affair was unconfirmed. The reality was that nobody would care. When a man is in cahoots with the mafia, people don't question if he's capable of infidelity.

16

After his weekly visits to Ray's Florist and Faith Cemetery, Anna's tombstone free of debris and replenished with a new $57 bouquet of red roses and white lilies, Ben read the article yet again and thought of Sally's desperately fierce denial. She was dejected and he understood why. But it was her question after he expressed doubt that consumed him.

What if someone had written that about Anna?

The unopened bottle of Golden Brown begged for his attention. He stared at it defiantly but knew every man could be broken. The smooth, aged whiskey sat still and quiet, silently offering reprieve. The glass next to it couldn't have been more appealing with sugarcoated rims.

Enough was enough.

He grabbed the phone and dialed the number.

"Hello?"

"Special Agent Benton, this is Ben Siebert."

"How did you get this numb —"

"Meet me at The Gage on Michigan Street. Thirty minutes. Come alone."

————

The Gage was an upscale restaurant near the Symphony Center in downtown Chicago. It had multiple exit points, private booths and good scallops. The darkened atmosphere was a plus, and it was only a few blocks from numerous side streets and alleys that could help him lose a tail. It was a bit of a hike, but he needed the time to refocus after reluctantly pouring all 750 milliliters of Golden Brown down the sink.

Nikki Benton walked inside, presumably alone. From where she lived, it'd take her the full thirty minutes to get there, and he knew she needed his help. His one rule was that she be alone. If she broke it, he was gone. And there was little doubt in his mind that she knew it.

He waved her over and she sat across the booth, wearing a pair of tight Lucky Jeans with a knitted black sweater and leather riding boots. She was more of a looker than he'd realized, her chestnut hair tied back in a high ponytail and slim 5'6" figure augmented by perky breasts. She wore no makeup, but her creamy skin didn't need it.

"How did you get my personal number?" she asked without so much as a hello.

"You have your files, I have mine."

"I'm an FBI Special Agent."

"And I'm a former Marine. Nice to meet you."

"I could have you —"

"We already played this game, remember? Only last time, it started with you spying and ended with me holding a gun. I thought we could try meeting under different circumstances. But if you're not up for it, just say the word and I'll never bother you again."

She sighed loudly and sat back into the leather cushion, eyeing him closely as he folded his hands in waiting.

"What do you want?"

"You do a lot of KenKen puzzles, at least five a day on the same bench in Navy Pier. That means you like games, and I'd like to play one."

"How did you know that?"

"My game is *quid pro quo*. Ever play it?"

"Huh?"

"Last time you told me that you knew me. Then you proceeded to tell me about myself. My turn."

"Okay?"

"Nicole Angela Benton. One sister, two nieces, but you don't make it down to Dallas much to see them. You just turned forty and celebrated your tenth anniversary with the FBI in the same year. But you didn't dream of being an agent chasing bad guys as a kid. You're a numbers girl. Graduated magna cum laude from Georgia Tech. Computer Science major with a minor in Statistics. Took your pick of job offers as a programmer for a reputable firm in Atlanta to be close to your fiancé. Worked there for six years until you were twenty-eight, then had your own bumps in the road."

"Go on."

"Excuse me?"

"That's what you said to me when I tried to gloss over your travesty. *Quid pro quo*, Mr. Siebert."

"Call me Ben."

"*Quid pro quo,* Ben."

"Two terrible things happened in the same year. You found out your fiancé was cheating on you and —"

"Wrong. I found out he was already married. *I* was the home wrecker."

"The file didn't say that."

"Someone once told me files are incomplete."

"Okay. That happened, which was tragic enough."

"Then what?"

"It doesn't matter."

"Say it, Ben."

"You lost your parents in 9/11."

"Four months after I caught that scum cheating," she added, her hazel eyes not blinking.

"And you needed a change. This is where my questions come in. You quit your job and spent a year travelling the world. You went to Europe and Australia and a few other places, but then you came back and decided to become an FBI Agent. What prompted that?"

Time to learn how much I can trust you, Nikki.

Just then the waiter arrived and they placed their orders. For him: scallops, fries, and a coke. For her: beet salad with goat cheese, hold the walnuts, dressing on the side, and an Arnold Palmer with Lite Lemonade. Men versus women.

"Well, I did travel," she said once the waiter left, "but a better description would be that I drank and just so happened to ride on airplanes. I went to some of the most beautiful cities in the world but spent more time holed-up in bars guzzling Long Island Ice Teas than I did seeing the sites. I tried the beach thing, but that only meant strawberry daiquiris and apricot stone sours instead. It became a vicious cycle. The only way I could shake the shame my drinking caused was to drink more, leading to more shame."

"So what tipped your scales?"

"Excuse me?"

"People who resort to drinking to deal with their pain don't usually fade out of it over time. It happens, but the more common path is that something occurs that snaps the person into shape. What snapped you?"

"I almost died."

"Tell me about it."

"This is getting a bit personal."

"We're looking at personal in the rearview mirror. Tell me."

"I was in Jamaica, in Negril. It was my last night and I went harder than usual. I'd already passed out in the bar after God only knows how many Red Stripes. When I came to, I decided I was fine to drive back to the hotel. But I was still really drunk. So drunk that I forgot to drive on the left-hand side of the road and almost got into a head-on collision, but swerved into a tree just in time. I don't remember much of the accident, but when I came to I was in a Jamaican hospital being told I was lucky to be alive."

"And almost dying snapped you out of drinking?"

"No, the regret I felt for not dying did. I spent two weeks in a third-world country's hospital with secondhand medical supplies and filthy floors. It was there I was forced to detox and face myself for what I'd become. Knowing that my immediate reaction was regret for not dying ... it consumed me. People all around me were fighting for life, and there I was sorry to have it.

"I met this little boy. I never even got his name, but he was emaciated and had an awful cough. Our beds were next to each other — hospitals in Jamaica don't have the luxury of sorting patients by illness. I lay next to him, watching those little brown eyes open for the first time every day, and every time I felt sad. But even more, I was ashamed. Ashamed of where my life was. I'd gotten to a point where I either needed to kill myself quickly or stop doing it slowly."

"What happened when you left the hospital?"

"I came back to the States, decided I wanted my work to prevent the next 9/11, applied to the FBI and did what I had to do to get in."

When the food arrived, Ben stayed focused on Nikki's eyes. Recapping her story from Jamaica had summoned some tears, as had mention of her fiancé and her parents' tragic death. Yet through all of it, she'd remained candid. He was a bit unsold on her rationale for joining the FBI, but he also remembered being surprised by how many young men and women enlisted in the Marines after 9/11 for the same reason.

"Your application was dated one day before your thirtieth birthday," he said before biting into the first scallop.

"That's right."

"You made it through Phase One and Two testing, survived Quantico and boom … a year later you were in Phoenix, doing what you'd said you'd do. Ambitious and impressive."

"Thank you," she replied, offering a slight but genuine smile, exposing paper white teeth.

"Spent eight years in Phoenix — far more than the average three for a first assignment — then got transferred here. Bit of a weather shock?"

Her responsive laugh was quick and firm. It seemed to surprise even her and she rushed to cover her mouth, but not before her bright white teeth reemerged. Considering the circumstances, her laugh made it seem that she was lonely, not that he was funny.

"Ben," she turned serious, as if reading his mind. "I'm flattered you're impressed, but why did you call me here?"

"Fair enough. I called because what you said makes sense. We are on the same team. We do want the same thing."

"What does that mean to you?"

"Funny, that's my question exactly. I made a promise I intend keep. I know you don't know what I do, and that's not an accident. But let's just say I have a knack for investigation."

"Obviously. I'm still wondering how you found out about Jamaica."

"What makes you think I knew?"

"You're not a man who asks questions he doesn't already know the answers to — not unless he trusts the person he's asking. And I think the reason you asked me was to find out if you can."

"Can I?"

"You tell me."

He let that sit for a bit while she chewed her awful-looking beet salad, dipping it one forkful at a time into the balsamic vinaigrette. She was trying to play it cool, but he knew that in her mind, this was the moment of truth. *Are we dancing or just talking?*

He broke the silence. "I was hoping you could get me Peter Hubley's laptop."

"What laptop?"

"The laptop your office confiscated from InvestSecure while I was in Brazil."

"Why?" she asked, inquisitiveness in her face implying she wondered something more than merely why he was asking.

"Because I'm hoping there's something useful on it."

"It'll be analyzed."

"Then what?"

"If there's a lead, we'll follow it."

"Are you sure? You may not even find out what the lead is."

"What?"

"You already told me you don't know why the FBI is involved. Doesn't it strike you as odd that you'd be assigned a case but not know why? Use your head for a minute. Someone is keeping your office in the dark. What makes you think you'll get any light from the laptop?"

"Interpol said —"

"Yeah, I got that part. But you don't know *why* Interpol asked for the FBI's help. That's the sixty-four thousand dollar question."

She froze, her silence confirming what she'd already admitted.

"I'm sure any of the PCC stuff will get identified and —"

"You're not listening, Nikki. I have a knack for investigation. All I want is to run my own analysis on the computer before it gets sent away to Interpol and we miss our chance."

"What makes you think it'll go to Interpol?"

"I actually have no idea what'll happen to it. But I do know that someone's not playing by the rules in keeping things from your office, and that the answer why might be on that computer. If it is, you sure won't get it playing by those same rules."

"There's no way I —"

"I'm not asking you to take any risks with the information. Copy the hard drive and back it up to keep the data safe. Make it read-only. Give me the duplicate if you like. Put a time lock on the compression files so I can't use it past twelve hours. I'll get it back to you in the exact condition you give it to me."

"It's against the rules."

"You asked for my help, now I'm asking for yours. All I want is to take a look. Give me twelve hours and I'll let you know if I find anything. Considering your own office doesn't know why it's investigating this case and there's no risk to the information, it's a better offer than you'll get anywhere else. What do you have to lose?"

"You're asking me to provide classified case evidence to a private citizen for no other reason than I don't like where my investigation is. I could get fired for that, and you could go to prison for espionage."

"I'm asking you to consult an expert who has already proven to you he can find things you didn't think were findable. And I'm suggesting it be done in a way that minimizes your risk and gives you the best chance to learn something useful."

She didn't respond, pushing her plate away and becoming restless in the booth. She craned her neck as if looking for the waitress. He knew he had about thirty seconds.

"I can't do it. It's against the rules."

"You're the one who asked me to work together. And we both know following me around isn't going to get you anywhere, but that my help can. This is my offer — if you're interested, I need twelve hours. Twelve plausibly deniable hours to look for answers in files that can be safely copied beforehand and easily destroyed after. I fill you in on anything I find and you decide what to do from there. If you're not willing to trust me now, I know you won't trust me later. And if that's the case, I wish you the best in your investigation."

"I have to go," she replied before quickly leaving the restaurant.

17

"Two hundred stacks of fifty $100 bills. Just as Mr. Riddle requested."

The man who'd identified himself as Adir Mousa placed the large black duffle bag on the table and gestured for him to accept it. At eighty-thirty on Sunday night, The Reef — a small oceanfront restaurant six miles north of St. Augustine, Florida — was otherwise empty. They'd ordered food, tipped generously in advance, promised to be out by nine and asked not to be disturbed. The teenage wait staff was happy to oblige.

Mousa fit the part, long black hair, shaggy and dirty, thick mustache and a scruffy chin and neck. Six feet tall, very thin, dark eyes. He wore a pair of jeans and a plain navy-blue sweatshirt.

Despite this, he of all people knew how easy it was to falsify an identity. Seventeen days ago he'd had a passport, driver's license and host of other ways to prove his name was Matthew J. Baker. But the Arab's identity was of little concern. His objective wasn't to ascertain if Adir Mousa was the man's name but to determine if he was capable of what he claimed. The money would answer that, and he took the duffle bag from the table and dropped it beside his feet, paying it little attention.

"You'll count it?" Mousa asked.

"In private."

The money would certainly be counted, as well as run through a half-dozen tests to analyze the bills and prove they were neither marked nor counterfeit. Scanning programs, dye tests, trace checkers, computer analyses … the works. And if any one of them concluded the money wasn't completely legitimate, Adir Mousa wouldn't live long to regret it.

"I expected Mr. Riddle this evening," Mousa whispered.

"You expected foolishly. This is what he pays me for."

"To be his puppy dog?"

He ignored the jab and rubbed his right hand over the top of his hairless head, glancing away from Mousa and the dining room's green walls, wood-panel ceilings and white fans and towards the large floor-to-ceiling windows. Through the night's darkness, he could still make out the white foam of the ocean waves as they turned and crashed towards the shore. He paused momentarily, and then shifted his complete attention back to Adir Mousa.

"You cannot provoke a man who doesn't respect you, Mr. Mousa. And if you continue to try, I'll advise Mr. Riddle of your efforts and let him decide what to do with you."

"I am not scared of you. Or of Mr. Riddle."

"Oh yes you are. You're *terrified* of him, as well you should be. You've heard his nickname mentioned in your circles, I'm sure."

"I have heard it."

"And I'm sure you've heard many rumors as to how he obtained it?"

"This is of little concern to me."

"Let me clear up any confusion you may have from the rumor mill. *Paraponera Clavata* is an ant species native to humid Central and South American rainforests. Victims of its fiery sting have compared it to that of a gunshot wound, claiming it to be the most severe pain they've ever endured. It takes every bit of twenty-four hours for a single sting's throbbing, all-consuming burn to subside. Consequently, *Paraponera Clavata* has been labeled 'Bullet Ant.' A few years ago, some of your kind —"

"My *kind?*"

"Rag-heads, roach-ranchers, sand niggers, take your pick."

Mousa's eyes grew angry, but he pressed on.

"As I was saying, some of your *kind* underestimated Mr. Riddle and stole $2,000 from him. Pennies to Mr. Riddle, but that's not the point. Of course, he was several steps ahead of them — just as he is you — and he'd anticipated their betrayal. To show his appreciation, he instructed the two gentlemen to sit in wooden chairs, much like the ones we're sitting in now. He first had their hands tied behind the chairs. Rope was then wound around their chests and backs, permanently affixing them to the seats. The last words they heard were Mr. Riddle's, telling them that both of their families had already experienced what they were about to.

"Then, two large sacks — each filled with one thousand Bullet Ants exactly, flown in from Paraguay and meticulously cared for — were untied and overturned on the two men's heads. I'm told the agony was so severe that they couldn't muster a single scream as the ants layered their bodies. My guess is that was because the insects had blocked their airways as they raced down their throats. Mr. Riddle's nickname 'Bullet Ant' was forged the next morning, when the men's wives and children were found at home, six thousand miles away, next to envelopes containing a combined $2,000."

Almost certain the Arab had heard the story before, he watched Mousa silently conceal the fear he was no doubt feeling. But, as before, it was of little concern. He was there to evaluate the man — it had simply become necessary to familiarize him with Mr. Riddle's tactics in order to do so.

"Now, back to our arrangement. As I said, Mr. Riddle will inspect this money very carefully. If he's satisfied with the results, I will contact you with the next steps."

Still no response from Adir Mousa. He *was* terrified. He could see it in the Arab's eyes … he'd finally grasped just how serious a game he was playing and just how serious the players were. Allah himself could not save him from Dominick Riddle.

"Relax, Mr. Mousa," he said. "If you keep your word, you'll be quite valuable to him. A million dollars cash in twelve hours is no small feat, and Mr. Riddle will be impressed with your resourcefulness. And don't forget that this will be your most important acquisition yet. Think of the possibilities Mr. Riddle's product will offer your organization and what it can mean for the future. If you do what you say you're going to do, Mr. Riddle will gladly give the product to you."

For an astonishing amount of money.

"I understand Mr. Riddle is not working alone on its development. Are his partners … reliable?" Mousa conjured up the fortitude to ask.

"They are subordinates, not partners. Mr. Riddle has no equals."

"But if they don't know about our deal, I need assurance they won't try to sabotage me. Given what this product can do, I imagine many Americans would be upset if they knew I was buying it."

"Your arrangement is with Mr. Riddle. Let him deal with his subordinates. Rest assured, however, none of them would dare threaten Mr. Riddle's deal. Even if they do find out a towel head is involved."

"How can you be certain?"

"Because they're just as petrified of him as you are."

18

"Good evening, Mr. Riddle," Terrance Smith answered late-night call.

"My contact just informed me the buyer passed the test."

"The million bucks? It's clean?"

"As a whistle."

"That's great news, sir."

"Indeed. And you know what that means."

"I'm ready."

Of course you are.

"But sir … ?"

"What?"

"Have you considered if this is really the best buyer? A million dollars is one thing, but I'm sure it's nowhere near your final price tag. I would've thought such a big-ticket item would go to a larger buyer. More organized."

Of course I considered that … over a year ago. That's why I'm in charge and you do as you're told.

"Like who?"

"Maybe a foreign government?"

Such shortsightedness was disappointing, but he'd also come to expect it. Terrance Smith had his moments. He'd proven himself a competent spin artist and had a knack for influencing public opinion, but he wasn't the brilliant visionary he imagined himself to be. His strategic thinking was far too localized and limited.

He resisted the temptation to put Terrance in his place. He'd been working on this deal for too long to lose focus now. And, he needed his spin artist to feel valued for a few more weeks. After that, Terrance Smith would be eliminated. As would the three gutless turds naïve enough to think they were equal partners with him.

"Governments have too much bureaucracy, and they're a bunch of pansies who might renege. Plus, a lot of them would have to get legislative approval for a transaction of this size."

"Not the non-democratic ones."

"Who'd you have in mind? China? Our national debt has the feds watching China like a teenage boy staring at a naked woman. Not to mention they're a bunch of cheap communist bastards. That typhoon that hit the Philippines … China only gave a hundred grand in relief. IKEA alone gave a million and a half."

"What about Japan?"

"Those squint-eyed monarchists are doing everything they can to keep the Yen weak just to make their economy look strong. They don't have the cash."

"What about —"

"Explain your concern with my buyer, Terrance," he said, purposefully using *my* instead of *our.*

"Terrorist groups live in caves in the Middle East. How can they afford to pay the kind of money you're talking? My concern is they either know now they can't or don't realize it because they're so fly-by-night. And that either way, we'll get stiffed in the end."

"You're underestimating their financial organization. Don't be a victim of your own craft. When UN peacekeepers raided an Al-Qaida facility in Timbuktu, they found more than a hundred receipts and post-it notes documenting every expense the North African branch incurred. All the way down to a buck-eighty bar of soap. The Associated Press confirmed similar bookkeeping methods in Afghanistan, Iraq and Somalia."

"That's Al-Qaida. They're bigger, more sophisticated."

"Don't try to tell me you weren't thinking of Al-Qaida when you mentioned caves. Besides, my buyer is similar to Al-Qaida. They're both jihadist organizations, they share the same doctrine and they both want everyone to think they're unorganized vagrants. Unsophisticated, living underground, lacking financial sense and independence."

"But —"

"It's part of their strategy, and it hinges on misdirection. After listening to you, I'm even more convinced it works. The fact is they manage their money exceptionally well. They account for every single expense, from a pot of mustard to a tube of super glue. They're not fly-by-night and they're anything but primitive. They're a hi-tech conglomerate with an organizational structure that rivals most Fortune 500 companies, with a CEO, Board of Directors and workplace departments. They also have access to multiple investors and use their strong networks very effectively."

"But —"

"Terrance, I have my buyer. I'm confident they'll deliver the payment. This conversation is over."

"Yes, sir."

That's right, you pathetic peon. Do as you're told.

There can only be one at the top, and there's a reason I own four Lamborghinis.

"Your tactics connecting Peter Hubley to the PCC were well-executed," he said, reluctantly building up his spin artist.

Only a few more weeks and it won't be necessary.

"Thank you, sir. They seem to have garnered attention."

"Your primary target was quite affected as well."

"I'm glad to hear it, sir. I thought mention of an affair would resonate with Agent Benton. It's nice to hear things have gone according to plan."

"She's unfortunately been influenced by someone else. If she hadn't been, I'm confident your strategy would have driven her entire investigation."

"Thank you, sir. Regarding this man, do you want me to see what can be done?"

Riddle had considered that as well. But immediately after he'd read Ben Siebert's background, it was apparent there was only one remedy. Once he'd learned how much Siebert knew and who he'd told, he'd send Matthew J. Baker to pay him a visit.

"No, we're going to have to deal with him the old-fashioned way."

"I understand, sir."

"Prepare the next steps for my buyer," he instructed, returning to the original reason for his call.

"Will do, sir."

"Terrance, no screw-ups on this."

"I understand, sir."

19

"Are you sure he's coming?" Nikki finally verbalized what Ben knew she'd been thinking for ten minutes. The golf club's lounge clock read 1:05 p.m., making Tom Fedorak officially twenty minutes late despite his choosing the time and location.

"He'll be here."

"Because it's —"

"We can leave anytime you'd like. You're the one who wanted to meet him."

Insisted would've been a better word choice. After sleeping on his request for Peter Hubley's computer, Nikki called at six in the morning. She'd told him she could provide copies of Hubley's files, but that she wanted to speak directly with whoever would be looking at them. Despite his attempts to convince her otherwise, she was unrelenting in the request.

So here they sat, waiting for Tom.

She was wearing tan dress pants and a red sweater that accentuated her figure nicely. She looked better every time he saw her, but it was her personal story of perseverance and drive that intrigued him. She'd been dealt a terrible hand and played a bad one, but then pulled it together quite impressively to get where she'd gotten. Not many people have the determination or resolve to propel themselves like that, even if they did get a swift kick in the ass. As he thought that specific word, he couldn't help but picture hers.

"Grasshopper!" he heard from across the room.

Both he and Nikki turned to see the man of the hour. Tom was 6'4," two inches taller than Ben. He was in his mid-fifties and had short brown hair — but longer than Ben's — combed straight back, no gel. Gel was for sissies, he'd once told Ben. He sported a long-sleeved blue-and-black checkered shirt and an unzipped red flannel vest. He wore brown-rimmed bug glasses, as Ben had comically referred to them, with lenses so large they stretched broadly across his face.

"This must be the lovely Special Agent Benton," he said when he reached the table, holding a small red basket with two hot dogs and fries in one hand and a twenty-ounce Coke in the other.

"Call me Nikki."

"Indeed I will. Already on a first-name basis. Damn, I'm good," Tom replied, glancing at him.

"It's nice to meet you," she said after a slight chuckle, extending her hand.

"Oh no. We're here on this beautiful, sunny Monday afternoon, it's mid-October and I just played golf, and we're on a first-name basis. That calls for a hug, girlfriend," Tom smirked, wrapping both arms around her curvy body.

Ben couldn't help but feel a twinge of jealousy.

When satisfied with the unusually long embrace, Tom plopped down into a leather chair without as much as a handshake to Ben. Instead, he offered his standard, condescending greeting:

"How are you, Grasshopper?"

"Grasshopper?" Nikki said.

The question was for Ben, but Tom had other ideas.

"When I first met this youngster, he was a baby-faced, first-year Marine who didn't know his ass from a hole in the ground. He needed *tutelage*. He needed the best damn Marine supervisor the world had ever known. I felt sorry for the kid, so I showed him a thing or two. I used my expert skills over the course of the training to observe that he didn't know how to do a *lot* of things, so I took him under my wing."

"And started calling me Grasshopper."

"And look what a fine Marine you became. Not as good as me, but hey, there can only be one who's the best. Am I right, Nikki?"

At this point, Tom had Nikki in a full-out laugh, something Ben had yet to accomplish.

Tom dove in to hot dog one, overflowing with toppings of all colors, dropping most of them as he bisected it in a single bite. A long sip of Coke later, he smiled.

"Best hot dogs in the state. Want one, Grasshopper?"

"Didn't the doctor put you on a diet?"

"He sure did. Good thing I didn't put myself on one. If I did, I wouldn't get to enjoy this fine gourmet meal. You want one,

Sweetheart?"

"No, I'm fine," Nikki replied, still laughing.

"You just let me know if you change your mind. The offer's on the table. My treat. You, Grasshopper … you get your own damn hot dog.

"Golf, fishing and hot dogs. That right there is the key. That's the secret to happiness all those philosophers are always talking about. Write that down, Grasshopper. I ain't gonna be around forever to teach you these things."

Ben nodded, pantomiming note-taking and eliciting Tom's large smile with nearly all yellow teeth due to a lack of dental care. Tom offered his view of dentists once as, "They're only good for the nitrous, and I have that at home."

Hot dog one down, Tom was onto number two.

"Grasshopper here tells me you wanted to meet me, Sweetheart. Like what you see so far?" Tom was an odd bird to begin with, but his direct and unexpected question caught her off guard. But she quickly recovered.

"Well, you *are* a character. He told me that about you."

"And you *are* beautiful. He told me that about you."

Now it was Ben's turn to downplay a Tom Fedorak comment. He didn't fare as well, feeling his face blush, and Tom didn't let anything slide. Ever.

"Ah, Grasshopper. Don't get your panties in a bundle. She knows she's beautiful. Don't you, Sweetheart?"

"I, I don't know —"

"Well of course you do!" he shouted, widely displaying his yellow teeth again for her. She could only laugh, then thanked him for the compliment.

"That's what I'm here for, Sweetheart. To call it like it is. Grasshopper deserves some of the credit. Just not as much as me."

Though Ben and Nikki were wearing forced smiles, Tom was unfazed. He must've had them where he wanted them because he then launched into business.

"So, Sweetheart … what do you think about Peter Hubley and these files you'd like me to look at?"

"Well, it's actually Ben who wants you to look."

"What? You don't *want* an unauthorized stud muffin poking around your most significant piece of evidence?"

Nikki chuckled yet again; Ben silently cursed Tom.

"Are you afraid I'm gonna cook it up and eat it?"

"No, it's not that. I just —"

"Don't you worry about a thing, Sweetheart. I'll take good care and get everything back to you in no time at all. But anyway, back to my question about Peter Hubley ... what do you think?"

"Well," she said, shifting her weight to shake off the levity. "Reports claim he had ties to the PCC and —"

"Reports! I don't trust reports."

"Excuse me?"

"You're excused, Sweetheart. But it's like I've been telling Grasshopper here. You never know both sides of a report, much less the whole story. Reporters aren't people, they're reporters. They write what sells and sell what writes. Truth is a luxury they can't afford."

"But the police have —"

"You mean the Brazilian police? The same outfit that has itself been accused of working with the PCC in the past? And is more corrupt than the Washington lawyers? Tell me you don't put a lot of stock in what they have to say. A police captain in *any* country — including America — will tell you whatever story you want to hear if the price is right. Cops are as gullible and impressionable as the criminals they seek. And this particular police captain decided to tell his story ... what ... sixteen days after the murder occurred? That dog don't hunt, Sweetheart."

"But it was —"

"And did you see those photographs? That's not the kind of evidence you obtain after someone's death. You either have it beforehand, in which case it wouldn't have taken a legitimate police force two weeks to reveal it. Or —"

"Or you never had it in the first place," Ben finished.

"Now you're thinking, Grasshopper. I guess you do listen every now and then."

"I'm confused," Nikki said. "You don't think it's true?"

"Did I say that, Sweetheart? No, I didn't say that. I said that a police captain would tell you anything you want him to. Right now, it's speculation. That's it. You want to give him the benefit of the doubt because he wears a badge? I guess that's reasonable. Crazier than a rat in a tin shithouse, but reasonable."

"You're making assumptions that —"

"No, *you're* making assumptions. You can't just take a report at its word and call it a day. Is that what they teach at Quantico these days? Let the media do the investigating? Too many honest people have been ruined by assumptions for you to make them too. And right now that's all this is. Assumption. You prove it out yourself … you dig up the *facts* to confirm that story … that's a horse of a different color."

"What about the terrorist video?"

"What about it? You're the investigator, Sweetheart. I know it looks real and all, but awfully convenient timing, don't you think?"

"I guess so."

Tom pointed to the computer case by her feet.

"What's on that isn't opinion or assumption. Whatever we find — we know for a fact Peter Hubley was involved with it. Let the facts do the talking."

Digging into his mound of fries, Tom still wasn't finished.

"But keep asking questions. The ones no one else seems to ask. I already posed the first. Why was the Brazil cop so late revealing what he knew?"

"Because it's part of an investigation."

"So?"

"So, there has to be some degree of secrecy."

"C'mon … there hasn't been anything secret about this investigation from the moment Hubley got shot. It's been as public as it gets — the killers wanted it that way. They wanted to use the public's speculation to misdirect authorities."

"You can't prove that."

"I don't have to. Last I checked the burden of proof lies with the prosecution."

"Only in a courtroom."

"Precisely my point, Sweetheart!" Tom lifted both arms in the air.

"Look at you, a trained investigator from the most sophisticated investigatory unit in the world, already drinking someone else's Kool-Aid. If *you* do that, how can anyone else be expected not to? People have been told what to think. And the evidence to support it just isn't there. It'd never fly in a court of law, at least not in the

U.S. But the public? The public's already made up its mind about Peter Hubley."

Tom's words reminded Ben of Sidarta's. Ben watched Nikki absorb them and try to make something useful out of them. It'd been clear to him that she had assumed the worst of Peter Hubley after the story broke, but he hadn't called her on it.

"And how about what happened to the shooters?" Tom continued. "Nobody's talking about that. Why? Did they both choke on a piece of food at the same time? Do you really think the PCC hijacked that ambulance?"

"How did you know about that?" Nikki asked of the information she'd assumed was confidential.

"Why is no one asking? Where's that in all these reports?"

No answer was offered and silence filled the room until all of Tom's fries and the balance of hot dog two were gone. He checked the wall clock and noted he'd better get to work, promising to have the computer back in twelve hours. Nikki sat silently next to Ben, pondering the assumptions she'd made and the questions she'd ignored.

———

The Glen Eagle Golf Club was a public course that branded itself private — using everything from its separate dining room to its ornate locker rooms to its two-course layout. The dress code and the courses' pristine conditions supported the branding initiative. But he didn't so much as have to provide Matthew J. Baker's driver's license to get on the grounds.

There was no gate, no guard, and no hassle.

Instead, he'd driven the rented Honda Civic up the long, winding blacktop path all the way to the clubhouse and sat unnoticed and undisturbed. The concealed camera then started taking continuous pictures of Nikki Benton and the man walking to their cars.

She looked younger than in her picture, her brown hair hanging down to her shoulders, draping over her ample breasts beneath that tight red sweater. Her toned figure and skinny waistline made him consider what he'd do if Mr. Riddle arranged a private meeting between the two of them. The mere thought of getting her alone in a room pumped blood to his extremities.

As Benton and the man drove off in separate cars, he grabbed the camera and e-mailed two of its images before using his phone.

"You were right, Mr. Riddle. I just sent you the photos."

20

Unsure why Redmond requested to see her after hours, Nikki entered his office and wrinkled her nose at Spot's ominous odor. Sitting down in front of her boss's desk after a very long day, she silently counted down the hours to Tom Fedorak's deadline.

"Who do you think you are, kid?" Redmond yelled as he entered, the vein in his forehead ever present. Wrinkled, rolled-up shirtsleeves, a loosened tie and a worn face indicated he'd had a long day as well.

"Sir?"

"Don't *sir* me. What makes you think you can copy Peter Hubley's computer files without asking me?"

She knew copying files wasn't standard practice — and she silently cursed Ben Siebert and his stupid logic for convincing her it was okay — but she didn't expect to be confronted like this. Lead investigators were given generous leeway to do what was necessary, to find the information and get the job done. Copying the files may've been a breach of protocol, but it didn't seem abominable. But despite limited interaction with Redmond, she knew right away she'd better choose her words carefully.

"Sir, with all due respect, I've been to Peter Hubley's house twice. I've spoken with his widow, I've visited his office, I've read every single page in his file four times, and I've gotten nowhere. Not one viable lead. A few days ago I read a newspaper article linking him to the same organized crime outfit that both you and the rest of the world believe killed him. Why *wouldn't* I copy his computer files?"

"Because that's not how we do things here. That's why!"

Redmond paced his office, sighing and swearing, rubbing his thick bush of a mustache before approaching his favorite office inhabitant and tapping the glass terrarium. The close up with Spot calmed him down and his volume followed suit, but his bulging vein verified he was still one pissed off boss.

"Agent Benton, you've disappointed me," he said while taking a seat behind the desk. "You've disappointed me so much that I called your old manager, Robert Stevens, to see if that kind of crap flies in the Phoenix office. Take a guess what he said."

"That it doesn't fly."

"That's right. And neither does keeping the Special Agent in Charge out of the loop. When you transferred here, all Stevens could talk about was how meticulous you were. How you were one of the best, most dedicated agents he'd ever seen. How he'd keep you another eight years if he could. What I want to know is, where is *that* person? Where's the agent who pulled back-to-back all-nighters to analyze financial records so she could nail a thief at the border? Where's the agent who turned in a co-worker for accepting a bribe her first year on the job?"

She didn't reply, and Redmond let his words linger for a while before finishing. His conclusion was worse than his introduction.

"In the past six months, I haven't seen her. And I *need* her, Agent Benton. *I* need to be the guy who eight years from now is singing your praises, pissed off that he lost you because you moved on to greener pastures."

Greener pastures my ass.

"I'm sorry I didn't discuss it with you first."

"Sorry doesn't cut it, kid. You don't beg for forgiveness instead of ask for permission in this office, understand?"

She nodded.

"*Do you understand?*"

"Yes, sir."

"I should suspend you. You violated procedure for copying confidential information and broke just about every rule we have for doing so. You've prevented the lab from fully analyzing the data first, potentially contaminated it, and could've jeopardized the entire case. My better judgment tells me you deserve a hard kick in the ass right out the front door."

She only stared, waiting for what now seemed the inevitable end of her ten-year FBI career.

"But at least you logged it, and that tells me you're not *trying* to be malicious. You were just being stupid."

In truth, she'd only logged it because she knew he'd find out anyway. The keycard access reader to get into the evidence locker

— not to mention the camera inside — would show she'd copied the files, logged or not. That became the second comment she refrained from making.

"Logging it doesn't make it okay. But I'm going to assume it means you just made the huge mistake of not asking me. As opposed to trying to sneak away unnoticed with confidential information."

"Thank you, sir."

The last comment she withheld was that in Phoenix — as well as in any other well-run office — the SAC didn't play cowboy and do the investigatory work. Rather, he or she assigned a duty like getting the computer in the first place to the lead investigator. But that seemed moot now.

"Look, kid," Redmond said in a softer voice, "I realize I gave you a tough case with limited info, and that I told you to do everything you could. But I also asked if you were up for it, if you could handle it. And you said yes."

"I am up for it and I can handle it, sir. I'm very sorry for not talking to you first. It won't happen again."

"It'd better not."

Redmond shook his head silently, looking down at the open manila folder in his hands, her anxiety skyrocketing with every quiet second. She tried not to move when she felt her armpits moisten.

"We're going to pretend this never happened. Just this once. I want the duplicate files on my desk first thing tomorrow, along with a detailed report of anything you learned and your *assurance* there are no other copies. You understand me?"

"Yes sir. Sir … thank you, sir," she said, conspicuous relief radiating from her face.

And she meant it, sincerely.

She'd realized over the course of their conversation just how right Redmond was. What she'd done was grounds for immediate suspension if not outright termination. She could be charged with a crime, since she technically broke the law. Yet even though she'd never seen eye-to-eye with Redmond and had many times rued the day she started working for him, he was cutting her a break. A large, undeserved break. He didn't owe her anything, and the grace he was showing smacked her in the face harder than any backhand could have.

Maybe he wasn't such a prick after all.

Knowing Robert Stevens, her mentor and friend, was aware of her actions made her feel even more ashamed and remorseful. Her anger towards Ben Siebert grew. She was so pissed at his smooth talk gibberish and convincing words and good looks. She started fantasizing about what she'd say the next time she saw him. But the fantasy was ephemeral, cut short by a game-changer.

"Take a look at this," Redmond said, extending the manila folder out to her.

―――

In contrast to most government dossiers the manila folder was relatively thin, and its contents explained its purpose without referencing a dozen others. There were three separate documents: a two-page, unsigned introduction letter, two BANK of CAYMAN ISLAND monthly statements, and two wire transfer receipts for those same Cayman accounts. After quickly reading them all, Nikki realized why the dossier was so straightforward.

This was no government document.

Redmond kept quiet, waiting until she flipped the final page and looked up before speaking. Hands folded behind his head, he leaned back in his leather desk chair.

"Believe it or not, kid, it bothered me just as much as it bothered you that we didn't know why this case made its way to our office. Interpol Brasilia for *some* reason contacted Interpol Washington, and I didn't appreciate not knowing why. So I made some calls to Headquarters and cashed in some favors to get this sent to me earlier today."

"Are these official?" she asked, holding up the bank statements.

"As official as it gets. Interpol confirmed that not only the accounts exist, but that both the wire transfers were executed on that date."

"September 29th," she read aloud.

"Yup."

"The account owners … is what the letter says correct?" she asked, holding up the two-page introduction.

"Brazil police verified it this afternoon."

She sighed and scratched the sudden itch on the back of her neck, dropping the letter, thinking through what it all meant. Redmond just stared, the vein no longer bulging, his eyes fixed on her.

"Sir, you're telling me that two days before Jose Luiz Lettnin and Floriano Felipe Pereira murdered Peter Hubley, money was transferred to both of their families' bank accounts?"

"That's what I'm telling you. Lettnin's wife and Pereira's cousin, both living in Brazil, both too poor to have Cayman accounts let alone money like this."

"What makes you say that?"

"Lettnin's wife is a homemaker and Pereira's cousin works in the mines. Best the Brazil police can tell neither was involved with the PCC. But even if they were, and they got some cash on the side, this kind of money is way beyond the PCC's purse strings."

"Is it true the names on the accounts are different than their actual names?"

"Brazil police confirmed both names are pseudonyms. But it also verified those pseudonyms belong to the shooters' wife and cousin. Turns out it's not nearly as hard to set up an account with a bogus name in the Cayman Islands as it is in the States."

"What'd the bank say?"

"That it's not their job to spot pseudonyms. And that all the appropriate documentation was there when the accounts were opened."

"Did we get *anything*?"

"The bank wouldn't give our agents in the Caymans much, even to aid an investigation. The criminals threw that privacy crap at 'em pretty quick. But our guys did learn that both the accounts are configured the same way. Four percent, continuously compounded interest rates, locked as long as no withdrawals are made for at least twelve months. After that, the funds are fully accessible by phone. All the account holders have to do is wait a year, make a call, and get the cash."

"False account names and a waiting period."

"It's perfect," Redmond replied. "Perfect if you want to hide a transaction and give the story time to blow over before family members get the money. Nobody down there will remember the

Hubley shooting in a year; much less connect it to a change in the relatives' lifestyles."

"Which means —"

"Which means someone paid these guys a ton of money to kill Peter Hubley. According to the letter, someone from the U.S.. One-and-a-half million reais. Just under $750,000 each, depending on the exchange rate. With their interest rate, the accounts will each grow to over 1.1 million bucks in ten years, plenty of money to live off for the rest of their lives. Whoever did this is clever and loaded. And far more concerned with getting rid of Hubley and framing the PCC than the money."

"And keeping the investigation in Brazil," she added.

"Yes, this was perfectly executed diversion. The only thing that doesn't add up is Hubley's connection to the PCC, but I'm starting to doubt even that now."

"Is the life insurance policy real? The letter says each shooter recently took out a five-million-dollar life insurance policy."

"That couldn't be confirmed because the insurance company won't disclose anything and legally doesn't have to. That privacy crap really pisses me off … these companies don't have to tell us jack squat. But based on the transfers we know to be legitimate, it wouldn't surprise me at all if the policies were too. Whoever this guy is, he sure knows his way around dirty money."

"Did they try to trace the wire transfers?"

"Of course they did. The letter claims the money originated from a U.S. source and was filtered through multiple offshore accounts, laundered so clean we wouldn't be able to trace it back to the source even if we knew where to look. But because of that, there's no evidence either. Right now it's just a claim in a letter, totally unfounded. When they traced the wire transfers to the Cayman accounts, the trace led to a small bank in Switzerland that doesn't have a single account holder on record."

"How's that possible?"

"The bank acts solely as a middleman for transferring money. Can you believe that? Its *only* purpose is to execute protected transfers … they're a bunch of crooks."

"Did they —"

"You don't survive in the banking industry by only transferring money unless the money you're transferring is as dirty as a soiled diaper."

Stevens had said the same thing once in Phoenix. That most banks in Switzerland were perfectly legitimate, but that the ones responsible for the stereotype really do exist. And they earn the label by facilitating the illegal flow of money, not just sheltering it.

"And because that's all this bank does," Redmond continued, "they know how sensitive the information is. If you think insurance companies are stingy with client information, try asking a Swiss bank. Last week a Senate investigation estimated Credit Suisse Switzerland has over 22,000 U.S. clients, yet the government only has record of 240 of them. These banks won't tell you a client's favorite color without sign off."

She withheld response, absorbing what Redmond said. The law was written to protect consumers, not aid the police. Even if they got a subpoena to force a statement or testimony, both would lack the details they really needed and most likely just regurgitate the facts they already had.

"What about this letter?"

"What about it?"

"How did we get it?"

"As I understand, the whole dossier was sealed in a standard brown envelope and left in a mail drop box. Mail routings confirmed the drop box is somewhere in the Chicago metropolitan area, and the USPS is trying to track down which one. But don't get your hopes up."

"Return address?"

"Did you know that if an envelope's return address and send to address are the same, the postal service is required by law to deliver them, even if there's insufficient postage?"

"Where was it sent?"

"Sao Paulo Civil Police Headquarters."

"When?"

"They received it five days after Hubley was murdered. When they did, I'm sure they were more than happy to call Interpol Brasilia and ask for our help. And here we are. The reason we're involved."

"Five days seems really fast for international mail," she replied, thinking of travel distance and customs.

"Evidently, mail marked URGENT AND CONFIDENTIAL in big red letters and addressed to Brazil Civil Police Headquarters gets upgraded to Global Express Guaranteed service and shipped FedEx. One-to-three days, door-to-door."

"If we can ID the drop box, we could look for surveillance —"

"We could look for surveillance cameras in the surrounding area to try to get a picture, and then run that picture through our database to get an ID?"

More angered than impressed, she didn't respond.

"Like I said, kid, don't get your hopes up. Even if the USPS can somehow identify which drop box was used, there are plenty of those things in residential areas nowhere near a camera."

"Well —"

"The next one you're going to ask about is fingerprints. Let me save you the time. Even if the sender's prints are on the envelope, which at this point is remote, can you imagine how many other hands have touched it? Global Express or not, the package went from Chicago to Miami, through customs, and then to a Sao Paulo sorting facility before it even arrived at police headquarters. And I'm sure the URGENT AND CONFIDENTIAL label and address garnered some extra attention in customs. Drop boxes and surveillance cameras might work in the movies, but this is the real world. The only play we've got here is to start with the sender's vantage point and work our way back. To follow the money trail, look wherever that person was looking, and see where it leads. And that's what I need you to do."

"Sir, I —"

"By the way, you can bet your ass the transfers weren't a simple one-two punch. There were probably at least three or four intermediates. Banks, wire services, holding companies, whatever. Whoever dished out a combined $1.5 million through a private Swiss bank that doesn't have accounts is certainly resourceful enough to add a few links to the chain. Find even one of them, and the floodgates might open."

"Sir, I —"

"It's almost seven o'clock. You're dismissed. Oh, and Benton ..." he said as she rose from her chair, "I want daily updates from now on. Everything you find, everyone you talk to. That crap you pulled with Hubley's computer files could've put this entire office in jeopardy. Don't ever do anything like that again."

21

"Where's Sweetheart?" Tom asked when Ben sat down in the only corner booth of Dick's Diner.

At ten o'clock, the restaurant was empty except for an elderly couple sipping coffee and reading their morning paper. It reminded him of Anna when they switched sections and smiled at each other, one of his old favorite morning routines.

Tom's table consisted of a full pot of coffee sitting on a potholder, a plateful of hash browns, a huge omelet and a gigantic glass of orange juice with a piece of apple pie and whipped cream on the side.

"Thanks for waiting." Ben smirked.

"You said you already ate with Sport."

"I still don't get why you call Joe that. He's not a dog, you know."

"There's a lot you don't get, Grasshopper. But let's not open that colossal can of worms. You're late."

"It's ten o'clock exactly."

"What do I always tell you? If you're early, you're on time. If you're on time, you're late. If you're late, you're screwed."

"This coming from the guy who made me wait twenty minutes yesterday."

"But you need me more than I need you," Tom said, cleaning his bug glasses with a napkin.

"Piss off, professor," he replied, revealing a cunning half-smile. "What the … " he said, pointing at Tom's plate, his mouth hanging open in disbelief.

"What, you've never seen a hot-dog-and-sausage omelet before?"

"Are you *trying* to kill yourself?"

"What are you talking about? My doctor's always barking in my ear about breakfast being the most important meal of the day."

"I'm sure this is what he had in mind." Ben gestured to the delicious-looking piece of steaming apple pie. It looked so good, in fact, that he grabbed Tom's unused spoon and cut into it. It was sugary and warm and had the perfect amount of apple filling.

"What do you think you're doing, Grasshopper?"

"Watching out for you, boss. This stuff will kill you."

With anyone but Tom, the timing was perfect for a jab about his age. Tom was sixteen years older and looked every bit of it. But Ben learned long ago that age teetered on Tom's line between sarcasm and respect. And as sarcastic as their relationship was, it was based on the latter, not the former.

"I appreciate your concern for my health, but why don't you let me take care of myself, Grasshopper. You've got your hands full with Beautiful Agent Benton."

"She's not —"

"Pipe down, Grasshopper. All I said was she's beautiful."

"Well she sure showed a different side of herself with you, I'll give you that."

"Oh?"

"All giddy and smiley, laughing all the time. It was a nice change."

"I have that effect on women."

"Don't get to excited. She told me you remind her of a late uncle."

"I'll take what I can get, Grasshopper. Speaking of which, I'll ask again: where is she?"

"I'll fill her in."

Tom stared through the giant bug glasses and didn't say a word. He didn't have to. Ben knew exactly what he was thinking and felt guilty for it. Nikki provided copies of Hubley's hard drive files and in doing so, demonstrated her trust in him. By not including her now, he was purposely not reciprocating that trust.

Tom didn't press, much to his relief.

"I started by doing a complete and thorough scan of the files. Most of it was pretty run-of-the-mill. He definitely didn't have stuff on the PCC or anything like that. I scanned his deleted browser history and looked at all his Cookies, even the archived ones, after the company's thirty-day auto refresh. No mafia hits, no police searches, no organized crime."

"That doesn't surprise me. Most companies track what their employees search on the web. Hubley was too smart for that."

"Well, I checked every single file and they're all squeaky clean. It's pretty likely he had stuff on the shared network, but I don't have access to that."

"That's just great. After all that hoopla about getting the files, they turn out to be useless."

"Not so fast, Grasshopper." Tom took the final bite of apple pie. "Like I said, 99.9% of his files were standard. .DAT, .PPT, .DOC, .XLS, .PDF, whatever. All those files were either on Hubley's desktop or in folders, easily accessible."

"Okay … " he replied, bending his fingers to invite more information.

"But just to make sure, I downloaded a data recovery program and connected it to Hubley's laptop via USB to run the application."

Ben was skeptical of data recovery programs. From Piriform's "Recuva" to SnapFiles's "Restoration" to Glarysoft's "Glary Undelete" there were tons of data recovery programs available to consumers. They vary in functionality, but they all make the same promise: to recover those treasured yet deleted files. Ben had worked with nearly all of them and none delivered on that promise.

"And?" he replied, openly pessimistic and well aware that Tom knew where he stood on those programs.

"I found just a handful of .LOG and .BLT files."

"A handful of *what?*"

"Exactly. My first thought was that I didn't know they turned a sandwich into a computer file. Even *I* had to look 'em up. You believe that crap?"

He did indeed. He'd never heard of those extensions, and he knew a lot of file types.

"Turns out they're AOL Instant Messenger files."

"AOL? I didn't think that still existed."

"Me neither. With FaceTime and Skype and all the other programs out there, it's outdated technology."

"Not to mention text messaging. Same concept but a lot quicker, and you don't need to be in front of a computer to do it."

"To make it even stranger, Hubley had Microsoft Office on his computer."

"Which comes with Skype," Ben said.

"That's right, Grasshopper. Microsoft converted its Live Messenger service to Skype years ago to roll with the times. Now every user has the newer program, including Hubley. So why did he have the archaic AOL?"

"To hide something." He finally saw where Tom was headed.

"That was my assumption, so I looked into the file types. The .LOG is a manage tool that allows users to save chats as text files. It's the behind-the-scenes version of the conversation users see in .HTML when they open a saved chat. The .BLT is a saved buddy list file that displays all the user's contacts."

"Were there any conversations saved?"

"It's not much. Hubley is the Bears."

Tom reached into his flannel vest pocket and withdrew a folded piece of paper, then slid it across the table. Ben unfolded it and read the short conversation:

Cubsfan 101 — Instant Message

Cubsfan101 (11:01:22 AM): been thinking about our talk. this is for real.

Dabears1985 (11:01:39 AM): not now talk later.

Cubsfan101 (11:02:45 AM): that stuff you gave me. been looking at it and its pretty high tech.

Dabears1985 (11:01:39 AM): dude not now

Cubsfan101 (11:04:01 AM): ok but when? if im right, we cant wait

Dabears1985 (11:04:58 AM): tomorrow. after work.

Cubsfan101 (11:05:12 AM): k ill call u

Dabears1985 (11:05:49 AM): no more chats like this

Cubsfan101 (11:05:12 AM): just be careful dude thought you were crazy at first but now you got me thinking

(11:05:34 AM): Dabears1985 has signed off

"Don't you hate how grammar goes out the window on those things? Pisses me off," Tom said as Ben looked up.

"Like I said … " Tom took a large swig of orange juice. "It's not much, Grasshopper. But when you consider that Hubley only had one contact on his buddy list and that he was using the dinosaur AOL when Skype was right there —"

"You have to figure he was trying to keep it under the radar."

"Exactly."

"But why? Look how cautious he is … he ends the chat before it starts. The other guy tries to talk to him and he shoots him down. If you're not saying anything important, why be so clandestine?"

"This is just the chat I found, Grasshopper. There could've been more that the software program didn't recover. Remember … another thing that proves Hubley wanted this secret is the fact that this whole conversation wasn't even on his desktop."

"But there's nothing —"

"*Confidential* InvestSecure financial documents and his personal Turbo Tax files from last year were right there — a few clicks away. He left them out in the open for anyone to access. Didn't even put a password on them. But this seemingly innocuous chat … *that* he deleted. Now why would he do that?"

"He didn't even want anyone to know he had AOL."

"You're missing the point, Grasshopper. AOL was just the medium. He didn't want anyone to know who he was talking to. And more importantly, what they were talking about."

"He only talked to one person?"

"There was only one user on his buddy list."

"Do you think there are other chats?"

"I'm almost sure there were, but Hubley probably deleted them as he went. Like you said, he seems pretty paranoid about secrecy."

"But we don't know why he's paranoid."

"Be that as it may, I'd be surprised if he didn't delete the chats right after he had them to keep his computer clean."

"Then why'd you find this one and no others?"

"Because this was the last one. Remember, when you delete stuff from your computer, you're not actually expunging anything. You're just telling the computer to re-write over it. That's why I downloaded the recovery program to my own machine. I wanted to make sure I didn't use up any memory because that could've wiped out these IM files. All the recovery program did was search for files that the computer hadn't already written over. Look at the date."

"September 14th."

"Pretty close to when Hubley left for Brazil, right?"

"Right."

"So let's play this out, Grasshopper. Hubley needs some help from someone but doesn't want anyone at work to know. The phone's out because someone might overhear him and he figures e-mail and the company IM are too risky. Too visible. So he sets up an ancient AOL chat account with a random user name and tells his buddy to do the same."

"Then he deletes the chats to cover his tracks. And when he saves other files, the system re-writes over the chats he just deleted."

"And that prevents the recovery software from getting the older chats."

"But then he gets killed in Brazil —"

"Only a few weeks after his last IM chat."

"And he hadn't saved enough other files to re-write over it."

"So the recovery program finds that last chat and the buddy list, because that opens automatically when someone sends you an IM. But it doesn't find anything else."

Ben fell backwards in the booth and stroked his smooth chin, playing it over in his mind. Tom punctuated his large glass of orange juice with an incredibly large belch into space previously occupied by soft whispers.

"It all makes sense, but what help is it?" Ben ignored the impressive burp. "There's nothing on this chat. No specifics, no hints at what they're talking about, no next move, no meeting place. We don't even know who Cubsfan101 is. And without that, we don't have anything to go on."

"You've got a lot to learn, Grasshopper."

22

"I know you're in there! Open up! Open this door right now or I swear I'll break it down."

She screamed like a madwoman in a quiet neighborhood after nine p.m., but only one thing mattered at the moment. Over the past ten years, emotion and logic fought many a battle in her mind. This time, emotion handily prevailed.

"Nikki, what are you doing?" Ben Siebert asked, opening his front door.

"You son of a bitch!" she cried, pushing herself inside.

"What's going on?" he said in that disgustingly-charming soft voice.

"Are we partners or not?"

"What are you talking about?"

"Don't pull that crap with me."

"How about we talk over a cup of tea?"

"How about you answer my damn question?" She threw her suede coat hard against the ugliest brown recliner she'd ever seen.

"I'm sorry I didn't tell you."

"You're *sorry?*"

"I should've —"

"You know what, Ben? I don't care. I really don't. If you don't want to help me, fine. If you want agents on you like white on rice, fine. If you want the FBI to consider your son an *accomplice*, fine. But you asked for my help and you can't have it both ways."

"I know, Nikki." His facial expression seemed so genuine ... but was he really just a slippery salesman?

"You lied to me. When you gave me back the computer, you told me it was a dead end. That Tom didn't find anything."

"I know."

"I was this close to getting fired for trusting you. And you looked me right in the eye. *And you lied to me.*"

He didn't respond.

"I met you halfway. I broke protocol and got you what you asked. And you treated me like your little bitch. Fetch this, fetch that. Now sit."

"I can't undo what's done. I was going to tell you though."

"I'm tired of your games." She snatched her coat and headed towards the door, determined to never speak to him again. But he grabbed her arm and held her back. He wasn't even trying, but she could sense how strong he was. His biceps pushed tight against his orange polo and his large forearms flexed.

"Don't leave. Please. I'm sorry for not telling you first. But hear me out. Have a cup of tea with me. I'll tell you everything I've got and why I didn't tell you sooner. If you want to leave after that, I won't try to stop you."

She pondered the offer and took note of his place. It was different than she'd expected. The living room had hardwood floors and dark-brown walls. There was no clutter and it was surprisingly clean. Neatly folded blankets sat in a large basket next to a comfy-looking couch. Two lamps on end tables illuminated the inviting space, and what had to be about fifty nutcrackers of all shapes and sizes sat atop shelves surrounding a wall-mounted flat screen.

"One cup of tea. But don't ever expect me to trust you again."

"I won't."

————

She followed him into the spacious kitchen, granite countertops wiped clean and an extensive tea collection displayed in an open cherry wood box. She selected her favorite — Sleepytime's Cinnamon Apple — and they sat at the light-brown kitchen table, Ben at the head. He offered her a cookie and she declined. Then he paused for a long moment, as if trying to decide whether or not to have the conversation.

But once he started talking, he didn't stop. He went on for nearly twenty minutes, telling her what he claimed was the full extent of Tom Fedorak's findings. She listened carefully and interjected questions as they came, trying the whole time to gauge his honesty. But she had no idea what to believe. He was so calm; so convincing and real. But she knew all too well that she had a weakness for convincing guys with a soft side.

When he finished, he took a sip of tea and waited for her response.

"Just so I understand … why was it you didn't tell me this sooner?"

"Because right now there's no proof. All we've got is a hunch from a guy who tends to be right more often than he's wrong."

"That's another thing. Since when is a sixty-year-old man who eats hot dogs for breakfast so proficient with computers? I had Tom pinned as Stone Age, not cutting edge."

"Tom's full of surprises. Deception's a big part of what makes him so effective."

"I'll say. But you shouldn't have lied to me."

"I get that, okay? And I've already apologized. My thinking at the time was that without this evidence — evidence you weren't supposed to have — talking to Hubley's chat partner would've compromised you."

"You expect me to believe you were watching out for me?"

"I don't expect anything. I'm just telling you the truth."

"So you say."

"Whether you believe me or not, the lead's pretty thin."

"Listen, you may be the rule breaker and I the rule follower, but it's my decision to make. Not yours. I could arrest you right now for interfering with an FBI investigation."

Ben extended his arms towards her, holding his wrists together as if waiting for the handcuffs.

"This isn't funny."

"I know it's not. And I know I should've told you sooner. And I'm sorry you got in trouble with your boss. But I can only apologize so many times. This is my story. I promise it's the truth and I'm sticking to it. It's your call to believe me or not."

"Did you say you *promise*? Don't you dare use that word if you don't mean it."

Every instinct she had told her to get out of there as fast as possible and put a tail so far up Ben's ass it'd tickle his throat. He'd lied to her before, and he'd done it with the same innocent face he now wore. His captivating blue eyes had deceived her then and there was no reason to think they weren't doing it now.

"I've got to go."

He nodded silently as she turned toward the front door and scooped up her coat without looking back.

23

He didn't believe his alarm clock: 3:12 a.m..

As the phone rang at what seemed twice its normal volume, Ben was convinced the time was off. Over twenty years of service had earned it antique status, and it must have finally reached the end. But SPARTUS clocks were indestructible. During his rehab — when he ran three miles every day and the alarm was permanently set for six a.m. — its infernal beeping often resulted in him throwing it against the wall. And that hadn't so much as dented that tank of a clock.

Maybe the power went out while I was sleeping. And took four hours to reset. Nope, the numbers weren't flashing.

"Hello," he said with a craggy voice.

"Hi, Ben."

"Nikki? Is that you? What —"

"I've been thinking about our talk."

"Do you know what time it is?"

"I have a proposition for you."

"Tell me tomorrow."

"It expires in thirty seconds, so I wouldn't hang up if I were you."

Balls.

He arose from bed and turned on his lamp, cursing that clock and its ominous display as his pupils adjusted to the sudden flood of light. Even in the Marines the earliest he'd started was five, and that was a long, long time ago. He coughed violently to clear his throat, doing so into the transmitter so Nikki could hear what she'd caused.

"Okay. What's your proposition?"

"If you ever lie to me again — and I mean *ever* again — I'm going straight to my boss and telling him you're my prime suspect."

"You know that's —"

"Let's look at what I know. I know you went to Brazil a week after Hubley was murdered. I know you took an interest in InvestSecure and have been to Hubley's house twice since."

"Sally asked me —"

"I don't *know* that. I only know that you went."

"What's this supposed to be?"

"It's a *promise*. You so much as fib about your birthday, you become the focal point of an FBI investigation. Something tells me once we start digging, we'll find you're more than capable of killing a man. Then you'll have the opportunity to prove your innocence under a microscope."

"You'd really do that?"

"There's only one way to find out."

He ran his hand over his head and gripped its short hair down to the follicle. He knew he didn't have much choice.

"I already promised you I wouldn't lie again."

"Then we have a deal?"

"Deal. Good night."

"Oh no, Benjamin."

"I don't like it when you call me that."

"Interesting. We're not done yet. You still have to make up for your lie."

"I said I was sorry!"

"That's nice."

"What else do you want?"

"You're a little flustered. I like that, Benjamin. It's nice to know you can lose your cool just like the rest of us."

"*What do you want?*"

"I want you to tell me something you'd rather not."

"What?"

"I want to know about Joe Leksa."

"What about him?"

"How did you meet him and how did he come to live with you? Someone's gone to great lengths to remove that information from your personnel file and his, and I think that someone is you. Since you dodged my question about him earlier, my guess is you'd prefer to keep that to yourself. So, that's my price. I think it's more than fair."

"It's three in the morning. Let's do this tomorrow."

"Actually it's 3:14. And Pi's my lucky number."

"A non-repeating, non-terminating decimal is your lucky number? What kind of childhood did you have?"

"A beautiful pattern of nature is nothing to sneeze at. Quit stalling. I've got all night and you've got as long as it takes to tell me."

This woman was really getting on his nerves.

"Fine. When Joe was eleven, Anna and I caught him trying to break into our house."

"Why didn't you call the police?"

He didn't answer.

"Ben … time's a wasting."

"Because he was only looking for something to eat. We had a hard time turning him in for that."

"What about his parents?"

"His mom died when he was five and his dad is a pathetic excuse for a man."

"That doesn't mean you can just keep him."

"After we caught him, we brought him inside and gave him our leftovers from the restaurant. My wife made him wash his hands first, and she saw the scars on his arm."

"Did you call Children and Family Services?"

"Yes, a friend of mine works there."

"And did they investigate?"

"Yes, and confirmed the abuse."

"What happened to Joe?"

"Anna felt sorry for him and wanted to take care of him until they found a permanent home. So he started staying with us."

"That's pretty unusual."

"She was a very generous woman."

"I meant that the courts would allow it so quickly. Foster care placement's a lengthy process."

"I have some connections that helped cut through the red tape."

"Of course you do. Then what happened?"

"After eight months Anna and Joe got pretty close, and she decided she wanted to adopt him."

"You were on board?"

"I'd never seen her happier."

"That's not what I asked."

"Joe and I weren't as tight as Anna and he were. But we were growing on each other."

"So you did it for her."

"No comment."

"And I'm guessing you used your connections to expedite the adoption process?"

"Yes."

"What happened to the father?"

"The courts issued a restraining order and he never saw Joe again. Six months later he got arrested for trying to rob a liquor store at gunpoint. Been behind bars ever since."

"How long after you adopted Joe did your wife —"

"Eleven months."

"And?"

"And Joe and I have been a duo since."

"Single dad … that had to be tough."

"I wasn't much, but I was all Joe had."

"And you knew that's what Anna would've wanted."

"Are you finished?"

"I'll see you tomorrow morning."

"You mean later *today.*"

"I'll give you an extra hour. Pick you up at nine."

24

Fall was definitely her favorite season. With the temperature in the high-fifties, many of the trees still hadn't lost their leaves but instead offered a collage of burning colors. The roads were dry, the air crisp, and Nikki felt rejuvenated after her late-night chat with Ben Siebert.

The daylight offered a much clearer picture of his lovely neighborhood. The lots were large, half-acre plots, allowing for plenty of space between homes. Trees lined both sides of the wide, freshly-paved asphalt streets. And a charmingly broad mix of houses — from tiny original-development ranches to four thousand square foot mega McMansions — diversified the subdivision nicely.

There was an abundance of green grass, no sidewalks or street lights, and the walking trail's parking lot at the end of the street recently repaved. She loved the smell of fresh asphalt. Overall, the neighborhood struck her as ideal for a family, but unique enough to avoid being classified as typical suburbia, defined by a smattering of cookie cutter homes on subdivided lots.

At exactly nine o'clock, Ben was waiting in front of his two-story, center hall colonial. The exterior was well-maintained: the shutters freshly-painted, beige siding almost completely dirt-free, and lawn immaculately mowed. He wore beige slacks, a charcoal long-sleeved button down, and a pair of black loafers.

"Hop in and it's yours," she yelled through her open window, holding up a large Dunkin Donuts coffee.

"What's in it?" he asked, climbing into her Chevy Malibu.

"Cream, no sugar."

He accepted it with a smirk and pointed to his wristwatch, tapping its glass cover.

"SEIKO — very elegant. And I *know* you're pointing at it to show it off, not to make light of the fact that you forced me to call you last night by lying to me. I lost some beauty sleep because of that phone call."

"Smart ass."

"Takes one to know one."

"I guess I deserved it."

"You sure did. I have a question."

"No more questions," he answered, rolling his eyes and bending his neck all the way back to show exhaustion.

"Nothing like that. Why do you wear your watch on your left hand?"

"Should I wear it on my foot?"

"Talk about a smart ass. You know what I mean. You're left-handed. Why not wear it on your opposite hand like the rest of the world?"

"I like to be different."

"That's for sure," she said, smiling.

"You're in a chipper mood today."

"A heart-to-heart conversation at three in the morning will do that to a girl."

"Whatever you say."

"About the watch … "

"It's something I learned from Tom. He told me once that anytime I'm in a foreign country where I might become a POW, I should wear my watch on my left hand to protect my trigger finger. Made sense at the time, and I just got used to it after that."

"Protect your trigger finger?"

"If they torture you, they often start with the finger that could do the most damage if you ever escaped. This way they'd cut off my right index finger, not my actual trigger finger."

Yikes.

"What?"

"There's a practical reason for everything you do, isn't there?"

"What'd you expect?"

"I don't know … either that there was no reason or that it was a silly one."

"Like what?"

"Like … you were riding a Ferris wheel with Anna and realized that when you wore it on your right hand, it dug into her leg. Something like that."

"Sorry to disappoint."

"Let's talk about Cubsfan101."

"His name is Eric Meyer. Forty-six years old, married for twenty-one years with three kids. Lived in River Forest the past eleven years and in the Chicagoland area all his life. No priors, not even a speeding ticket. Graduated from the University of Illinois and started work at the same software firm he's with now."

"That's where he met Peter Hubley?" she asked.

"Yup. They worked in the same department for nine years, doing high-level programming. They got to know each other at the office, became friends, and stayed in touch after Peter left two years ago to be Vice President at InvestSecure."

"What kind of programming does Meyer do?"

"Mostly corporate security systems, from what Tom's research shows. But basically he programs whatever's asked of him. He's brilliant — off the charts analytical skills and deductive reasoning. Could've moved into management years ago but never wanted to. He's a numbers person, like you. Wants to be left alone to write his programs."

"And he only recently set up his AIM account?"

"Five months before Peter got killed."

"And you're sure he set it up just to talk to Hubley?"

"They created their accounts on the same day and neither had used AOL for years before then."

"Do you think Tom will be able to access their previous chats?"

"He's looking into it but told me it's unlikely."

She turned at the ramp and revved up the engine to rapidly merge onto I-290. Traffic was light and she zipped into the express lane quickly. Ben sipped his coffee and stared ahead.

"Nice wheels," he said.

"Thanks. I call her Bu. Her automatic engine stop/start feature is pretty cool," she said of her recently-purchased, four-cylinder baby.

"Do you know how Tom gets his intel? Some of the information he finds isn't easy to get."

"I asked him once and he told me not to concern myself with things over my head. I took that as a 'don't ask' type answer."

"I would too."

"But it's legit. Tom's got more connections than you can imagine. And like you said yesterday, he's far savvier than meets the eye. In all the years I've known him, he's never been wrong when it comes to intelligence. Not once. And when it's speculative, he always upfront about it. You can bet the farm that Eric Meyer is who Tom's research says he is."

"And that is?"

"Best I can tell, he's a boring family man with a mundane job who's never so much as broken the rules, much less the law. A model citizen who pays his taxes, works hard for his family and coaches Little League. Outside of his AOL screen name, there's nothing that suggests we should have any reason to talk to him."

"And he doesn't know we're our way to see him right now?"

"Not unless you told him."

"What a nice little surprise he's in for," she replied, pressing down on the accelerator.

25

"They're on the move. Eastbound towards the city."

Dominick Riddle didn't immediately respond. Back in his North Carolina mansion, he rose from the leather-studded desk chair and paced past the basement's walkout doors, gripping his Scotty Cameron putter and pondering his next play. This news was disappointing, but he never let that show.

"You're certain Siebert didn't spot you?"

"Yes, sir."

"Continue following them, but make sure you remain unseen. Remember, Siebert is smarter than you think."

"I will, sir."

"Report back to me in an hour."

"Yes, sir."

Matthew J. Baker disconnected and Riddle ripped the headset from his ear and violently threw it against the wall before unleashing a string of expletives. After the outburst, he tried to consider the situation from different perspectives.

The malware was progressing very well, and that was paramount. Each of the developers was on track, in the debugging and checking phases, and the sum of their work would be revolutionary. Nothing would matter once it was complete, and that milestone was less than two weeks away. After that, Siebert and Benton could drive around together all they wanted.

Adir Mousa proved the terrorist organization could and would pay his price, and Mousa appeared high enough up the food chain to negotiate the deal. Negotiation, of course, was just a word. He'd tell Mousa what to pay and the sand nigger would pay it. The beauty of the free market is that if you create a product people want badly enough, you set the price. That's why he went to the lengths he did to validate the project at the beginning, before his investment. Adam Smith would be so proud.

The recent partnership between Agent Benton and the former marine was a concern. He wasn't worried about the FBI agent; he had her under control. But she obviously had some reason to work with and perhaps even trust Siebert, and Siebert was a wild card. He didn't follow the rules; he wasn't bound by the system and he'd already proven he was smarter than the feds.

But there was *always* a wild card, Riddle reminded himself. No matter how well planned an operation was, there was always something that popped up. Human nature is impossible to entirely predict. Even the Indian sugar project had a wild card. Sure, influencing the government to purchase cane at below product cost had cornered the market and driven the dollars where he wanted. But those Indian farmers were more resilient than expected, and that took unforeseen violence to rectify.

Wild cards were inevitable. The key was how to deal with them.

His spin artist, Terrance Smith, again offered his services on Siebert. And for five million dollars, he could see why. But the reality was Smith's approach with Hubley's PCC ties and affair didn't work on Agent Benton. Trying Smith again at this point was a waste of time and money. It was best to keep him focused on Plan X. Sand niggers had proven before that if caught, they'd either sing like canaries or be too stupid to prevent authorities from finding what they wanted on their own. And even though there was — of course — no connection to him, he needed Smith's Plan X just in case. No loose ends, no margin for error. The way winners did things.

Siebert couldn't be bribed. Even if that was a possibility in the short term, there was no telling how long it'd last once he realized who purchased the malware. He was smart, and he'd put the pieces together, and that might cause a crisis of conscience.

He also couldn't be threatened. Not even through his son, Joe Leksa. You didn't threaten a man like Ben Siebert. You didn't tip him off or give him time to react. You eliminated him quickly, without warning. And Matthew J. Baker was the man for the job. Docile as they came, Baker wouldn't ask questions. He'd say kill and Baker would say when.

But that couldn't happen until he knew the extent of the wild card problem, and that was taking too long to surmise. He needed to know who else should be eliminated, and Benton and Siebert would provide the answers. Patience was a virtue and he was virtuous.

Then, he'd kill them all — the three wimps who didn't support his brilliance, Terrance the haughty spin artist, the attractive Nikki Benton and the elusive Ben Siebert. The bloodbath would begin and end in the same day.

It was lonely at the top for a reason.

26

"Eric Meyer?" Nikki asked once they'd reached cubicle H8.

"Later," a high-pitched voice answered.

Meyer kept his back to them, typing on his computer with classical music playing in the background. His two-screen display had at least ten open windows and his entire workspace was layered with papers and empty Mountain Dew bottles. A black-and-white picture of a man in a suit Ben didn't recognize was pinned to the grey-cloth cubicle wall, above the quote:

YOUNG MAN, IN MATHEMATICS YOU DON'T UNDERSTAND THINGS. YOU JUST GET USED TO THEM.

Then, Meyer — still facing away — lifted both arms from his keyboard to eye level and bent each of his ten fingers simultaneously, knuckles cracking. Ben could hear him mumbling over the symphonic tunes but couldn't make out any words.

"I think he's in the zone," Ben whispered to Nikki, who was unimpressed.

"No, *now*," she said. "I'm Special Agent Nikki Benton of the FBI. We'd like a word."

The forty-six-year-old programmer swiveled his chair to face them. He wore a pair of dark blue jeans and a gray sweater with no collar, his white undershirt sticking out too far at the neck, and a pair of worn Asics. Black-rimmed glasses covered part of his face and mild acne covered the rest.

"The FBI? What do —"

"Is there somewhere private we can talk?"

"Um. Uh, yes. Follow, follow me."

Stuttering and almost falling out of his seat, Ben noticed Meyer left his coat and didn't lock his computer; even he knew that was a no-no for programmers. He wasn't an inch over 5'6" and walked so fast it was more comical than hasty. His tiny legs motoring ahead, combined with short, stiff arms locked down his side and a bulging head pointed straight towards the ground made Ben chuckle to himself as they followed.

Meyer paraded them down the hallway to a door that led into an outdoor quad smattered with concrete tables and uncomfortable-looking white benches.

"We'll try to make it quick, Eric. The reason we're here is because we're investigating the murder of Peter Hubley. I understand you knew him well."

"Well, I didn't know him well or anything. I … well … he worked here. I knew him from work. We weren't close or anything."

"You worked with him directly?"

"Yeah. I mean, a little. We were in the same department before, before he left the company."

"What department was that?"

"Advanced algorithms," Eric answered with his first stutter-free response.

"Was he a talented programmer?"

"Peter? Oh, he was very talented. I mean, I don't know. That's subjective. But I think so. He was very smart."

"You enjoyed working with him?"

"I, I guess."

"Did you ever see him outside the office?"

"No! Well, I mean, we had lunch. He liked burritos. I like burritos."

"That's nice. But did you ever see him socially?"

"Like at the movies?"

"I suppose. Or in any other non-work setting?"

"We maybe went to the movies once or twice. After work. I didn't see him on the weekends. I have a family."

"I understand, Eric. And please, relax. We're just gathering information. Peter didn't have many friends at InvestSecure since he was relatively new. So we're trying to get a sense about him from people who knew him."

Ben noticed Meyer's eyes widen when Nikki said InvestSecure.

"I was so sad when I heard what happened."

"A lot of people were."

"Yeah. He was … he was a really nice person."

Nikki didn't respond right away. Instead she merely nodded as a gentle breeze stirred the few un-raked leaves on the quad, spiraling them into each other to form a tiny cluster near Ben's feet. Meyer shivered, and Ben was almost certain Nikki had only a few minutes to do whatever it was she planned to do. She must've been thinking the same thing:

"I know your time is valuable, Eric. So let me get to the point. The reason we're here is because of your AOL screen name, Cubsfan101. It's come to our attention that you had several IM chats with Peter in the months leading to his death."

Meyer literally got up from his stone seat and then sat back down immediately. He started folding his fingers together and then separating them, and Ben wouldn't have been surprised if even in fifty-degree weather he started sweating.

"Here's a printout of the last chat," Nikki withdrew a sheet of paper and handing it to Meyer.

"Oh, that was nothing. He just, well he asked me to chat with him."

"I understand that, Eric. What I don't know is why?"

It was the smart move. Further beating around the bush was an exercise of futility at this point. Meyer wasn't going to calm down and he wasn't going to collect himself. Obtaining more information was quickly turning into a pipe dream. It was best to push him now and get whatever was to be gotten.

"He asked me about malware and stuff."

"By malware, you mean malicious software?"

"Uh, yeah. But I didn't do anything."

"No one is saying you did. But why do you think he was asking about malware?"

"I, I don't know. He had this mobile software project … I mean, I don't know why he was asking."

"What software project? Was he programming something at InvestSecure?"

"No, he was like, like an executive there. He didn't code."

"So why was he asking you about malware?"

"I, I don't know why he was asking. He only said it was important. He wanted me to look at it, look at it as soon as I could. I just … well he asked me and I...I was talking to him. That's all."

"Did he say where it came from?"

"No."

"Did he mention the PCC organization?"

"Oh, Heavens no!" To Ben, it seemed the first honest answer to Nikki's long stream of questions.

"Do you still have the malware code he sent you?"

"He didn't … *know* it was malware. He just asked. He asked me. And he was my friend. So I looked."

"And was it malware?"

Meyer became noticeably upset with himself for leading her there.

"I … I don't know."

"Back to my question, do you have it?"

"No, I threw it away."

"Do you have the e-mail he sent it in?"

"He just gave me a sheet of paper. Like that." Meyer pointed to the printout. "No e-mail."

"Eric, I need to know what he asked you. You're not in trouble; we're not here to interrogate you. But we need to understand why he came to you in the first place."

Meyer shifted his focus between Nikki and Ben, who remained silent. The wheels were definitely spinning in the quirky programmer's head. Nikki was on the right track, but Meyer didn't want to give more. The question was *why*.

"Peter was married with two kids and considered you a friend. Don't you want to help us figure out why he was killed?"

"I do want to help! Peter was such a nice person. He was my friend. I was so, so sad when I heard and I … " his voice trailed off. Ben noted Meyer's second escalation of his status with Peter, from its initial mere "co-worker he had lunch with" to "friend."

"You what, Eric?"

"He sent me some code and asked for my help. Like, if it looked okay."

"What do you mean, 'okay?' Do you mean 'legal?'"

"No. Well, maybe. But that's it. That's all I did. I … I looked at the code, and I tried to help Peter. That's it; I just tried to help my friend. Honest."

"Was it malware? Was it mobile malware?"

"No. I mean, I don't know. Peter didn't say much. He just asked for my help, and then he got shot. I felt terrible about what happened."

"Eric, there's more than you're telling us. Look at this printout. You're warning him, for Heaven's sake. We're the good guys here. You can help us here on your own terms … or you can make me go back and get a subpoena, drag you in front of a judge, and be forced to tell us on ours."

"And watch us interrogate your family," Ben chimed in with his first and only comment.

Meyer stirred noticeably and Nikki held up her hand, conspicuously displeased that Ben had spoken at all. She shot him a look and he merely stared back.

"Eric, don't you think it's best we just talk now? You're not in trouble. We just need to get to the bottom of this."

"I … I'm sorry. Really, you have to believe me. I'm sorry. I wish I could help more. I just … have to get back to work. I have to go."

27

At Ben's request, they made a quick stop at Larry's Joint, a pizza-by-the-slice establishment a few blocks from Eric Meyer's office. Given her frustration and hunger, she was in no mood to argue. Larry's offered pick-up and delivery only, less a tiny two-person table in the corner of the grimy tile floor. The "Dining Room," as identified by a handwritten yellow sign taped to the window, was next to filthy countertops in front of an open kitchen, affording her the opportunity to watch men without gloves prepare her food.

"This place is the best," Ben said.

As if that wasn't enough, her hunger eviscerated as she watched Ben manhandle three slices of greasy pepperoni and sausage pizza with extra cheese and extra sauce on top of enough deep-dish crust to exceed her weekly Weight Watchers limit. Ben didn't so much as come up for air, much less try to talk, so she picked at her crappy boxed salad with packet ranch dressing in silence. Then Ben paid the bill at the register and they headed back to Nikki's car — in and out of Larry's in 20 minutes flat.

"You could've pushed Meyer a little harder," Ben said, gesturing that he'd drive.

"Excuse me?"

"Excuse you. He was right there, kept saying how he wished he could've helped more. You could've nudged him along."

"I don't need you telling me how to interview a witness."

"We don't even know if he is a witness. For all we know, he's a suspect. What was with all that stuttering?"

"He was *scared*. He came to work this morning like any other day, then all of the sudden he's got an FBI Agent and a scary dude putting him through the wringer about his dead friend."

"The *wringer*?" Ben chuckled. "He doesn't have the first clue what the wringer feels like." Ben accelerated harder, pushing the speedometer to near seventy in a forty-five.

"Want to cool it at the red-lights? I don't need a hundred-dollar ticket to my FBI name," she said after yet another close call at a red-light camera intersection.

"You let him off too easy."

"What'd you want me to do, break out my water torture kit?"

"You're an FBI Agent. I wanted you to find something between that and holding his hand the whole time."

"I wasn't going to coerce him. We do this the legal way."

"Who said anything about breaking the law?"

"You're implying —"

"I'm not implying anything. I'm *saying* Meyer knows more than he told us. You had him by the balls, caught off guard and no help in sight. That's why he was scared. Piece by piece, he was filling in the blanks. If you'd leaned on him, he would've folded like a cheap card table."

"He also could've reported me for harassment. And then he'd *never* cooperate."

"He's not going to cooperate anyway. He already told you more than he wanted to. All you did was give him time to think about how not to next time. You lost the element of surprise and that was your best weapon."

"That's your theory."

"Right now he's calling an attorney and getting his ducks in a row. Next time you try to talk to him, he'll have a script in his hand and a suit by his side. Good luck getting anything from him then."

"I'm not going to harass the guy."

"I'm not saying you should. I'm saying sometimes you can't just accept what you're given. You have to go get more. Something I learned in the Marines."

"The Marines you got kicked out of, macho man?"

Ben didn't respond and she immediately felt regret. His face, as always, showed no emotion. But the sudden halt of conversation made her curse herself for a blow that she knew was below the belt.

What pissed her off the most was that he was right. She'd always played it straight and safe, personally and professionally. Rules were there for a reason and were most certainly *not* meant to be broken. But while that mantra might've worked in college relationships and computer programming, she'd found it to be a poor approach with fiancés and FBI fieldwork.

"I'm sorry, Ben. I didn't mean that."

"Don't worry about it."

"I just —"

"I said don't worry about it." He slowed to the speed limit.

"Thanks," was all she could manage, the car descending into uncomfortable silence.

"Did you recognize the picture in Meyer's cube above the quote about mathematics?" Ben asked.

"Sure, every Comp Sci major knows him. John von Neumann, inventor of CPU."

"That's one strange cat to put on your wall. Would a Derek Jeter poster kill the guy?"

The unexpected joke both eased the tension and caught her by surprise, prompting her to fling her head back and laugh.

"You've got a nice smile. You should wear it more often."

A few moments went by that felt like an hour.

"So, Ben ... do you mind telling me where you're taking us?" she finally asked.

"To find out why Peter Hubley was asking Eric Meyer about malware."

She thought for a brief moment.

"InvestSecure?"

"Yup."

"Not a bad idea. Not much else to do. I'll call their office to let them know we're coming."

"No, don't."

"Why?"

"Because you're about to see the element of surprise used to its fullest."

28

Karen Hovey, InvestSecure's kind, mid-fifties receptionist, greeted Ben and Nikki on the other side of the floor-to-ceiling glass doors. After passing the ornate fountain in the lobby and getting off a shiny, gold-colored elevator, Ben was reminded that image was critical to private equity firms.

"Why, hello Agent Benton," Karen said, removing her black-framed glasses.

"Good afternoon, Karen."

"And you're Ben, right? Mrs. Hubley's friend?"

"Hi, Karen," he answered, impressed by the recollection.

"What a surprise. How can I help you?"

"I need a word with Mr. Bodie," Nikki replied.

Good. Like I told you. Tell, don't ask.

"Let me page him. You can have a seat in the corner. It'll be just a moment."

Ben eyed two plush leather chairs that looked like they cost a small fortune. But once he sat down, he concluded they were worth it. As Karen dialed Bodie's extension, he noted numerous framed awards and newspaper stories lining the walls. One was a plaque commemorating twenty years of InvestSecure's sustained growth. Another highlighted the firm's local hiring presence, labeling it one of Chicago's "Best Places to Work." A third was a *Daily Herald* article, one of the suburbs' biggest newspapers. The Business section headline read "Special Q&A with Mr. Bodie Himself" and preceded a two-page interview regarding InvestSecure's founding and presence in the community.

"Let me show you to the conference room," Karen said once off the phone. "Mr. Bodie is just finishing up a meeting and will be right with you."

Inside the lavish conference room, an elliptical twenty-person, granite-topped table — while likely functional for board meetings — was more of a statement piece. Coffee pots stood at the ready atop the wet bar at the rear of the room, flanked with InvestSecure-logo coasters. A glass pitcher filled with something clear and carbonated sat on the table next to a pad of paper and a gold pencil jar.

Karen pressed a button and the projection screen at the front began to retract, exposing double east-facing windows with a clear third-story view of Interstate 90. The tollway exchange had a long queue of cars where the lanes merged, even at the low-traffic one o'clock hour. Taxis, most likely from O'Hare Airport, dominated the stream of vehicles creeping through the plaza.

"Can I offer you something to drink? Coffee or sparkling water, perhaps?"

"No thank you," Nikki answered for both of them.

"Very well. Mr. Bodie will be here shortly."

———

Ten minutes later, InvestSecure's Chairman, President and CEO Ryan Bodie III walked through the frosted glass doors wearing a pair of tan dress slacks, a long-sleeved pink button down and a white tie with a silver clip. The founder's short, salt-and-pepper hair was combed impeccably straight back, and his clean-shaven face had not even a freckle out of place.

"I'm sorry to keep you waiting." He greeted them with a smile.

"No problem, Mr. Bodie. You're a busy man," Nikki replied.

"Too busy it seems. I'm Ryan Bodie. And you are?"

"I'm Special Agent Nikki Benton of the FBI. And this is Ben Siebert, a family friend of the Hubley's."

"How is Sally?" Bodie asked, revealing the first-name basis he was on with his employees' spouses.

"Some days are better than others," Ben answered.

"I can imagine," Bodie wiped the smile from his face and replaced it with a solemn stare.

"I understand you founded this company. Stayed with it the whole time, huh?" Ben asked. He wanted Bodie back the way he was — comfortable, gleefully smiling, not thinking about Peter or preparing for the next question.

"Twenty-two years."

"Wow. You've seen a lot of change."

"Incredible amounts. Unforeseen amounts. When I first started, my sole motivation was to not have to pay my old employer fees out of my commission. Why give away so much of the money I sweated for, you know? I ran the numbers and calculated I could sell half as much stock and make twice as much money. So I decided to take the plunge and get a piece of the technology sector for myself. I knew the market from my years at the Merc and at the time, all I wanted to do was model a typical boutique investment firm. Make a little money and call it a day. I didn't even have an assistant. But one thing led to another and we've evolved into a much bigger operation than I ever imagined."

"You do a lot of M&A?" Another question to which Ben already knew the answer.

"That's the bulk of our business. I tell my employees to think of themselves as diamond hunters. There's a lot of rough out there and diamonds are hard to find, but when you do, it's worth it."

"I'll say. Pretty amazing you've grown as much as you have."

"We've worked hard. And we've got really great people. But we also caught a lot of breaks along the way. Some of the companies we acquired early on turned out to be even better bets than we thought. It just goes to show you that when you give good people the resources they need and let them do their jobs, they can surprise you."

"But you don't retain ownership, right?"

"Not our specialty. We find companies that need capital investments and usually a fair amount of restructuring. New ideas, new blood, that kind of thing. A lot of the companies we work with are past the entrepreneurial phase but not quite into execution. So they're caught between aggressiveness and steadiness, struggling for direction. That's a dangerous place to be, because it tends to result in upper management focusing exclusively on the company itself and not paying attention to what the broader marketplace is telling them. When you do that, you miss opportunities."

"So you set them up, get them back on track."

"We provide a timed plan, usually three years, and then give them the cash they need to meet that plan. But once the pieces are in place and they understand the strategy, we don't offer them much value. That's typically when we look for a larger organization that believes in their product and wants to manage the execution phase as a part of its overall operation."

And when you make a boatload of money.

"But anyway, I'm sure you didn't come here to listen to me talk about our business. How can I help you two?"

"As you know, I'm investigating the murder of Peter Hubley," Nikki said.

"Absolutely tragic what happened to him."

"We're trying to get as much background as we can, and I wanted to ask you a few questions about his work at InvestSecure."

"Anything you need, Agent Benton."

"Thank you, Mr. Bodie. Was Peter a good employee?"

"No. He was a *great* employee. Brilliant guy. One of the brightest software minds I've come across, and he also knew his way around a balance sheet. That was critical for us. Too often, the technical folks don't understand the business side. Peter was the perfect mix."

Ben thought of Eric Meyer and knew it to be true.

"How long did he work here?"

"About two years, give or take."

Ben reassumed control from Nikki.

"How'd you find him?"

"We outsource our recruiting to a third party. It's just too expensive to do it in-house, and we don't have the industry connections. We were getting pretty involved with some high-tech software companies we didn't fully understand. So I told Capital Search to look for electrical and computer engineers that had strong business acumen. Gave them a pretty stringent requirements list. Experience, education, career moves, things like that. They headhunted the market for six months and came back with one name."

"Did he come aboard right away?"

"No, I was actually surprised at how long he held out. Four interviews and almost three months of phone calls and lunches. The more he resisted, the more I wanted him."

"Why were you surprised? He'd been at his previous company for a long time, right?" Nikki asked.

Nikki's first mistake wasn't all that bad. Even so, Ben watched Bodie's reaction and knew exactly where his answer was headed.

The high-nine-figures-net-worth tycoon smiled, as if trying to decide how arrogant he wanted to be.

"Everyone has a price."

"And you're willing to pay that price," Ben quickly said.

"For the right people, you bet I am. Look, we've got 109 employees here, and I've interviewed every single one of them. They all went through a rigorous hiring process and they were all working somewhere else when we found them. Did everyone get the attention that Peter got? No. Did everyone get the same offer or signing bonus he got? Of course not. He was hired as a Vice President. A position like that usually takes a bit more … convincing. But everyone has a price."

"Do you always get your man?"

"That depends on how badly I want him. With Peter, I was determined to make it happen. But I didn't play Vito Corleone. He made his own decision."

"But you did make him an offer he couldn't refuse."

Bodie smirked. "Yes, I guess I did."

"What companies were you working with when you decided you need someone like Hubley?" Nikki snapped.

Ben tried not to reveal his disappointment at the naïve question, but found that task more difficult the second time around. Bodie's response reiterated why.

"I'm not at liberty to discuss that."

"Why?"

"Because we're still in negotiations with them, and you're not privy to what you're asking."

"I'm investigating a murder, Mr. Bodie."

"Tell that to the SEC."

Nikki paused and Ben tried to seize the opportunity to change subjects.

"Mr. Bodie, with regards to the —"

"Hold on a second," she said. "Just to make sure I'm clear on this. Mr. Bodie, are you saying you don't want to discuss your reasons for hiring Peter Hubley because you're worried about the Security and Exchange Commission?"

Bodie grimaced at Nikki, who had clearly identified herself as his opponent. The CEO kept his calm but Ben knew tension was building. She was losing the ground he'd made and while he understood what she was trying to do, her aggression was misplaced. She should've used it on Meyer; it was no match for Bodie. Not here and not like this.

"No, Agent Benton, that's not what I'm saying. In fact, I've already answered the question. What I don't want to discuss are the specifics behind the possible acquisitions of publicly traded companies. That's a conversation the SEC certainly doesn't want me to have and would probably consider insider trading if not fraud. And frankly, it's a conversation you're out of line for even asking me to have, much less feel entitled to be a part of."

"All I want to know is —"

"Agent Benton, *for the third time*, this is not a topic I'm at liberty to discuss. If you feel you have the right to force me to reveal this information, I suggest you contact the Bureau's team of lawyers and take the matter up with them."

Just then, a knock on the door was followed by Karen Hovey's reentrance into it, holding a silver coffee tray. Instantly silencing the room, her chipper personality clashed hard with the tension Nikki's question created. All three of them could only gawk at the receptionist, who couldn't have picked a worse time to offer beverages.

"I'm sorry to interrupt, but I thought you might like some refreshments. I know you said you didn't want any earlier, but maybe you changed your mind." As she picked up the metal server to begin pouring, Bodie revealed he was thinking the same thing Ben was.

"Thanks Karen. But they're about to leave and we need a moment."

"Oh, I'm so sorry," she said, dropping the server and quickly exiting, now aware of her inappropriate interruption.

"Unbelievable!" Bodie said. "She's a nice lady, but Heavens to Betsy, does she interrupt at the worst times. She's always doing that crap."

"She's just trying to be nice," Nikki replied.

Her comment catapulted Ben from annoyed to furious. What on earth was she doing? Was she *trying* to piss Bodie off? Did he not tell her to follow his lead? She was ruining everything, and that was bad enough. But on top of it, she chastised the CEO for comments about his own employee after she barged into his private meeting unannounced. *What was wrong with this woman?*

Every word out of her mouth further ruined his chances of getting somewhere with Bodie. If he let her go on, he'd have no shot whatsoever. It was now or never, under far less than optimal conditions.

"Agent Benton, I think it's time for you to leave."

"Mr. Bodie, let me get to the point," Ben sternly replied.

"I wish someone would! I'm tired of being lectured on what I can and can't say. And being accused of —"

"Cut the shit. No one's accusing you of anything. We're trying to get answers to tough questions and you're going out of your way not to help us."

"What did you say?"

"Did I stutter or are you deaf?"

"Just who do you think you are?"

"Agent Benton already told you my name."

"What business does the victim's family friend have with an FBI investigation?"

"None, thank God."

"Then what are you —"

"I'm here because I know Peter Hubley was doing something illegal. And I know he was doing it for you."

"I'm not going to stand for this."

"That's right ... you're not going to stand. You're going to *sit* there in your preppy-ass slacks and *listen* to what I have to say. You want to play games with her, that's fine. But try to play them with me and I'll cram that pink shirt so far up your ass you'll gag on it."

29

Ryan Bodie III was no longer cocky, no longer unfettered. In a matter of seconds, Nikki watched him shift from being in control — decisively particular about what he would and wouldn't say — to startled and intimidated. He wasn't used to people talking back, but that alone wouldn't have caused the shift she witnessed. He was a strong-willed Type A who'd enjoyed tremendous success doing things his way; folks like that didn't back down from conflict.

What caused the shift was Ben. His sheer intensity sent Bodie running for cover in a suddenly dangerous game of tag. And Ben was *it.*

She couldn't reconcile how intense he'd become. Aside from his choice of words and delivery, the first thing she noticed was his eyes morph into a darker blue. Once calm and innocent, they now demanded attention and emanated danger. His angled lips and pointed eyebrows completed the transformation; gone were his charm and pleasant smile. All that remained was a badass vibe that told even her it was time to shut up and follow his lead.

"I'm going to call you Ryan from now on," Ben continued. "I'm not here to threaten you, but it's time to start telling the truth."

"I've been telling the truth the whole ti —"

"Save it, Ryan. Your plaques and your money don't mean a thing to me. But finding out who killed my friend does. And since I don't think you did, I'm giving you the chance to tell me about Peter's malware project before I pry it out of you."

Bodie's face shifted again and this time froze, giving Ben and Nikki time to study his pronounced surprise. Bodie sat there — eyes wide, mouth slightly open — like a deer that scampered into the street only to be blinded by the truth of the oncoming headlights.

"Malware?"

"You know … malicious software often disguised as legitimate that's used to break into secure computer systems and steal sensitive information or crash operations. Worms, Trojan horses, dialers, keyloggers, spyware, govware … there's a whole list of possibilities."

"I don't have the faintest —"

"Think very carefully about what you say next. You really don't want to find out what happens when I'm lied to twice."

Another pause.

"What makes you think Peter was —"

"I didn't ask you one question to get another."

Bodie stared back with now fearful eyes, resting his fingers over his lips. He then started, ever so slightly, nodding his head. Ben stared back, his dilated pupils growing even darker, and Nikki shivered with the cold sensation of quiet terror when the heat kicked off and the room fell silent.

But then she saw something she didn't expect — a soft but evident smile creep across Bodie's face, just before he reached for the leather portfolio and gold jar of pens on the table. He tore a single sheet and with painstaking slowness laid the Mont Blanc pen diagonally atop it, all the while looking at Ben.

"Ryan, I'm not getting any younger."

Bodie's face revealed little aside from being scared, but it now seemed he was in deep thought as well, as if his mind was in many different places at once. Bodie's eyes, in stark contrast to Ben's, looked uncertain and sad.

"Ryan, maybe I did stutter after all. You've got five seconds to start talking or you'll get to see firsthand what happens."

Bodie turned to the paper, scribbling something for about thirty seconds. When finished, he turned it over and half-rose out of his chair to slide it across the table before falling back into the leather seat and folding his hands on the chilly granite.

Ben turned the sheet of paper over and quickly pocketed it as Bodie began to speak. Ben's expression remained, but Bodie's confidence returned and his voice projected sternness.

"You're barking up the wrong tree. I feel terrible about what happened to Peter, I really do. And I wish I could help. But I have no idea what you're talking about and threatening me doesn't change that. I'm absolutely certain you have no evidence to support your claim, because it flat out isn't true. Am I right or am I right?"

"That's beside the point."

"No, that's precisely the point. Am I right? You have no proof whatsoever?"

"That doesn't mean it's not true."

"Mr. Siebert, Peter was our technical liaison. He ran sanity checks on software engineering firms we'd considered acquiring. If he'd so much as speculated one of those firms was involved with malware, he would've disclosed it immediately and InvestSecure would've reported it to the authorities. The very notion you're suggesting otherwise is both completely asinine and defamation.

"And if you ever do it in public — as I believe you're threatening to do — you'll be hearing from our corporate attorney. We've been in business for twenty-two years and have a stellar reputation. From day one, we've done it by the book. And if you try to insinuate or imply otherwise, I'll sue your sorry ass and show you the true meaning of the phrase *public embarrassment*."

"Your threats don't scare me."

"You know I'm right."

"If you're so squeaky clean, why did your VP get gunned down on a business trip you sent him on?"

"You're asking me why two foreign gangsters killed my employee? Why don't you ask her? I'm a businessman. I conduct *business*, legally and legitimately. My employees do the same. If you don't believe me, get the Bureau's lawyers to force me to disclose our records and see for yourself. But until you do, there's nothing else to talk about and I have to get back to work."

Ben sat quietly for a few seconds before nodding at her and rising from his seat. His 6'2" figure towered over the sitting Bodie like a skyscraper, and he looked down on the CEO with forceful posture.

"You're right. We don't have proof … *yet*. But Peter didn't get killed for selling Girl Scout Cookies and I have my intuition. It usually steers me pretty well, and it's telling me Peter was killed because of something he was doing here. Since I knew the man, I know he wouldn't have done that by choice, and that narrows the options down pretty damn quick. You might've called my bluff on the malware, but there's something there. And you can bet your sorry, pompous ass I'll find it. And when I do, if I learn you're lying to me now, I'm coming for you. You hear me? And I *will* find you."

"Your intuition has taken a wrong turn, Mr. Siebert. A very wrong turn. I encourage you to investigate. Doing so will only prove my point. But until then, you'd better refrain from making idle threats towards me or my company without any evidence. If you don't, you're the one who'll be sorry. Are we clear on that?"

"You'd better not be lying to me."

"*Are we clear?*"

"We're clear."

"Karen can show you out."

Bodie rose from his seat and so hurriedly exited the room that she felt a breeze from his abrupt departure. By the time they were in the hallway, he was nowhere in sight. She couldn't believe Ben let it go at that. She stared at him angrily but he didn't return the glance. Instead, he ordered her to follow him out the door, which she didn't much care for.

After saying good-bye to Karen and getting into Bu, she turned to Ben in rage.

"What the hell was that?" she yelled as he headed towards the interstate. "What ever happened to *using the element of surprise to its fullest?* I can't believe you lectured me and then didn't have the balls to do it yourself!"

Without a word, Ben handed her the sheet of paper Bodie gave him in the meeting. She unfolded it quickly and read it twice.

Play along for now and make it <u>CONVINCING</u>. Then get out and don't come back. Be at the payphone at 1137 W. 18th Street in Chicago at 1 a.m. TONIGHT. Come alone and wear gym shoes. Destroy this note as soon as you leave.

30

Twenty minutes until two and still no sign of Tom.

Nikki's suggestion to call him from the car after they left InvestSecure resulted in the disaster Ben knew it would. A constant humming in the background and the in-car Bluetooth speakerphone drifting in and out of service meant missing every other word.

"Ultimate sound quality my ass," he lamented aloud, referring to the bogus claim in Bu's manual. State-of-the-art or not, he could barely hear what Tom was saying. Taking the call off speaker would've meant having to regurgitate the same conversation back to Nikki, so he suggested they all meet instead. Tom agreed and told them he'd be in the lobby of The Renaissance Hotel on Wacker Drive at one-thirty. After weaving around several SUVs cruising ten miles per hour under the speed limit in the passing lane, they arrived at a quarter after one.

As people buzzed around all directions of the brightly lit, elaborate hotel lobby, he kept his eyes peeled for a man who would stick out like a porcupine in a nudist colony. The place cost three hundred bucks a night and charged for every accessory imaginable. Three ornate chandeliers hung from the thirty-foot ceiling and about twenty paintings that cost tens of thousands of dollars each lined the walls. The setting suited Tom like a formal ballet suited an offensive lineman. Most folks were well dressed — overdressed by Ben's standards and *way* overdressed by Tom's — and consisted primarily of "suits" headed to their next meeting.

As one of those suits rolled his bag past them en route to Reception, the soft hum of the suitcase's wheels on the lobby carpet soothed him. Nikki had been anxious since reading Bodie's note, but he hadn't yet opened the door for them to discuss it. He was too busy thinking through the CEO's request to meet, and to do so on the Lower West Side at one o'clock in the morning.

Finally Tom arrived, wearing camouflage pants, a black jacket and brown boots. After walking through the door labeled "PLEASE DO NOT USE. USE REVOLVING DOOR" he dragged one of the formal red armchairs from one end of the lobby to the other, positioning it opposite them. A bellman curiously eyed him as he did, but Tom paid no attention. When finished, he collapsed onto what felt like a red cinder block.

"Sweetheart!" he nearly shouted.

"Hi, Tom," said Nikki with a smile.

"Making this running late thing a habit, are we?" Ben said with a straight face.

"Cool your jets, Grasshopper. Wacker Drive's an enigma wrapped in a labyrinth inside a mystery, or whatever the hell Churchill said."

"I read somewhere it's one of the most confusing streets in America," Nikki added.

"See, Grasshopper?"

Ben signified his shift into *go mode* — a term they'd started using together years ago — by clearing his throat and leaning in towards him. Tom returned the gesture, Nikki tried to match it, and Ben spent the next ten minutes recapping the conversation with Bodie. Tom stared intently and Nikki didn't speak. Finally, Ben withdrew Bodie's note and handed it to Tom, completing the recap. Tom studied it for two solid minutes, then gave it back to Ben and urged him to follow its instructions to destroy it.

He submerged the paper in his glass of water and then tore it into several soaked pieces, the ink starting to run, before crumbling it all up and tossing the wet mess into the trashcan by his feet.

"So … what do you think?"

"I'll tell you one thing, Grasshopper … "

"What's that?"

"If there is some sort of connection to malware, you'd better buckle up."

"What's that supposed to mean?"

"Malware's one of if not *the* fastest growing security threats in the world. It's like Moore's Law — it gets twice as dangerous and twice as effective every year. And mobile malware in particular has a lot of room to grow. According to a recent Cisco report, only about one percent of all malware out there is mobile. And over ninety-nine percent of that is targeted specifically at Android devices."

"That's a lot of iPhones waiting for a problem."

"You bet it is."

"He's right," Nikki said, conspicuously trying to help but coming off more as a tagalong. "We spend more incremental defense budget money on cyber security than any other kind."

"That's fine," Ben said. "Obviously cyber threats are very real and very dangerous. But what's that supposed to mean for us now?"

"I'm not sure you grasp how big this is, Grasshopper. So let me give you some more free tutelage. Sweetheart here can probably tell you. All fifty-six FBI field offices now have a special Cyber Task Force, or CTF. These sons of bitches don't do anything but work on cyber threats. All day long, 365 days a year. Not to mention the NCIJTF, which the FBI is executive agent of and —"

"What's that?"

"The National Cyber Investigative Joint Task Force. Nineteen different intelligence, law enforcement and military agencies that all teamed up to coordinate cyber investigation efforts. *Nineteen*, Grasshopper. It's one of the biggest coalitions in history. Bigger than anything we ever saw in the Marines," Tom concluded, widening his eyes behind those bug glasses.

Nikki nodded, impressed that Tom knew as much as he did.

You have no idea, Ben thought.

"Maybe that means whatever we do doesn't have as much of an impact as we're assuming. With all the attention cyber security already gets, maybe one little situation like this isn't that big of a deal," Ben replied. "If there's really a problem, I'd think the task force or the FBI's CTFs would head it off. I would hope the outcome isn't dependent on what *we* do."

"Hope in one hand and shit in the other and see which fills up first, Grasshopper."

"What's that supposed to mean?"

"It means start using your head like I know you can. The fact is it's all that attention that actually makes this situation an even bigger threat."

"How do you figure?"

"Go back to the basics. The real kicker about malware — spyware in general for that matter — is how broad it is. There are countless number of ways it can be used to do bad things to good people. And there's no way the authorities can stay ahead of the people creating it."

"What makes you say that?"

"Usually malware is transmitted through apps that people voluntarily download. You believe that? People actively invite this upon themselves. They get tricked or baited into clicking *here*. And when they do, the malware penetrates their computers and gives hackers access to sensitive information. Credit card info, social security numbers, you name it. Then the hackers sell that info on the black market to make a buck. It's hard to trace but even harder to head off. Usually by the time the crime has been committed, the hackers are long gone."

"That happens all the time, Tom. Department stores and banks get hacked every other week. People file their claims, get new credit cards, and the world goes on."

"That's exactly right."

"So ... what's your point?"

"Grasshopper, those are just the *usual* examples of malware, and they're all consumer-targeted. People don't like it, but to your point the damage is relatively minimal. Folks who get hacked have a pain-in-the-ass process ahead of them. Companies are held accountable, get embarrassed and lose customers, maybe even a few bucks on the stock price. But it happens so often that authorities have learned how to deal with it and can minimize the damage. So overall there's not a huge impact."

"And ... ?"

"And while consumer malware might be the only kind you hear about, it's certainly not alone. Malware comes in all shapes and sizes. There are plenty of potential targets out there that don't show up in the newspapers."

"Such as?"

"The military, for one. With certain access, a hacker could use malware to jeopardize military markets or government agencies."

"Why would they do that if they don't make money?" Nikki asked.

"There are always ways to make money if you can expose confidential information, Sweetheart. It's *Mission Impossible* only for real. Undercover CIA agents, key operations in the works, suspects on the watch list, surveillance systems, you name it. These things might not directly affect the everyday Joe, but they pose a much bigger threat than department store hacks. The soldiers playing video games online at a remote base could be painting a real-life bulls-eye on their backs if someone uses malware to hack their network and pinpoint their location through GPS. Imagine if one of our ops back in the day had been exposed and our unit walked into an ambush, Grasshopper."

"Military systems are more secure than department stores."

"That doesn't make them safe. The competition is a lot better too."

"What makes you think this malware is targeting the military?"

"Nothing, right now. But I plan for the worst and hope for the best."

Ben leaned back and crossed his right foot over his left knee, considering the possibilities. On paper, InvestSecure didn't work with any government or military outfits, though he knew that paper didn't always tell the truth. Still, if Hubley had caught wind of malware at his position, it was likely to be more sophisticated — and hence more dangerous — than an everyday scam. But Ben wasn't convinced. There was no evidence to support the doomsday scenario Tom was alluding to and such scenarios were extremely rare. It didn't mean he could dismiss it, but it called for a different angle. Tom, who had the uncanny ability to read people's minds, then provided him one.

"Food for thought, Grasshopper. It could still be a commercial industry target but a less common one, that's more dangerous than what you hear about. The feds have only recently started working with the private sector, and they've got a lot of catching up to do. Operation Clean Slate is the FBI's collaborative effort to fight cyber threats. It's the most comprehensive public-private approach ever, but it's still relatively new."

"What kind of industries?"

"It could be a lot of things. Take the airlines. United, American and JetBlue all recently replaced their old-fashioned paper flight logs with iPads. Makes a lot of sense on the surface. It gives pilots access to the latest weather conditions and provides real-time navigational data. And it does it all with a one-pound, nine-inch device that spares airlines tons of paper and printing costs, not to mention the trees."

"So?" Nikki asked, leading Tom down the primrose path.

"So now the entire flight plan for every trip those airlines take is out there for the taking. Think about what a hacker might do with it."

"These are extremely secure systems, Tom. Even if hackers somehow got in, the security codes and anti-spyware get updated daily."

"It only takes one, Grasshopper."

Again, he had no response. Tom leaned in further and he followed suit. Lobby traffic had picked up and there were even more people bustling by them, rolling their bags towards the elevators, thinking about the next part of their days rather than military malware targets or airline vulnerabilities.

"You might be right, Grasshopper. But I bring it up is because as usual, the risk is in the unknown. The only way you stop an attack like that is if you know about it beforehand. And you're right, anything at this level is probably already on someone's radar, pun intended. CIA, NSA, whatever. That said, I'd think the FBI would be involved too. And from the look on Sweetheart's face, it isn't."

Nikki solemnly languished, not trying to hide that Tom's what-ifs were rummaging her mind.

"So you think I should answer Bodie's note?"

"I don't think you have a choice, Grasshopper. If you don't, you're throwing darts blindfolded at a moving target a hundred miles away. But be ready for anything. It could be a trap."

"How encouraging."

"We'll go through it, Grasshopper. For now, I've got to take care of a few things. Call me later and we'll run through the game plan."

Tom rose from the fine red leather armchair, left it right where he'd dragged it, and exited the hotel lobby without so much as a good-bye. He'd wanted Tom's help at first but now regretted asking.

———

You have to tell him; tell him now.

She'd thought about it the whole time. Really, ever since she'd read Bodie's note. She meant to say something sooner but every chance she got disappeared twice as fast as it had emerged. Still, that didn't change what she had to do.

"Ben ... "

"Don't you hate it when he does that? He comes here, throws dangerous scenarios around like he's playing catch, then leaves. I'm meeting Bodie in less than eleven hours. Why can't he talk about it now?"

"There's something I haven't told you that you need to know."

He wore a frozen expression the entire time she revealed the wire transfers to the killers' families' accounts, and how she found out about them. She spared no details, from the letter that had been sent to the Brazil police to the holds on the accounts to Redmond's theory on the Swiss bank.

"Where's the letter?" he finally asked after a painful, awkward silence.

"Secure in the evidence locker."

"I need to see it."

"Impossible."

"You're impossible."

"I was going to tell —"

"You bitch me out for meeting Tom without you, but all the while you're withholding the only actual evidence this rotten case has."

"I'm trying to say that I was going to tell you!"

"Oh? When? Before or after I got shot standing at a payphone tonight?"

"You didn't exactly walk through the door of trust either, Ben. And it swings both ways. I almost got fired because of you."

"And you think this makes us *even*?"

"I was —"

"Bodie could've written that letter in the first place. Did you even consider that? We could've asked him about it. We could've —"

"Look, I was going to tell you in the car, but you were too busy yelling at me for not pushing Meyer. And I was pissed, okay? I was pissed at you and at myself and I didn't tell you when I should have."

"You should've told me before we even met Meyer."

"Maybe so, but I didn't. I wasn't sure if I could trust you after the computer files, and this was the *one* thing I had that you didn't. So I kept it to myself and that was a mistake."

"You think?"

"Ben, I was going to tell you. I'm not going to try to convince you of that anymore, you just have to believe me or not."

"Some trusting relationship we have."

"Yeah … we both offered each other our trust and we've both broken it. I forgave you and we moved on. I'm asking you to do the same."

"Have you told me everything? I mean every, *single* nugget?"

"I promise."

"Don't be a hypocrite with your own word."

"I'm not being a hypocrite. I swear to you. That's everything I've got. There hasn't been any luck with the Swiss bank and Redmond said there wouldn't be. The postal service can't trace the package but knows it came from Chicago. There's almost zero chance of figuring out who made the wire transfer. And the money itself can't be withdrawn for a year. We can't afford to wait that long. I *promise* … you have all the facts I have. You know everything I know about why the FBI's involved."

"I have to go."

He rose from his seat and left the hotel just as quickly as Tom Fedorak. She reached for his arm but he pulled his away. She yelled *wait* but he stormed out of the lobby.

Dejected, she slumped back into the leather seat and closed her eyes. Her pride had gotten in the way, and now her best chance of solving the case was gone.

She just *had* to one-up him, and now he was done with her. She didn't even get the chance to explain why it was urgent she tell him now. Her attitude ruined that and now she was alone. *Again.* Alone and even more pissed at herself than she was at Ben when he lied to her. She didn't even get his take on her theory.

That Eric Meyer, not Ryan Bodie, wrote the letter. And that Ryan Bodie III, Mr. Big Shot CEO, murdered his own employee.

31

The world was still talking about *brazilexpert101*'s original blog post and the controversy that followed. Frenzy swarmed the online community instantly and, within twenty-four hours, the print industry as well. Substantiation of *brazilexpert101*'s claims, initially labeled bogus, funneled in from multiple sources. In less than forty-eight hours, Peter Hubley's credibility had gone from tenuous to nonexistent. The everyday American dismissed him as a jerk that got what he deserved. Prominent members of the media used the public's newfound animosity towards him to fuel debate about whether authorities should allocate precious resources to investigate a case that clearly occurred on Brazilian soil. And local politicians spoke out against the deceased's involvement with the PCC. It was, in a word, beautiful. A cunning display of strategic marketing that had changed minds and convinced the world. Nobody questioned *brazilexpert101* anymore. That was yesterday's news, as was the notion that Hubley might be innocent. By almost any measure, it was a screaming success.

Yet Terrance Smith, the man behind the blog name, was terrified.

Terrified because the one person he was ordered to influence had instead been influenced by a former marine. FBI Special Agent Nikki Benton not only continued her investigation unbiased, she became partners with Ben Siebert. Mr. Riddle was not pleased.

Smith knew enough about Dominick Riddle to know his years of dedication and service were of little significance. All that mattered was what he did lately. And lately, he changed the minds of everyone in the world except the one person Riddle told him to.

When he spoke with Riddle earlier, his employer didn't say anything and actually complimented his work. But he wasn't fooled. He knew Riddle didn't forget. Riddle never forgot. He might struggle to recall the hundreds of success stories throughout a man's career, but his one failure would be forever remembered and never forgiven.

Plan X was most definitely his final assignment.

And it was progressing smoothly. Adir Mousa surprised him. In addition to procuring a million dollars cash in twelve hours, the Arab had passed his thorough background screening. Mousa was third in command of the small but cash-rich terrorist organization and seemed more than willing to pay whatever Riddle was asking.

He'd worked the contingency stories from every angle, dotting the "Is" and crossing the "Ts" as always. Considering the target audience and the plethora of booby traps surrounding this particular message, the emergency plans were impressively comprehensive and, as of this morning, complete. Every stone was overturned, from the slimmest possible tie between Riddle and Adir Mousa to Mousa's "connection" to the President of France and recent bombings in Pakistan. A laudable collection of misdirection, diversion, coincidence and flat-out fabrication would undoubtedly rescue Riddle if called upon. Rescue him even in the highly unlikely event that the worst-case scenario played out after the transaction was complete.

But he knew it wouldn't rescue *him* from Riddle.

Which was why he had a plan of his own.

He used the prepaid cell phone to place his calls. First the offshore banks, then his contact in Bermuda, finally his friends in Australia. The money had grown even faster than he hoped. He could live off the interest alone. His arrangements were in place and a team of people was waiting to serve him and only him. The life of luxury Riddle lived was about to become his own.

After a few more phone calls, to the transportation service and newspapers, he'd be ready for the final step.

That final step was to call Mr. Riddle for the last time, which he'd do in a few minutes. His boss would want to discuss Plan X — the pathetically unimaginative name Riddle coined — in painful detail. And he'd do so with a smile on his face, a willing employee eager to please.

Because it didn't matter. *None* of it mattered. He didn't care what Riddle thought of him and he could give two craps how much he liked Plan X. He just needed the boss off his back for a few more days. As long as it shut Riddle up for seventy-two hours, Plan X would serve his purposes just fine.

32

There wasn't a soul around and every window in sight was pitch-black. But that didn't stop Ben from carefully scanning the area from his car, parked on 18th Street. This particular stretch of road had the honorary name of Juan A. Velazquez Street, a testament to the neighborhood's predominately Mexican population.

The payphone in question sat on a heavily cracked sidewalk corner just east of the May Street T-Intersection, a half-mile west of the Dan Ryan expressway and two miles south of I-290. The area seemed abandoned and isolated beyond the effects of the late hour. Most of the commercial buildings along 18th were dilapidated and boarded up. Those still in use were comprised of either permanently stained, crumbling brick or cheap, brightly colored siding with pervasive chipping and graffiti. In either case brown and yellow streaks ran from the roof down the sides of every building, augmenting cracked windows and aged exteriors.

All the businesses still in operation were closed for the evening, black metal gates over doors and windows to prevent break-ins. Blue light surveillance cameras, formally known as Police Observation Devices, were located at two intersections within Ben's line of sight. Distinguished by flashing blue lights atop a box covered with the Chicago Police Department's checkerboard logo, the cameras operated 24/7 and transmitted footage to an adjacent district station. There, police officers viewed the footage from the comfort of personal data terminals. Introduced in 2003, the idea was that if the cops were always watching, crime would decrease. However, the cameras' effectiveness was questionable and over time had become so commonplace they'd lost whatever effect they may have once had. They certainly didn't offer Ben any comfort. Instead, they merely reminded him he was in a neighborhood deemed dangerous enough to warrant constant surveillance.

He'd tried to sleep earlier to no avail. Much too wired and way too pissed at Nikki to drift, instead he called Tom to discuss the "game plan." As expected, he wound up reluctantly accepting — as opposed to agreeing — that backup was a bad idea. Not only did Bodie's note reference gym shoes, implying this wasn't his only stop, but Tom had added that Bodie would most likely be watching. And that backup at this hour would be too obvious to be worth the risk. Easy for Tom to say.

Fatigued, he got out of the car and approached the payphone. As he walked around the front of the Taurus, he noted that the surrounding retail goods would've offered him far more comfort than the blue light cameras. There was an El Trebol liquor store, cheap tacos promised at Taqueria Iguala, and an Imperial Stress Reduction Center.

When he reached the payphone, he knew he was beyond exposed. He was a sitting duck with a bulls-eye on his back. If this was a setup, now was the perfect opportunity. Bodie had him right where he wanted him and there was nothing he could do about it. He checked his watch and waited for the quick pop of a sniper rifle.

Then the phone began to ring.

"Siebert."

"We do this my way from start to finish. No questions, no complaining. Deal?"

"Ryan, we don't —"

"It's a yes or no question."

"Yes."

"Stick your arm out and hold up some fingers."

"Um, okay."

"You're holding up four fingers."

"Is that supposed to impress me?"

"No, it's supposed to tell you I'll be watching. Do exactly as I say or I'm gone."

"I said I agree."

"You'd better be alone or I'll know."

"I'm alone."

"There's a black duffle bag sitting against the building just south of you that used to be May's Laundromat. Get it and come back to the payphone without looking inside."

Ben did as he was told and held the typical carrier in his right hand when he returned. It was about five pounds and fully zipped.

"Good. Now open it up. What do you see?"

"Clothes. And shoes."

"Change into them. Start with your top. Strip down and do a slow, full 360-spin before you put on the shirt. Then do the same with your pants. Do your shoes and socks last. Don't take anything out of your pockets and put the clothes you're wearing now in the bag when you're done."

"Here?"

"Here."

"There's underwear in here!"

"Very perceptive."

"This is a public street."

"Well aren't you lucky it's late enough that there's no one around."

This was a first, he told himself. The nighttime drop in temperature and his unexpected nudity implored him to change quickly, but he did a slow turn to prove he wasn't wearing the wire Bodie was concerned about. Once wearing the loose-fitting blue jeans, Bears sweatshirt and one-size-too-small Nikes, he picked up the receiver.

"Good. I apologize for that, but I had to be certain we'd be speaking in private."

"You could've just asked."

"I can't afford to make assumptions. How are you feeling?"

"How am I *feeling*? Gee, let me think. A phone call woke me up at three in the morning and you've got me here past one, so I haven't slept in twenty-two hours. I'm tired. And cold … you just had me naked in fifty-degree weather."

"Perfect. I've got something that'll wake and warm you right up. One-fifth of a mile down May Street is Dvorak Park and a Little League baseball field. In precisely three minutes, the cell phone sitting under the bleachers on the first base side will start ringing. If it makes it to voicemail, you might as well catch a cab home."

"Wait, what —"

Dial tone.

———

A full-out sprint and painful reminder of his age later, Ben reached under the first row of bleachers and withdrew a black cell phone. It was an archaic blast from the past — a simple Samsung flip phone with no touch screen, Internet or apps. He got about twenty seconds with it — enough to verify there was no call history — before it started to ring.

"Siebert."

"Keep going south on May until you hit 21st. Then head west. After six blocks, turn right on Ashland Avenue. Once you pass Cullerton, you'll see St. Pius V Church. Take a right just south of the main entrance and let yourself in through the side door. All-told it's about three-quarters of a mile, so I'll give you six minutes. And since the phone you're holding can't place outgoing calls anyway, go ahead and destroy it now. Be at the second pew in six minutes and bring the phone's internal circuit board or our deal is off."

"We have a deal?"

Bodie hung up on him for the second time, prompting him to kick the dirt hard towards the bleachers. The small pellets ricocheted off the metal with clinks and clanks and one of them recoiled, narrowly missing his face. Frustrated as he was, he didn't have time to pout. A run only a third as long had just sucked the wind out of his lungs, so he needed every second he could spare. He stomped the phone to pieces and picked up the small green circuit board that used to be its brain. Then he bolted for the church, wondering aloud when the Dirty Harry act was going to end.

It seemed he was running into the wind regardless of his direction. Dragging himself through Chicago's Near Southwest Side, he pumped his arms to generate as much speed as he could and finally crossed the border into Pilsen.

Pilsen, originally settled by Irish and German immigrants, was now a predominately Mexican neighborhood. So he wasn't surprised to run past businesses with Spanish-only advertisements in the windows, or to see numerous fliers void of English stapled to telephone poles.

He was, however, a bit surprised at the artsy feel of the neighborhood and the colorful murals he came across. Compared to near the payphone, the buildings were in slightly better condition; not *every* business had metal gates stretched across its entrance. He didn't see any blue light cameras and there was far less gang graffiti.

Sprinting on the sidewalk along the usually hectic Ashland Avenue, he saw only two moving cars at the late hour. Truth be told, he was glad that few witnessed his alternating rhythm of yanking baggy jeans upwards and using his oversized sweatshirt sleeve to mop his dripping forehead as he ran.

When he reached the church, exhausted from the sprint, he noticed immediately that the building was quite old. Deteriorating red brick was splattered with black stains throughout and white streaks covered almost the entire frontal area. The shingles on the church's green roof were noticeably warped and the paint on the three crosses atop the steeples flaked like dandruff. He checked his watch and saw he only had forty-five seconds to get to the second pew. Hardly enough time to question the broken padlock lying next to the side door.

Upon entering, he made his way down the center aisle, four aged stained glass windows on the right, prayer candles on the left. The brownish tile floor was dirty and slick and there was a strong musty smell throughout. Ryan Bodie III was sitting in the second row pew, waiting for his arrival.

33

The CEO was dressed much differently than before. Gone were the tie and fancy clip, pleated slacks and lavish pink dress shirt. In their stead was a pair of dark blue jeans, a loose-fitting brown sweater with no collar and a pair of black gym shoes. His sleeves were pushed up as opposed to rolled, and his hair was neither gelled nor combed.

"You made it," Bodie nearly whispered.

"I didn't know payphones were still around."

"Not many are. But I've had my eye on that one and its number memorized for some time now."

"Why?"

"Because I always thought this day might come."

"What day is that?"

"Do you have what I told you to bring?"

Ben sighed at the change of subject, then took a seat next to Bodie in the pew and handed him the flip phone's circuit board. Bodie accepted it without response, quickly shoving it in his pants pocket while looking towards the front of the church. Ben followed his eyes to the slightly elevated sanctuary. There, a large altar with a white tablecloth draped over it had already been set with glasses and bowls in preparation for Friday night's Communion.

Having thankfully — and *barely* — met Bodie's six-minute deadline, he took a minute to further familiarize himself with his surroundings. He didn't see anything to indicate they weren't alone, but there were a lot of places to hide. If this was an ambush, he didn't have a prayer … even in a church.

The church itself looked like any other Catholic Church would at one-thirty in the morning. A religion that prides itself on standardization — *catholic* literally means *universal*— this church reminded him of all the other catholic churches he'd been in over the years. Small track lighting along the end of the aisles provided just enough illumination to guide parishioners to their pews. There was a podium to the right with three altar boy chairs beneath it, small holy water dishes mounted on the walls next to the side entrances and a rectangular display board posting hymnal pages. About the only distinguishing characteristic he noticed was that both the hymnals and mass guides were in Spanish.

"Were you really up at three this morning?"

"Three-fourteen, actually."

On the run over, he'd contemplated confronting Bodie head-on about the letter that *someone* had sent to the Brazil Police to catch him off guard and see if his reaction revealed that *someone*, but had decided it was best instead to see where Bodie led the conversation.

"That makes for a long day."

"It's an even longer day when I have to change clothes out in the open on the Lower West Side."

"Just be thankful I didn't send your dumb ass to Englewood."

"Dumb ass?"

"You show up at my office with an FBI Agent and no plan? My sources told me you were shrewd and adaptable ... not some run-of-the-mill dimwit who thinks it's okay to barge into my conference room and try to intimidate me like some punk-ass rookie cop, asking questions you don't know the answers to that are gonna get us both killed."

"Maybe you should enlighten me."

"Good. Keep your calm, keep your wits. You're gonna need both if you plan to see this through."

"See what through?"

Bodie paused slightly before responding.

"You know why I like this church?"

"Why?"

"Because it caters to the hopeless."

"What?"

"For over sixty years, this church has been a symbol of promise for people who didn't have any. Even its shrine, The Shrine of St. Jude Thaddeus, is labeled 'Patron of Hopeless Cases.' Irish immigrants may've founded it but it now serves a Mexican community that's been crapped on since the sixties, when it got displaced from the Near West Side because The University of Illinois at Chicago was being built. The church doesn't give up on them. It feeds promise to the Mexican community through faith, community and dependability. Qualities that make people proud to live where they live."

"Dependability?"

"People can come here and know they're safe. They know these walls will always be here for them. They've been around since 1874 and aren't going anywhere. That's dependability."

"I'm sure the church appreciates your admiration. But how do you think it feels about your breaking the lock and sneaking in?"

"They'll feel better about the lock when they find the hundred grand in the confessional. As for my sneaking in, I already told you. This church caters to the hopeless."

"You call yourself hopeless? Feel sorry for yourself some more, *millionaire.*"

"Shut your damn mouth until you know what the hell you're talking about."

"The church wouldn't approve of that language, Ryan."

Bodie sighed, uninterested in witty chitchat.

"The church wouldn't approve of a lot of things I've done. Neither would God, nor my family."

Bodie's face filled with sadness, emptiness. Lethargy and fear radiated from his eyes like a confused child. It was as if he'd been fighting for too long and had finally given up. And it was an expression that was difficult to respond to. Push him too hard, he'd curl into a ball and simply stop talking. Give in too much, he'd walk all over the conversation without saying anything significant.

But Bodie needed something from him, and sooner or later it would surface. Otherwise, he wouldn't have asked Ben to meet him.

"I can't change the past, Ryan. But I can help with the future. You ran me almost a mile in clothes that don't fit past one in the morning, but I'm here now. You might as well let me try."

"I don't want your help."

"Then what do you want?"

"I want my family safe."

"Are they in danger? Are you in danger?"

"Danger?" Bodie chuckled. "No, I'm not in danger. I'm well past that."

"Why?"

"Because you're talking to a dead man."

"What makes you say that?"

"The moment you came to my office and started asking questions about malware, you signed my death warrant."

"Why?"

Bodie shook his head ... seemingly to himself. It was as if he was in a mental debate, contemplating the situation, desperately looking for any other option; but that after searching, he'd come to the difficult conclusion there wasn't one. Eyes on the altar, the business tycoon faced Ben, a deep breath preceding a very difficult conversation.

"Here's my offer, Ben Siebert. I tell you exactly what I'm prepared to tell you. I don't know everything you'll want to know. And some of what I do know, I won't be able to share."

"Why?"

"For two reasons. One, telling you some of what I know would put other men's families at risk. Two, it would mean even more exposure for my wife and children."

"If talking to me puts your family in jeopardy, why are you doing it?"

"You've got to start listening. I'm not going to be alive for very long to repeat myself."

"How about one last time?"

"They're *already* in jeopardy. You put them there when you came to my office."

The notion involuntarily paralyzed Ben's mind like an electric fence would his body. His brain felt tight, unwilling to accept his actions contributed to innocent lives being put at risk. To shake the feeling he told himself Bodie was making it up. But he knew he wasn't. The CEO's eyes were honest for the first time in what he guessed was years.

"Do you think I wrote that note as some sort of game? What did you think was going to happen after your cavalier shenanigans at InvestSecure?"

"How was I being cavalier?"

"If you really thought Peter was murdered by the PCC, then I'd chalk it up to ignorance and give you the benefit of the doubt. We also wouldn't be talking right now. But you're too smart for that. You know that whole PCC story is a sham. And because you know, your questions weren't ignorant. They were arrogant. And you, Mr.

Vigilante justice administrator, you of all people should've known the office was bugged."

"Why should I have known that? I don't even know what got Peter killed. I didn't even know about the malware until yesterday. For all I actually know, you're the one who gave the order."

"Don't you dare say that again. I did everything I could to save Peter's life. Everything I could think of short of ending my own and now I wish I had. Keep your mouth shut as to what I have and have not done. I've done plenty I'm not proud of, but you don't have the first clue. Got it?"

"Got it. Sorry," he said, trying to keep Bodie talking.

"Back to my offer. On my end, I finish this conversation and fill in as many blanks as I can without jeopardizing more lives. I don't tell you anything that I think might endanger my family and I don't ever hear you doubt me again like you just did. You'll get the chance to decide whether to believe me or not, but you *will* show me the respect of not doing it in my presence."

"That's fair."

"In return, I have two conditions. First, get my family into the Witness Protection Program as soon as possible."

"I can't do that."

"Nikki Benton can."

"Then why aren't you talking to her?"

"Because she can't fulfill my second condition. Frankly, I'm not sure you can either, but you're the only chance my family has."

"You just said you wanted them in Witness Protection."

Bodie emitted a laugh loud enough that its echo ricocheted off the walls and filled the church with ominous cackle, flinging his hand dismissively.

"You think it's that easy? Just throw them in Witness Protection and call it day?"

"That's what you —"

"Witness Protection can't save them. That's like the FDA competing with big tobacco in advertising. But if it's done right away, just maybe it'll buy enough time."

"Enough time for what?"

"For you to deliver on my second condition."

"What's that?"

"Kill Dominick Riddle. Stand there and physically watch him breathe his last breath. Unless and until that happens, my family isn't safe."

———

"I've never heard of Dominick Riddle."

"Of course you haven't. I don't even think that's his real name."

"How am I supposed to kill him if I don't know his real name?"

"You'll have to figure it out."

"Sorry, but I take issue with killing people I don't know."

"Allow me to modify my condition."

"Okay … "

"I'm confident a man of your reach will find a way to learn about him. When you do, you'll see that he's *pure evil*. A monster. A scornful barbarian who can't be reformed or saved. A thousand times worse than Barry Lee Richard."

Picturing the 6'8" wife-beating stockbroker who got away with it again and again, Ben was impressed by the reference. He nodded slightly at Bodie, a form of tipping his cap to the CEO.

"Barry Lee Richard was a pig and he deserved what you gave him. All I ask is that you look into Dominick Riddle and react proportionally."

"By react, you mean kill."

"The more painful the better."

"I can't agree to that."

"I'm not asking you to kill a man you don't know deserves it. I'm asking you to not run away from someone whom you know does. Seems pretty reasonable, considering your track record."

Ben eyed Bodie, a man no one would ever expect to be desperate. He was almost begging for Ben's help. All that power, all that money, and he was pleading for Ben to kill another man. Whether Bodie was telling the truth or not, he could see that Bodie honestly felt this was it. This was the end for him, his last chance to save his family.

"If I determine — on my own — that that's what Riddle deserves, that's what I'll administer. That's my counteroffer. Take it or leave it."

34

"Dominick Riddle has been orchestrating high-level, high-intelligence scams and terrorist acts for years. He's gotten filthy rich by taking advantage of people all over the world. He's influenced foreign governments, stolen from and blackmailed wealthy individuals, and used his power and connections to get wealthier and wealthier."

"How do you know all this?"

"I'm ashamed to say I've helped him do it. Not because I've wanted to, but to protect my family."

"He threatened your family if you didn't help him?"

"Not the first time. But after that."

"How'd you get involved with him?"

"It started six years ago because I was stupid and greedy and did him a favor. I broke the law and it was the biggest mistake I've ever made. I'm ashamed to say I invited Dominick Riddle into my life.

"What kind of favor?"

"I used some offshore accounts InvestSecure had worked with during an acquisition to launder his money from a transaction. Nothing upfront, no guarantees until the transaction cleared. I just didn't think it actually would."

"But it did."

"I have no one to blame but myself. Ever since then, Riddle's forced me to do things I can't believe I've done."

"How did he force you?"

"Once my hands were dirty, he started by blackmailing me, threatening to turn me in for what I'd done. I'd take that deal in a heartbeat now. Over time, his threats shifted to my family. The more I've done, the more I've wanted out.

"But the steeper the price."

"Now I'm in so deep it only ends with his death or mine."

"Or if he stops needing you."

"When that happens, he'll kill me."

"Why does such a powerful man need you?"

"He's manipulated hundreds of people, through bribes and blackmail. But he's gotten the most help, the most strings pulled, from three of us. With us in his pocket and everything else he has, he has more control, power and connections than the President. And far fewer restrictions."

"Who are the other two people?"

"I can't tell you that. But they're incredibly powerful men with niche connections that Riddle needs right now."

"And it was one of these scams that got Peter Hubley killed?"

"The worst one yet. Probably not his last, certainly ours."

"What makes you say that?"

"Because he's going to kill all three of us."

"Why don't you kill him first?"

"I don't want my family to be buried alive."

"If he's dead, how can he do that?"

"He's got plans for our families already in place if one of us ever gets him."

"What if no one knows it's you?"

"Hence my second condition."

"What's the scam with Peter?"

"You were on the right track earlier, I just couldn't say it in the office. It's a convoluted, esoteric malware that can specifically target advanced computer systems. It could go after Defense networks, but it could also hit the Federal Reserve, stock market, Homeland Security and a host of others."

"He's writing the malware himself?"

"Fat chance. He's got over twenty different groups of expert software engineers and hackers that I'm aware of, all writing a piece of it. They've got to know it's illegal — but they have no idea their work feeds into a much bigger product that can do considerable damage. He's using piecemeal development code from each to create the ultimate hacker's tool. No computer system in the world will be safe, to hear him tell it."

"You believe him? Something that sophisticated would be very hard to build."

"I'll give you that. But yes, I believe him. He's been working on it for over two years and we've seen a few simulations of the completed portions. It makes the stuff you read about look like a joke. And why shouldn't it? He's got the most brilliant computer minds and hackers in the world developing it."

"What makes you so sure?"

"Because I know the man. He's made billions the past six years alone by creating products I swore couldn't be made. That's why I helped with the offshore accounts in the first place. My greedy ego got the better of me and I took a huge payment because I didn't think there was a chance he'd pull it off. There was no risk if he failed. But he didn't fail."

"That doesn't mean he'll succeed this time. You said yourself this was the biggest one yet. Maybe he's met his match."

"I've been telling myself that for six years."

"That doesn't prove he's got it. You haven't seen the finished product?"

"No."

"Even if he did pull it off, the systems you're talking about are ultra-secure and experts learn from their weaknesses. If he manages to hack them once, they'll find him. I don't care how many smart hackers he employs. You break into the Defense network, they're going to find your ass."

"I couldn't agree more. And he certainly knows that."

"So … ?"

"So that's why he's not going to use it."

"What?"

"He tells us, the three of us, that his plan is to use the malware to steal financial information from the consumer market. Kind of a glorified Ponzi scheme, only it runs in the background. He goes on and on about how companies using technology to track consumer data plays right into our hand. About how susceptible those companies are when they report their earnings; says it'll be like taking candy from a baby."

"But you don't believe him?"

"I've heard him talk about the malware. It's different. To him the software's too valuable to limit it to the consumer market. And I know for a fact he's not planning to steal credit card info. He hasn't said he has a buyer, but he does. He's gonna sell the malware and run like the coward that he is."

"Do you have any proof? Do you know who the buyer is?"

"Nothing after months of digging. He's too smart, he's impeccably covered his tracks."

"You're not smart?"

"Dominick Riddle has backup plans for backup plans. He keeps the facts close to his chest and spawns off gibberish. You never know what's true and what's not. The three of us ... he's just using us. Feeds us line after line about making money, stealing fractions of a cent a billion times a day, but there's no way he's planning to use the malware for that. He's going to sell it for a bundle and walk away. To your point, whoever does use it will get caught. But not before Riddle cashes in, and you can bet your ass there won't be any connection back to him."

"Why is that?"

"He's got the whole world convinced Peter was in the PCC, doesn't he?"

Ben paused at the reference.

"I couldn't believe it at first. Well, scratch that. I could believe it ... I just didn't want to. I was so pissed that Riddle did it again."

"Did what again?"

"Gotten people to believe an outrageous lie. He's got someone spinning the story for him. Someone I've never met. But I know he's there. And whoever he is, he can make the world believe whatever Riddle wants it to. It's just like ... "

"What?"

"Never mind."

"I need to know."

"What you need to know is the real reason Peter Hubley is dead is me."

"You?"

"About six months ago, Riddle made me give Peter some of the malware for evaluation. It was masked as legitimate software and Riddle said he needed to be sure it was concealed well. So he made me have Peter review it to see if he found anything that tipped it off as malicious."

"Why Peter?"

"He was one of the most brilliant programmers out there, for one. Plus, he'd look beyond the code itself and Riddle knew it. He'd look at its possible applications and see if there was anything — no matter how small — that jumped out as sketchy. There just aren't that many people who can do that."

"What'd you do?"

"First I told Riddle it was a bad idea to bring Peter into it. I begged him to vet it through someone else, someone who didn't work for me. But Dominick Riddle has me and the rest of the world by the balls."

"What happened?"

"I did my best. I tried to protect Peter by pawning it off as a potential acquisition's developmental software still in beta testing. I asked him to run an analysis and see if any red flags in the code popped up before it went to market. I specifically told him to report back to me alone, and I prayed that he wouldn't find anything."

"But he did."

Bodie put his head down and nodded silently.

"Peter said the code was 99% legitimate. And that made sense. Riddle's programmers are very good, and he pays them extremely well. But it's very sophisticated, lots of moving parts and integration, and there was a small problem. Riddle knew if anyone could find it, Peter could. That's why he made me give it to him."

"What'd Peter do?"

"At first, just what I asked. He told me the code had a suspicious execute file that could be combined with other software to hack into networks. He didn't use the word *malware* but he told me something wasn't right about it."

"What'd you say?"

"I told him good job, and that he should let me take it from there. That I'd terminate discussions with the company and that it was time for him to move on."

"But Peter didn't leave it at that."

"No." Bodie sighed. "He didn't."

"What happened?"

"He started looking into it on his own. Said we couldn't just ignore it. That it could be dangerous, and we should report it to the authorities."

"And you said ... ?"

"I tried to get him to back off. I told him it wasn't our job to play the police. I said I'd hand it over to the FBI and that he needed to stay focused on his other projects. But Peter was too good of a man.

He couldn't just dismiss it. Once he had a hunch it was illegal he had to find out if it was."

"How?"

"He started researching malware and asking around. A lot. When I first found out, I chewed him out. You know, to scare him. Make him think he'd lose his job. Tried to guilt trip him with his new baby, told him to stop disobeying my instructions or I'd fire him for insubordination. It seemed to calm him down, but all it did was make him look quietly."

Ben thought of Eric Meyer and the IM conversations. The secret talk, the clandestine meetings, the paranoia in his message. It made sense. He'd been cornered at work so he turned to an old buddy for help but tried to keep it on the Down Low.

"Of course, Riddle found out about it. I'm still not sure how. Like I said, he's got his sources. He had the malware fixed but then had to deal with Peter. I tried to tell him it was okay, that I had Peter under control. That I'd make sure nothing got out … "

"But Riddle didn't buy it."

"It's not about buying it. Or making money. Or protecting interests. It's about power. He'll *never* stop. That's why you have to stop him. He warned me that Peter was a threat and said I needed to deal with him. But I knew that was a load of crap; I'd heard him say that before."

"What do you mean by that?"

"The point is, I knew Peter was in trouble. I didn't know when and I tried again and again to get him to let it go. But it didn't work. So I sent him to Brazil to get him out of the office, keep his calendar so full that he wouldn't have the time. But then I saw the news that night … "

Bodie's voice trailed off as he looked up towards the large cross, mounted above the altar, begging for reconciliation but his face showing he didn't feel he deserved it.

"Riddle just *did* it. No warning, no indication, nothing. He just had that good man desecrated in the middle of an airport. In front of hundreds of people, right there for the world to see. Afterwards, Riddle told the three of us that Peter's killing was an example of what happens when people get careless. He said it was my fault; that no one was safe and that he did it in such a public place to prove a point.

"And that freaked me out even more. I started thinking about all the people I come into contact with, how I could be putting them in danger. From my wife and kids to my employees to my driver. That's why I freaked out on Karen when she barged in earlier today. Anyone who poses even the slightest possibility of a risk, he kills. And that's exactly the message he wanted us to get after Peter was murdered. He'd done it before … he'd do it again."

"And then he got the world to think it was Peter's fault."

"The PCC? Brazilian mafia? Are you kidding me? I get depressed when I think about it. Such a good man, doing the honorable thing, getting what he got. And then on top of it the world thinks it was his fault. His poor wife … his kids … But he's not Riddle's first innocent victim."

Bodie sighed deeply and held his head down, pressing his fist into his forehead so hard Ben could see his knuckles turn white. He was infuriated with himself. For more — Ben deduced — than Peter's death.

"Riddle told us the Brazil police would chase his red herrings around in circles for months. Said that was why he had Peter killed down there. Said the world would forget about Peter just like it'd forget about us if we ever crossed him. And he was right.

"Then why'd the FBI get involved?" Ben asked, hoping to provoke a response about the letter.

"I can't get into that. But that's the one thing Riddle didn't plan on happening."

"You said the malware isn't complete?"

"Not yet. But it's close. *Very* close. I don't know exactly how much time you have, but I'd guess a week at best. You've got to find Riddle and stop him."

Ben noted that Bodie had made it *his* problem, *his* responsibility.

"You said that wasn't even his real name?"

"What's your point?"

"How am I supposed to stop him if I don't know his name?"

Bodie reached into his pocket and withdrew a folded piece of paper, pausing before handing it to him. When Ben opened it, he saw a man with light-blond, almost white hair in a maroon turtleneck. The picture was cut off at the chest, so there was no sense of height or weight, but the man looked to be in his sixties, clean-shaven with dark eyes. He had a small scar on his right cheek but no other distinguishing characteristics.

"This is him?"

"You can't ever let him see that picture."

"This isn't much."

"The reason you're the last chance my family has is because you're a guy who finds answers no one else can."

"How do you know that?"

"It doesn't matter."

"It does to me."

"Well, we'll have to agree to disagree."

"Do you even know where Riddle lives?"

"He has hundreds of places around the world."

"Do you have a way to get in touch with him?"

"He calls me, not the other way around."

"I'm assuming caller ID is a pipe dream?"

"It's always either BLOCKED or a scrambled number. And he knows if anyone tries to trace his calls."

"If he's that sophisticated, how do you expect me to find him in a week?"

"I can only hope you're as good as I'm told you are."

"No, you can do more than that. You can arrange a meeting. You can —"

"I will not put my family at further risk."

"You're not giving me anything."

"I wish I could help more. And believe me, if I could, I would. But I've already gotten Peter killed and I can't afford to risk others."

"But —"

"I've given you an alias, photograph, details on the malware project and the fact he's trying to sell it to someone with enough money and motive to buy it. That's all I have to offer you."

"You haven't told me about anyone else. Who does —"

"This completes my end of our deal. As a man known for keeping his word, I hope you honor yours. Good luck Ben." Bodie stood up from the wooden pew. "For me, for you, for anyone connected to Peter. And for the millions of people who don't even know they're counting on you."

35

"Hello?" Nikki answered in a hoarse voice, yanking herself from a nebulous drift that resided somewhere between intentionally sleeping and accidentally dozing off. She couldn't be sure how many times the phone rang but it felt like only once. She was on the couch, the computer powered on but asleep on the coffee table, her sockless feet and bare legs exposed because the bottoms of her pink pajama pants had bunched up around her knees.

"It's 3:14, your lucky number, as I recall. So I'm going to consider letting you cash in some favors to pull some strings."

"I think my favors are all used up, Ben," she responded, trying to hide the fact she wasn't fully awake and alert.

"Maybe just one more. Not for me."

"What happened tonight?"

"I thought about what you said. About how we'd both earned each other's trust and then pissed it away."

"I didn't say that."

"But that was your point."

"Okay."

"Then I thought about something else. Something Tom said."

"Are you going to tell me or are we playing Twenty Questions?"

"You're awfully sarcastic for someone who wants information."

"I've learned I can't smooth talk you. I can only give you a choice and let you decide. No amount of sucking up will change your mind, so why give you the satisfaction?"

"I knew you were a smart woman."

"So are you going to end the suspense or can I go back to bed?"

"When Tom was talking about cyber security, he mentioned Cyber Task Forces."

"Okay."

"He said all CTFs do is investigate cyber threats, 365 days a year. And that every FBI field office has one. And you agreed."

"So?"

"So it dawned on me: you're not really playing things by the book. If you were, you'd already be off the Hubley case. You would've turned over what you knew to the Special Agent in Charge and he would've reassigned it to someone in Chicago's CTF."

This was not unexpected. She knew Ben would figure it out and was actually surprised he didn't mention it at The Renaissance. Lacking the energy and conviction to try to convince him otherwise, she instead submitted to his accurate assessment.

"I guess you have a point there."

"Why don't you want to hand the case over, Nikki?"

"I don't have time for —"

"No, you need to tell me. You've got a mountain of mystery with very little help, a pain-in-the-ass former marine poking around, telling you how to do your job. You almost got fired. You're pissed Bodie wanted to talk to me tonight when you're the FBI Agent, and the whole case has frustrated you from the beginning because you're not getting the facts you need to solve it. It's over your head and you know it. Plus, it's not the kind of case or consequences you signed up for in the first place."

"It's not over my head."

"Save it. I know you."

"You know me?"

"I know that all your life you've played it by the book but had to fight adversity along the way. I know that when people tell you that you can't handle something — anything — you want nothing more than to prove them wrong. Even if you know they're right, you'll never admit it and will do whatever it takes to show them otherwise. You've spent the last ten years in a job that doesn't really make you happy for that very reason."

His assessment was once again humbling and impressive. As usual, he had her number and as usual, it pissed her off. But she'd never let him know that.

"Is there a point to all this?"

"Yes and you know what it is. You've got your way out now. You could take this to your boss and get it off your plate and the only thing you'd be guilty of is doing your job. Doing the right thing, as far as the book is concerned. No one would doubt you or say you couldn't handle it. In fact, you're probably jeopardizing the case and position by *not* turning it over. Which leads me to ask, why are you doing this? Are you just trying to prove some point that nobody but you would understand, or is there another reason?"

"I'm doing my job. I'd appreciate it if you would stop harassing me about it."

"Cut the crap. I'm the one holding the cards and we don't have time for *quid pro quo.*"

She lowered the cordless receiver and pushed it into her chest, staring ahead at the picture of Mom and Dad resting on the tiny gas fireplace mantle. Their once-encouraging smiles now just reminded her of the pain she'd tried so hard to forget. Her mind flashed to that little boy in the Jamaican hospital, to the pivotal moment that'd defined the next decade of her life, and to Ben's painfully accurate statements about her need to prove people wrong.

"I want the case because I want to find out who killed Peter Hubley. And I want to deliver justice to his widow. I want the case because I think I can solve it. I do need your help, which pisses me off. But I want the case because when I look at Sally Hubley, I see myself twelve years ago. I see a woman desperate for answers and not getting them. And I believe I can help. I believe I can hunt those answers down in the middle of the night and hand them over to her the next morning. And I want to give her that closure.

"Yes, I also want to prove you wrong, just like I proved everyone who said I couldn't make it in the FBI wrong. Yes, I want to finish what I started, because that's who I am. And yes, I want to stop whoever is doing this from doing it again. But my motivation is to give Sally Hubley what she deserves. And frankly, I don't care if you approve or not. I'm done trying to impress you."

Ben didn't answer and she savored the immediate relief after finally speaking her mind. She honestly didn't care what he thought — it was past three in the morning and he was right, the games had to stop. It was liberating to call it like it was to *someone*. Even if that someone was a guy she'd only just met who'd caused her more harm than good.

"Feels pretty good to speak from the heart, doesn't it?"

"Yes, it does."

"You should do it more often. You're much better when you do. Get dressed. I'm picking you up in ten minutes."

"What?"

"I've got to fill you in on my conversation."

"With Bod —"

"Not now. We'll talk when I pick you up."

"Can it wait until morning?" she replied, half surprised she'd even suggested waiting for what she'd spent weeks hoping to get, half hopeful he'd say yes so she could get some sleep.

"No. Start thinking about my favor."

"Can you give me a hint?"

"Know anyone in the Witness Protection Program you trust?"

In contrast to the CTF comment, this was unexpected. She flashed through the past ten years and recalled one of her first cases in Phoenix.

"Yeah, I do."

"I'll be there in ten."

36

"I'm impressed, Bill. The office doesn't even open until eight."

The chilling voice that Bill Knoble would never forget came from the visitors' seat of his newly redesigned office before he'd so much as flipped on the lights. Standing silent in the doorway with a briefcase in one hand and a cup of coffee in the other, his body returned to the temporary state of paralysis it'd experienced only once before.

"Please, come into your own office," the man said.

Knoble entered delicately, opting to keep the lights off because the man didn't say otherwise. He also didn't bother to ask how he got in; such a question seemed irrelevant at the moment. As he gingerly walked towards his desk, the suspicious character remained motionless in the leather chair, his right leg resting on his left knee, hands folded in his lap. He wore a white shirt and what looked like navy blue slacks, but he couldn't be sure in the dark.

"Bill, I have to say … kudos to you. Tomorrow marks two weeks since our last conversation, and in that short time you've made a lot of positive changes. Tell me about them."

Standing behind the desk, he eyed the man cautiously. Still holding his briefcase but the coffee now on the desk, he struggled to find the right words.

"Bill, take a seat. Relax. You have nothing to be afraid of."

Easing into his new desk chair — simple, wooden, and slightly uncomfortable — Knoble felt quite terrified despite the man's complimentary words. He seemed like a man who would speak favorably until he was ready to pounce. And when he did pounce, there wouldn't be time to evaluate or react. Like a tiger on the prowl, he came across as keenly alert, even as he leisurely leaned back.

"I scrubbed my client list."

"Indeed you did. Got rid of all that crap baggage you were carting around and started looking for people who actually need help."

"That was the idea," he replied, withholding the fact that that "crap baggage" also paid the bills.

"Were your old clients upset?"

"A few. Most were just curious and maybe a little afraid."

"I'll bet they were. They were all guilty as sin."

"Perhaps you're right."

"How's business now?"

"Um, it's okay," he replied nervously, not wanting to insinuate that the firm's abysmal balance sheet and cash flows might prompt a return to old practices.

"Give me twenty business cards before I leave. Things will pick up."

"Um," he answered, surprised by the offer and not quite sure what it meant. "That's okay, we'll be okay."

"Let me help you. Honest help for an honest man."

"Well, thank you."

"You changed your office dress code, I see. Out with the Hawaiian shirts and jeans and in with the suits?"

"That's right."

"You even got your secretary … what's her name?"

"Genie."

"That's right, Genie. You even got Genie into night school. Isn't that so?"

"Yes, she's taking community college classes. She wants to be a paralegal."

"You're sponsoring her?"

"Yes."

"That's great, Bill. And I hear you've stopped drinking."

"Yes," he said, which was merely the tip of the iceberg. Beyond ditching the booze he'd also joined a gym, swore off greasy foods and started volunteering weekly at a local food pantry.

No matter what the skeptics might say, people really do have religious awakenings. Moved by the spirit, they get inspired to turn their lives around instantly. And while he couldn't say his was a positive epiphany from the Big Man Upstairs, he did very much have a life-changing moment of his own. And it happened in the same room he sat in now, thirteen days ago exactly. Redemption really did begin for him that day, just as the mysterious man in his office now said it would.

"You've also redecorated a bit."

"Just some spring cleaning," Knoble played off one of the most expensive two weeks of his life.

The fact was the office of William T. Knoble, Attorney at Law looked completely different. There was brand new carpet in the lobby and his private office, new window treatments throughout, and the old liquor cabinet was gone. The walls were painted and redecorated with inspirational posters and degrees that had collected so much dust in their old boxes that they needed individual scrubbing. Combined with the power-washed sidewalks and squeaky clean exterior windows, the office experienced an aesthetic transformation that cost him over thirty grand all told.

"It looks great in here, Bill. Really, it does."

"Thank, thank you."

"I heard Barry Lee Richard still hasn't turned up."

Forced casual conversation converted to terribly awkward serious dialogue didn't help his heart rate or momentary paralysis. The man's blue eyes were somehow both piercing and nonchalant, making it hard to know how to respond.

"That's correct."

"Have you tried to contact him?"

"No. Genie sent his office a termination letter just like all the others, but I haven't heard back."

"Something tells me you won't."

"Okay … "

"And soon Barry Lee's widow will receive her ten-million dollar death benefit payout from the insurance company. It's little consolation for what she's put up with, but at least she'll be financially set to move on with her life."

"Her lawyer called me the other day to discuss that. The process can take up to seven years in Illinois for missing persons."

"That's just the default without a court order declaring the missing person dead. A judge I happen to know will issue one well before that. What else did her lawyer say?"

"Not much. I told her I didn't represent Barry Lee anymore and she asked why. When I didn't tell her, she said okay and that she'd contact the insurance company directly. I haven't spoken with her since."

"Did Barry Lee have a will? And please, don't feel pressured to tell me anything that violates attorney-client privilege. I understand you *now* take that very seriously ... "

Knoble thought of the journalist who came to his office ten days earlier, offering him eight grand for information about an old client that was completely innocuous but also confidential. He'd felt more than tempted but said no. Was that a setup to see if he'd divulge privileged information?"

"He did have a will. No trust though, which is odd for a man of his net worth."

"Why?"

"Most high net worth individuals want to bypass probate, so their beneficiaries can collect as soon as possible. Trusts are the easiest way to do it."

"Well, usually they don't send their spouses to the emergency room six times."

"That's true."

"I don't think that'll be a problem either, Bill. Something tells me her case is headed to the top of the list and it'll get in and out pretty quick."

He processed the comment and what it implied, scratching his forehead. His eyes still on the man in the chair, who'd remained in the same sitting position the entire time, he started to wonder about this man's influence. Where, if anywhere, did his reach end and the BS begin? Based on what'd happened with Barry Lee — from his mysterious disappearance to the lack of evidence to everything else — he could only guess it was as far as advertised.

"Well, I hope so. She deserves it."

"Indeed she does. But listen, I'm on a tight schedule. And happy as I am to talk about all the positive changes you're making, I'm actually here on business."

"Oh?" he said, raising his eyebrows in an attempt at nonchalance. Even to him it sounded more like a whimper than a matter-of-fact comment.

"Remember when I told you that one day I might need a favor from an honest man?"

How could I forget?

"Yes."

"Well, I wasn't sure it would ever come, but today's the day."

"What … what can I do for you?"

"It's all in the envelope sitting on your desk."

He checked the desk and saw a plain white envelope propped against the black touch lamp. Reaching for it, he looked at the man as if to ask if he should open it now.

"You can read it when I leave. It's all there. But I did want to ask one thing."

"Yes?"

"If possible, could you give it your immediate attention? I'd really appreciate it. I'll owe you one. I know how hard you're working to revamp the office, all the balls you have in the air. Trust me — I'm a good guy to have in your debt."

"I'll look into it right away. No need to repay me."

"That's very generous. Thank you."

"Don't mention it."

"Bill," the man said, rising from the leather chair to his full 6'2" stature, "my name's Ben, and I can honestly say it's been a real pleasure this morning. I'm pretty sure the pleasure's been all mine this time around, but bear with me. I'm not a bad guy to be in business with. And if you keep doing what you're doing, I have a feeling you'll find that out for yourself sooner rather than later. I know we got off to a rocky start, but sometimes that's how these things go. You keep doing the right things, maybe one day you'll actually look forward to my visit."

Yeah, and maybe next year the Bears will win the Super Bowl.

37

At just before ten o'clock in the morning, Nikki's body was running on the caffeine from her fourth cup of coffee. Her brain, on the other hand, was sprinting around the endless loop of her conversation with Ben six-and-a-half hours ago.

There were plenty of things to think about, but initially only one thing stood out. Even with Bodie's confirmation that treacherous malware was involved, his request for Witness Protection and Ben's insistence that she take extra precaution, all she could think about was the name Dominick Riddle.

Ben instructed her to *not* search the FBI database, though she still didn't fully understand why. Said he had his own sources and would get back to her by day-end. He also said she shouldn't Google the name or in any other way draw attention to the fact she knew it. Even not knowing his reasons, that request felt extreme. But he only asked her to hold off for twenty-four hours and despite the strong temptation, their renewed trust wasn't something she wanted to jeopardize again. After all, he didn't have to tell her about his conversation with Bodie in the first place.

So she instead tried to stay focused on her other key takeaway of his conversation, the fact Peter Hubley was innocent. Uninvolved with the PCC, unassociated with the malware, unattached to any heinous wrongdoing. In fact, he was the only person who did the right thing. And it was that decision that had got him killed.

She preferred not to dwell on the macabre irony, but rather the soon-to-be fulfilled promise. Sally Hubley was right the whole time. Even as bloggers, reporters and pretty much the entire country — including Nikki — doubted Peter Hubley, Sally had remained faithful to her husband. She defended him, refusing to give in to what the world was saying. If there was any lemonade to be made of this rotten lemon of a case, it was Sally's dedication to Peter.

Which was why Nikki was surprised but more disappointed when Ben said they should hold off telling her the good news. When she asked him if she could be there when he did —

acknowledging that it should come from a family friend, not an FBI Agent — he suddenly got in a hurry at four in the morning. He turned the car around and minutes later pulled up to her apartment building, handed her a prepaid cell phone and told her to use it whenever she called him. Then he peeled out, spouting off something about a meeting he had and that he'd call her later.

So there Nikki sat … at her tiny, painfully unorganized desk, re-reading the case file for the umpteenth time. Having already called her friend at Witness Protection, it was the only thing she could do while she waited to hear back from Karen Hovey.

She'd asked the InvestSecure secretary for a copy of Bodie's schedule over the past three weeks, hoping to ascertain who the other two men Bodie mentioned were. Karen said she'd get back to her, so after hearing Redmond say there was still no luck tracing the wire transfers to the Cayman accounts, she returned to the Hubley case file she now almost knew by heart. She could hear Robert Stevens telling her the answers were in those pages. But she couldn't find them.

That's when the prepaid cell phone started ringing.

"What's the secret password?" she said with exaggerated seriousness.

"Are you alone?" Ben answered, unamused.

"Is this clandestine talk really necessary?"

"Where are you?"

"Work."

"Are you alone?"

"Yes, yes. I'm alone. What's going on?"

"Meet me at Sally Hubley's house at noon."

"It's about time we paid her a visit. I was thinking we —"

"Stay where you are until then."

"Ben … what's going on?"

Silence.

"Ben!"

"Eric Meyer is dead."

———

"That's so terrible," Sally Hubley said, covering her mouth.

Ben nodded and lowered his head, acknowledging the horror of the news he'd just delivered. Sitting in Sally's living room for the third time in as many weeks, he caught a glimpse of *Acceptance and Gratitude*, a book in the *Everyday Matters Bible Study for Women* series. It sat next to the same open Bible he'd seen before and the pot of tea Sally brought out for their unannounced and — judging by the mess — unexpected visit.

Nikki sat next to Sally on the couch and rested her hand on Sally's shoulder as the poor young widow absorbed the news that her husband's old co-worker died in a house fire.

"Do they know what caused it?"

"All they know now is it started sometime in the middle of the night. Neighbors saw house lights on at eleven and the Fire Department was called just after five."

That wasn't *all* they knew. According to Tom's contact in the River Forest Fire Department, the Victorian-style home was engulfed in flames at a rate almost twice as fast as expected. Typically, the source said, it would take a fire originating on the ground floor about forty minutes to reach a two-story home's roof of about the same square footage. In the Meyers' case, flames covered their entire *three*-story home by the time the Fire Department got there, after only an estimated fifteen minutes. The plausible explanation was that the fire originated in multiple rooms and the flames worked their way up in parallel. And that was a telltale sign of arson.

"The Meyers ... they had children. Three children."

"Yes."

"Did they ... ?"

He sighed uncomfortably.

"They didn't make it."

"Oh my God," Sally said, looking towards the ceiling, praying or mumbling, he couldn't tell which.

There was nothing easy about what came next, but it had to be done and time wasn't his ally. He'd been thinking about how bring it up since Tom called about the fire, but he still didn't have a good segue.

He swallowed the pain and said it directly. "Sally, there's reason to believe this wasn't an accident."

"What? You mean … someone … *murdered* Eric Meyer and his family?"

"I don't have time to explain. But yes, it's a strong possibility the house was set on fire intentionally. That's why we're here."

"I don't understand."

"We want to make sure you're protected, Sally," Nikki interjected.

"Why would *I* need protection?"

Nikki looked in his direction but he didn't look back.

"It's probably an over precaution, but our investigation has indicated that it's possible the people who … the people responsible for what happened to Peter might now be coming after his acquaintances."

"You think this happened because of Peter? Because of something he did?"

"No, it's not that at all. Nothing Peter did wrong. And we can't even confirm there's a connection. But we'd rather be overcautious and would like you and the children to come with us just to be sure."

"Oh my Lord … "

After enough silence as Sally contemplated the request, Ben knew he had to move this along. While Nikki was right about the lack of confirmation, his gut was telling him otherwise.

"Sally, I know this is a lot to take, but you have to be strong now. Strong for Peter, and for Timothy and Samuel. Where are they now?"

"They're with the Gordons."

"Good, they're safe there. Why don't you get a few things and give Nick a call. Tell him you'll be by in a few to pick up the kids and we can all head to the —"

"Where would we live?"

"I'm sorry?" Nikki asked.

Sally seemed to regain energy, sitting up, running her hand through her long, red hair. Ben knew she was doing what he'd asked … focusing. Just not the way he wanted.

"Ms. Benton, I've lived here ever since Peter and I got married. I have Thanksgiving every year in that dining room. I gave birth to both of my children in the upstairs bathroom. I've laughed and cried in this very room for years and I've shared the Gospel in that kitchen more times than I can count on two hands. This is my home and you're asking me to leave it. So I'm asking you, where would I go?"

"We'd take you to a hotel at first. Just for a week while they conduct an investigation on the cause of the fire."

"That can take longer than a week."

"Sometimes, but I don't think it will."

"And then what? What happens after the investigation?"

"It depends. If it confirms this is an over precaution, you'd come back home."

"And if not?"

"We'd put you in temporary housing owned by the federal government. You'd have access to whatever you needed — clothes, food, toys for the kids, everything. I'd personally ensure you and your children have enough space, privacy and anything else you need. You'd be as comfortable and safe as possible."

Sally looked at Ben, arching her head slightly, even nodding a bit. But it wasn't a nod of agreement.

"Ben, this is my home. I'm not leaving."

"Sally, be reasonable. It's just to make sure you're safe —"

"I am being reasonable. I understand what you're saying, but this is my home."

"What about the kids?"

"You said they were safe at Nick and Lisa's. And believe me, I am thinking of them. This is our home and we're not going to be pushed out of it."

"Sally, don't make this any more difficult than it needs to be."

"I'm not the one making it difficult."

"You're in a lot of pain, and there's so much going on it's hard to think straight. But you need to take precaution. I've got Joe staying with a friend of mine, too. You think I want him out of the house? No, but it's the smart thing to do. You can come back when it's over."

"As soon as what's over? What else has to be *over* before I can try to move on with my life?"

"As soon as —"

"Ben, I understand all you've done for me. The Lord used you to help heal me. And I know I'd be in terrible shape without you. You, on the other hand, wouldn't be in trouble at all if it weren't for me.

I'm so grateful for you. I asked for your help and you've been so generous with it. And I realize that because of your generosity, your own family may be in danger. I am so, so sorry for that. I hope you can forgive me."

"Sally, I —"

"But you're asking me to leave the only consistency I have left. People are talking about my husband like he's a monster, about affairs and mafias and things that I've only seen in the movies. If I hear all that garbage in person, I might start to believe it. My home is my refuge. It's not much, but it's my shelter from the world. It's where the Lord wants me and I'm not leaving. I know that's not what you want to hear, but it's final."

Her eyes were now dressed in a conviction that said only by force would she leave. And Ben couldn't bring himself to invoke coercion. Not after all she'd been through. No matter how he felt, it wasn't his place to take her free will away.

"Okay, Sally."

"Thank you."

"But before we leave, there's something you should know."

"What?"

He proceeded to inform her of Peter's innocence, from start to finish. Holding nothing back and telling her the information couldn't leave the room, he shared everything Bodie said. And that Peter's only part was the virtuous one.

Nikki kept quiet but occasionally nodded her head when Sally looked at her to nonverbally confirm what she was hearing wasn't too good to be true. She didn't care about malware or wire transfers or InvestSecure's CEO. The only thing that mattered was the fact that she'd been right the whole time to remain loyal to Peter. That Peter was an honest, loving husband who'd neither cheated on her nor done anything illegal.

"I'm not sure when or even if the world will ever say it, but you had a right to know the truth."

"That doesn't matter. I heard it and knew it was true. The Lord has delivered closure through you. Thank you, Ben, for seeking the truth and telling me."

Sally rose from the couch and leaned down to embrace him in the chair. She hooked her arms around his neck and pulled him tight. Her smooth face pressed against his and he could smell her fruity shampoo as she thanked him for taking care of her while he waited to see Anna in Heaven.

38

Of the thirty-two identities he'd used since meeting Dominick Riddle thirteen years ago, Matthew J. Baker was definitely his favorite. It had a certain ring to it. A soothing charm that nicely complemented the genuine-sounding name under which he performed his duties.

But as he hunkered down under the shrubbery, gigantic pine trees surrounding him, he was happy that no identity was necessary today. It wasn't that airports scared him — the documentation Mr. Riddle provided was always more than sufficient — it was that he just didn't like them. People were the worst, and there were always so many of them in airports. They hustled from one place to the next, totally engrossed in their own, busy lives. It was all too chaotic and messy for him. He much preferred today's setting: quiet, isolated and unknown.

The beautiful five-bedroom, two-story brick house he stared at through binoculars from across the street was on Cunningham Lane in Cadiz, Kentucky. It was built only three years earlier and sat five minutes from the Cumberland River. Its large, concrete circle drive and centrally located twenty-foot flagpole made a powerful opening statement. It was only a half-mile from Highway KY-274 and thirty miles north of the Tennessee border. That, combined with its close proximity to I-24, made it a perfect location for a quick getaway.

Cadiz on the whole was a small town at best, with three thousand residents, little commerce and virtually no recognizable downtown. It was rated one of the safest towns in Kentucky, its violent crime rate index nearly one-fourth of the average U.S. city.

This particular part of Cadiz was even smaller and safer. The nearest neighbor was a quarter mile away on a very quiet street, blocked by hundreds of large pine that would remain full of leaves even through the winter. The homes in the sparse neighborhood all had open backyards leading to the river, where boats were docked for fishing. Shotguns could be heard during deer hunting season, but aside from that the area remained still throughout the year. Folks minded their own business and expected others to do the same.

Perfect.

After Mr. Riddle gave him the address, he'd learned that the six-acre property belonged to Terrance A. Smith. Mr. Smith owned a small marketing firm and worked from home when he wasn't traveling. Financial information was hard to come by, but judging by the $750,000 house and three luxury automobiles, he did all right for himself.

He'd been divorced for eleven years and built this place as a retreat. No kids and no immediate family in the area. No friends either, for that matter. The man fit into the rural Cadiz mentality well and it seemed very few people even knew who he was.

And that was it — the extent of his research stopped there. It wasn't his job to know the target beyond knowing what might impede the operation. Mr. Riddle told him who, when and where. He took care of the rest. He did a quick background check and identified potential threats, then moved swiftly to finish his work. Based on what he'd learned, this operation would be easier than most.

Adorned in cheap but effective camouflage and a brown hat covering his bald head, he lay down on his stomach and stared through the brown binoculars. The work had already been done, now it was time to wait. The leftmost of three garage doors opened four minutes ahead of schedule at 8:46, and Mr. Smith walked outside and paused. It was as if he did so to inhale the fresh air and listen to the silent serenity of nature. Squirrels chased each other in the large uncut yard and the sun peeked in and out of thick clouds as he looked up at the sky, perhaps surveying those clouds to determine if the convertible was an option.

Of course, it didn't matter — he'd visited each of Mr. Smith's three vehicles. But as always, there was room for a game. This time, it was a bet he'd made with himself regarding which car Mr. Smith would choose. It'd been an unseasonably warm fall in a place that averaged a high of seventy-one degrees in October, so he had his money on the grey Chevrolet Camaro ZL1 convertible. He figured Smith would try to get as much use out of it as he could before winter. And when Smith went back in the garage and the first door closed behind him, he knew he'd guessed correctly.

The moment of anticipation suddenly upon him, he rested his hand on the shotgun by his side. He did it purely for comfort, his own little pacifier. The birds above singing and creek behind flowing, less than thirty seconds later the middle garage door opened.

Seconds later, the starter turned and the explosion occurred.

He'd very carefully built and planted the bombs so they wouldn't destroy the entire house or make a loud noise that would draw unwanted attention. Rather, the near silent whiff of fire would ignite inwards towards the driver and instantaneously engulf the front seat in quiet flames.

It was so gentle in fact that the garage door continued opening, completely unaffected by the blast. When the door was fully ajar, he looked through the binoculars and saw the once beautiful, highest performing Camaro of all time engulfed in flames. The top was still up and the fire had already overtaken Mr. Smith. The side windows had shattered, no doors had been opened and no signs of life were present.

Satisfied, he reached inside his camouflage jacket pocket and retrieved his cell phone. Two calls needed to be placed, the first to Mr. Riddle. The second would go to his man standing by in a tow truck waiting for his call.

His contact would arrive at Mr. Smith's home less than five minutes later. He'd haul the hunk of metal that used to be Mr. Smith's car away from civilization. What was left of it would eventually end up in a mobile car crusher, a special type of baling press compactor that would turn the previously valued $75,000 automobile into a large cube of recyclable metal.

Terrance Smith's charred body inside it.

39

"That's good news," Dominick Riddle spoke into the receiver.

"Thank you, sir."

"It's such good news I've just doubled your fee."

"That's very generous of you, sir."

I can more than afford it.

"You'll get back to Chicago this afternoon?" he asked more as a directive.

"Yes, sir. I'll leave as soon as the target's car is removed from the premises."

"When will you arrive?"

"It's roughly six hours from Cadiz, sir."

He checked the Thomas Tompion Clock sitting atop his desk next to the crystalline hourglass and pewter Bullet Ant paperweight. Six hours. That meant Matthew J. Baker would be back in the Windy City by three, plenty of time.

"You're clear on your next assignments?"

"Crystal, sir."

"And you realize the significance of their timing?"

"They will be completed in order by the end of the day."

"Another doubled fee will be in order once they are."

"Thank you again, sir."

Riddle hung up the phone and unleashed a gigantic belly laugh to his own amusement. He didn't often afford himself such luxuries, but he took a moment to reflect. The master spin artist, the self-labeled strategic marketing genius, the latest fool to underestimate him, was now dead.

That's what you get when you try to cross me.

He'd been tracking Terrance Smith's calls for weeks, both on the prepaid cell phones and otherwise. He knew of Terrance's conversations with the offshore banks and his contact in Bermuda. He knew about the $20 Million socked away, the interest it was earning and the spin artist's plan to disappear into Somerset Village.

Terrance almost made it too; less than eighteen hours away from paradise.

Too bad, so sad.

Terrance's retirement had of course always been inevitable. He'd tried to tell the spin artist that when the time came, it was in his best interests to do as he said. He'd always taken care of Terrance as an employee and might've done the same in retirement.

But no, Terrance had to have his own plans; plans that included sneaking off to Bermuda behind his back and only pretending to care about the malware project and Plan X. Plans centered around his own confusion and false impression of docility while Terrance secretly plotted an escape. Most importantly, plans that had gotten Terrance killed. His spin artist tried to outsmart him and had to pay the price for that mistake.

"Well, Mr. Genius Marketer ... how does it feel? I beat you in every way, you faggot pond scum. You told me about Plan X on Wednesday. Today is Friday and you're dead. You almost made it to Saturday, you pathetic little lepton," he shouted, emancipating another belly laugh.

The irony was that Plan X was truly outstanding. The distance Terrance had inserted between Adir Mousa and him was impressive and believable, and the misdirection would work wonders if called upon. Terrance had taken steps to ensure the terrorists would be swallowed up by the press and while that was happening, he would fade away unscathed. All things considered, it was Terrance's best work yet.

A perfect way to go out.

The Thomas Tompion Clock reminded him of the perfection that drove him. Like Lamborghinis, it inspired. It also was known — albeit to a smaller degree — for its extreme rarity and value. Given the fact there were only three such clocks available in the entire world and that they were assembled by a British clockmaker in the seventeenth century, the two million dollar price tag was appropriate. The status the clock's red tortoiseshell exterior and Grande Sonnerie chimes offered was worth every cent.

Exclusivity, the reason I own it and others don't.

As if the news about Terrance wasn't enough, the day still had a lot to offer.

The malware was nearly complete and before midnight he'd have $700 Million he didn't have before. Adir Mousa hadn't so much as flinched at his fifty percent down request, and why should he? The malware would deliver well over $1.4 Billion worth of intelligence the first week.

The terrorists would use it once, become immediately infatuated, and inevitability would take over. The towel heads would get greedy and aggressive, a dangerous yet surefire combination from Ahab the Arab. They'd use it too quickly, fail to cover their tracks, get traced and eventually caught. By then Plan X would be implemented and he'd be well on his way to the next project with another billion-five to invest.

He still had to arrange the early retirements of his three "partners." That would be almost as much fun as it was arranging Terrance's exodus from the workforce. Then he'd have Matthew J. Baker seal the deal with the terrorist group. Delivery and final payment would be confirmed. He'd set the rules and Mousa would adhere. It was as simple as that, just like always.

The only remaining question was what to do with Matthew J. Baker. He'd planned to clean house — Terrance, the three partners, everyone. Wipe them all out and rebuild fresh. Such spring cleaning was necessary ever so often and Baker was part of the clutter.

But the man had continued to impress. From going to Brazil to ensure Hubley was eliminated, to negotiating with Adir Mousa, to following Nikki Benton unseen, to disposing of Terrance Smith ... Baker had exceeded his expectations each time, something very few people did.

"Maybe I'll keep him after all. As Terrance proved, pet projects can be fun."

40

Nikki turned off Bu's ignition and downed the 5-hour ENERGY like a shot of tequila. Her taste buds immediately objected, but her droopy body savored the flavor after hours of protest that coffee alone wasn't getting the job done. The bitter flavor meant the cavalry — two hundred milligrams of caffeine packed into two fluid ounces — was on its way. She dropped the small, multi-colored bottle in the cup holder and chased the shot with a swig of Dejà Blue canned water.

It'd been over twenty-four hours since she'd called Karen Hovey requesting Bodie's schedule. At the time, Hovey made it seem like she'd call back soon, but a day later Nikki simply couldn't stare at the case file anymore. If Robert Stevens was right and the answer was in those pages, she'd have to tip her hat to whoever could find it.

She'd called Ben and he said he was "busy," whatever that was supposed to mean. The guy was a modern day John Wayne, running off doing this, doing that, expecting the audience to sit good-naturedly awaiting his heroic return. She told herself "busy" didn't mean investigating her case without her, but that logic got harder and harder to swallow.

Bu parked in the visitor spot on Clark, she looked up towards the modern office building's third-story windows. Ben had made it clear she shouldn't go back to InvestSecure, but he also said he couldn't control her and was done trying.

With no new leads and the malware threat exposed, she licked her lips at the thought of Bodie's schedule. Her focus on identifying those two other men, she figured Bodie's schedule crossed with a database of "powerful" people was her best bet. When she explained her logic to Ben, he noted she was making a lot of assumptions but that overall it wasn't her worst idea.

Gee, thanks Ben.

No, she told herself after replaying that conversation. *You're the Special Agent, not Ben Siebert. You have a case and an idea and you need to do something about it. Stop worrying about what he says and do your job.*

Dressed in a beige suit and light-brown shoes, she motored through the lobby past the elaborate fountain, pumping her arms for speed. She held in the CLOSE DOOR button on the gold-colored elevator like a kid imploring it to move faster. She stormed through the fancy glass doors to get in front of Karen Hovey, using the anger she felt for the lack of callback as courage to demand the respect she'd been denied.

But when she looked at the receptionist, Karen's reddened eyes reminded her of Sally Hubley. A box of tissues on her lap, she blotted tears away with obvious sadness. At first, she didn't even notice Nikki was there. The office was eerily quiet, so quiet the cliché saying about a pin dropping came to mind, and she drew attention to herself by clearing her throat.

"Agent Benton … I was supposed to call you yesterday."

"That's right," she snapped, fortifying her authoritative position. *I'm no pushover.*

"I'm sorry for not getting back to you," Karen replied, fighting tears to choke the words out.

"What's wrong?"

"It's just terrible," Karen replied just before a burst of tears erupted from her like lava from a volcano.

"What is it?" she repeated, folding her hands on the top of the desk and already regretting the *tough girl* act.

"It's Mr. Bodie … "

"What about him?"

"He took his own life this morning."

———

"I thought I said not to go to InvestSecure?" Ben replied to the disturbing news.

"Aren't you glad I did?"

He clenched the phone tightly, fully aware why Nikki visited the private equity firm. Defiance. To send the message that she didn't have to listen to him.

"You keep doing things like that and you're going to get hurt."

"You can't tell me what to do."

"That's not the point."

"It is for me, Ben."

"What exactly is your point?"

"That I'm not some cow you can control with a feeding trough and a cattle prod."

"That's an odd image."

"The shoe fits. Like you said, if we're partners, we're partners. What are *you* up to? Why wasn't I with you?"

"I'm glad you enjoy making your points. Just don't get yourself killed doing it"

"My question still stands. What are you doing? Let me come do it with you if I'm endangering myself otherwise."

"I just got back from visiting Joe."

"Joe, your son? At Tom Fedorak's house?"

"Yes. Nothing case related."

"Why?"

"Because he wanted to see me. When that happens, I try to be there."

"And you're saying it had nothing to do with the case?"

"That's not what I'm saying. That's what I said."

"You expect me to believe you?"

"Sure do, *partner.*"

Nikki didn't respond and frankly he didn't care. They didn't have time to bicker about her going to InvestSecure or him visiting Joe. The situation was escalating at an alarming rate and would continue to do so until eventually it'd come to a crashing halt and die. Die instantly and in a telling way. A way that said they'd missed their chance, that Dominick Riddle and the malware were gone forever.

"What happened with Bodie?" he asked.

"I talked to a friend of mine at the local PD. Bodie had a couple of pretty important meetings this morning. When he didn't show, Karen called the house."

"Bodie's wife wasn't home, was she?"

"No, out running errands, so the phone just rang. Same thing with his cell. After four hours, Karen got nervous and called 911."

"Seems a bit extreme, doesn't it? He's a busy guy and my guess is it's not her day to watch him."

"According to her statement, Bodie's lack of response was highly unusual. Typically he at least sends a text within minutes."

"Still seems bizarre, but oh well."

"Anyway, dispatch sent a black-and-white to his house. When no one answered, the cop noticed the garage was open and peeked inside. He saw Bodie's unconscious body reclined all the way back in the passenger seat, next to an open vial of prescription painkillers and a half-empty bottle of Jack Daniel's."

"That's original."

"Not funny."

"I'm not trying to be funny."

"What are you trying to be?"

"I'm trying to figure out if it was really a suicide."

"What?"

"Was there a note?"

"No note, no calls to his wife or kids, no warning."

"Where's his family?"

"At the police station. My friend tells me the wife's hysterical. Can't stop crying. This was definitely a shock to her."

Ben silently replayed Bodie's words in St. Pius V Church, less than two days ago, questioning how much of a surprise it should be to him.

The moment you came to my office and started asking questions about malware, you signed my death warrant.

"Anything else?" he asked, a tad frustrated.

"You mean aside from the fact that the one guy we knew who had knowledge of Dominick Riddle is dead? No, there's nothing else."

"What do you make of it?"

"There's no indication of foul play. The garage was wide open and Bodie was sitting in his own car, wearing sweat pants and a T-shirt. They're still dusting, but my friend tells me his prints are all over the vial and bottle. His blood alcohol content confirms he took down at least half the bottle — that's 375 milliliters of 94 proof whiskey — and I'm guessing the toxicology report will confirm he took the pills as well. More than enough drugs and alcohol to kill a man and there's no evidence of coercion. We won't know for sure until the autopsy's done, but it looks like a legitimate suicide to me."

"Agreed."

"Anything to add?"

"Only that my guess is if Dominick Riddle had him killed, he would've arranged it to be done a little more privately and a lot more painfully."

"But Hubley's murder wasn't private."

"Yes, but Peter wasn't killed on American soil. Two random Brazilians executed him and his body was stolen from an ambulance before an autopsy could be performed. According to Bodie, the reason for that was to throw the authorities off and make everyone think Peter's death had something to do with Brazil. Very intelligently planned and executed misdirection."

"What does that have to do with Bodie's death? It's a totally different situation."

"Precisely my point … it doesn't add up. Why plan Peter's execution so carefully, so meticulously, down to the finest detail, and then just knock Bodie off in his garage and leave the body there? Riddle wouldn't have done that. Convincing the world Bodie committed suicide wouldn't be as easy as convincing the world Peter was tied to the PCC. Bodie was a prominent member of the community, Man of the Year at that. If this was a murder, Riddle would've covered his tracks."

"Or maybe that's what he wants you to think."

"I could be wrong, but I still agree with you. This doesn't seem like a murder."

"Speaking of Riddle, did you get anything from your sources?"

"Not much. The guy's a phantom. I've never seen anything like it. There are rumors about him in certain circles but nothing concrete to follow up on. People don't know him, they know *of* him. Unconfirmed reports say he eliminates people he works with every so often, which would explain why he's so elusive. But it's all speculation."

"Address, phone number, anything we could use to find him?"

"No."

"Maybe I should take a look at —"

"Don't check the FBI database."

"Why?"

"Give me a little more time."

"What are you not telling me? I thought we were partners."

"We are."

"Eric Meyer and Ryan Bodie are dead! Why should I trust you and back off from using a database that's going to nail the bastard? What are you not telling me?"

"I know they're dead, Nikki. You don't have to remind me. And you don't have to trust me, but that's what I'm asking. Sit tight for forty-eight hours, let me check some things. You didn't listen to me when you went to InvestSecure but I need you to now."

"My visit is what —"

"I don't have time for this, Nikki. Hold off on the Dominick Riddle search, okay? I realize I'm being cryptic, but I'm not asking you anymore. Trust me; you'll get the whole story once I have it. I promise. And I'm using that word deliberately. Telling you what I know now would do more harm than good."

"What's that supposed to mean?"

"I have to go. Just trust me."

41

Welcome to Bizarro World, Joe Leksa thought.

Tom Fedorak's log cabin, three-story home — with its man-made pond surrounded by duck decoys and fishing benches in the backyard, hot-dog-in-a-bun-shaped mailbox at the end of a mile-long gravel drive and large YOU ARE NOT WELCOME HERE front door floor mat — was straight out of a comic book.

Located in the far west suburbs of Illinois, Maple Park felt light years away from Chicago. On both private well and septic with no neighbors in sight and not a sound to be heard, Tom's hand-built mansion was desolate and uninviting to a twenty-three-year-old from the city. When Joe stepped outside to look around, all he could see was farmland and sky. With binoculars, during the day he could catch a glimpse of Howard Road, but it was just as empty and he hadn't seen a car in days.

Tom's home was also without a doubt the most fascinating juxtaposition of cutting edge technology and relics Joe had ever seen. Most people were young or old, hip or outdated, connected or detached. The notion that someone could be both was unfamiliar. But Tom Fedorak was an odd bird; he knew that now more than ever. If anyone marched to the beat of his own drum, it was Tom.

When he first set foot inside the dimly lit abode two days earlier, he froze when he saw Tom's family room. On the coffee table were two iPads, a MacBook Air laptop and an external Hitachi G-DRIVE Slim, all linked to Apple's Time Machine. What was next to that table? The only item Tom paid attention to: a twenty-five-inch, brown-framed RCA tube television from the eighties, the volume knob missing.

Over the next few days, he noted the family room devices were just the tips of a gigantic-ass iceberg. Tom had a nifty portable speaker unit that could interface via Bluetooth with any mobile device or computer to stream music. Its battery offered ten hours of playtime and the range was incredible. But Tom's media of choice was a vintage Gramophone record player. A giant flower-like speaker stuck out of it so far it almost poked Joe in the eye twice.

Tom had offered him the holographic alarm clock on the bedroom nightstand, which could project 3D images of the "Hottie of the Month" — in Tom's words — for a happy wake up. Tom's reason for giving it to him: "First off, Sport, I don't do wake-ups often. But when I do, I like *Old Reliable*," which turned out to be an all-white vintage analog alarm clock with extra-large black numbers and two gigantic bells on top.

There were all sorts of fancy kitchen gadgetry. Examples included an electronic smoking gun to infuse food with the unique flavor blend, a rice cooker that automatically regulated temperature and heat distribution and an iGrill cooking thermometer that wirelessly sent raw meat's internal temperature to a smart phone. Yet Tom's favorite utensil was an old wooden spoon with a cracked handle called into action whenever mixing, mashing, poking, flipping or stirring was required. "One size fits all, Sport."

"Mr. Fedorak?" he said softly.

"What did I tell you, Sport?" Tom said as Jeffrey the dog sipped Fiji water from his golf-ball-shaped bowl. "*Mr.* is for geezers. Call me that again and you'll have to answer to *Betsy*," he jabbed, holding up and affectionately staring at the fishing knife.

"Sorry."

"While we're at it, Grasshopper doesn't like *Mr.* any more than I do. You could always just call him *Dad*."

Before Joe could respond, *it* happened.

It was the occurrence Tom made him prepare for when he first arrived for over two hours. The "very unlikely" situation that at first terrified him but he eventually handled by harnessing Tom's assurance that *it* probably wouldn't happen.

Yet here *it* was, happening. The beeping came from Tom's laptop, sitting on the wall cutout desk behind the couch. He turned and stared at the computer, Tom doing the same for a few seconds before walking over to it. He caught a brief glimpse of a black box with red and green lines when Tom unlocked the screen but didn't know what any of them were. After a few second seconds, Tom faced him. He had a look — a serious, focused look that he'd never seen in all the years he'd known Tom.

"Joe, it's time. Just like we planned, son."

42

Dayam, the house was dark.

But then again, there weren't no windows either.

He'd never seen a house without windows. Log cabin or no, weren't windows some sort of requirement from the Fire Department or whatever? Maybe there were windows in the back, but it was some strange shit seeing the front of a crib without no windows. Maybe he shoulda gone around back, but the bald dude who hired him said he had to go this way. When he told the bald dude he usually did this shit from the back, baldie got pissed and chewed his ass out. *His way*, he'd said. Take it or leave it.

He didn't care then, at least not too much. But that was before he knew how dark it was gonna be out in the sticks. Moon might've been full, but that shit was behind the clouds. It was *really* friggin dark out here. No streetlights, no cars, nothing.

Whatever. Not that bigga deal. This wadn't his first rodeo and he knew his shit. Whether downtown Chicago or out in the boonies, a job was a job, score a score. And after this one … *man* … after this one he wouldn't do no others ever again. He'd use the cash to start his bar, like he'd always wanted. Get his homeboys and lil' sis to help, you know, waitressing and all that, build that shit from the ground up.

After barely getting by in some cold-ass winters for twenty-three years, he finally got a break. They don't come around much in Englewood, so he sure wasn't gonna piss it away cuz he couldn't come from the back. This score wadn't normal. This was his last one. Plus, baldie was a little scary. Had that creep-o look, those weird eyes. But for the kind of dough baldie was dishin out, he could deal with it

Just do what baldie says, get the cash and start your bar.

But as he crawled hunched down in the grass next to the gravel driveway — just like baldie said — the no windows thing bothered him. It was bad enough he had to walk all the way from that weird hot dog mailbox. And the two-hour car ride with baldie *really*

201

sucked ass. But no windows … he didn't know what to make of a crib with no windows.

Gripping his M1911 Colt pistol, he told himself no sweat. Baldie told him how easy it'd be. There was a grandpa, sixty or so, retired, slow, and a white college boy, early twenties. Both would probably be sleeping, baldie said. So he could go get the diamonds — third kitchen cabinet, second shelf — and get the hell out. If they weren't sleeping, he'd wave the gun in grandpa's face and make him shit his pants and give him the diamonds. Either way, baldie told him he'd have the stones and be on his way in ten minutes. In and out, wadn't nothing to it.

Woulda been better to know for sure they were sleeping, but when he asked baldie about waiting 'til four in the morning the guy said no. Said he had to get the stones before midnight. Said it was important and handed him ten grand on the spot. Said it was for his trouble. He flipped through that shit 'til his eyes almost popped out. Tens and twenties, clean and crisp.

Eleven-thirty it is, boss.

When he got to the front door, he took a look around and pulled the piece close. Real quiet and dark, he whipped around to go inside and get it over with. His bar, his empire, was waiting. Dollar signs dancin' in his head.

Just like the boss said, the door was unlocked. He couldn't believe that shit. Not only was he worried how he'd get in, with no windows and all, but what kind of dumbass leaves his door open? White farm-boys who live out in the sticks, that's who. Gramps here had over a hundred g's worth of stones in his kitchen and leaves the front door open. *Jamal*, he said to himself, *you been in the wrong business*. He kept his piece aimed straight ahead and walked inside.

It was real quiet, just like outside, no lights on. Didn't hear a TV or voices or nothing. Good, they were sleeping. The crib was nice. Wood floors, tall ceilings, a nice hutch in the foyer. To his right was a big-ass living room with a big-ass couch, couple recliners. To his left, a smaller room with a piano, wood bench and a fancy chair. Bunch of deer heads on the wall. Country boy did him some hunting. But straight ahead was where he was headed, long hallway to the kitchen.

As he started walking, he felt cold steel on the back of his head. Then he heard a gun cock. And a voice that didn't sound like no friggin grandpa.

"Drop the gun before I make a window out of your head."

———

The intruder couldn't have been more than twenty-five on a good day. He looked the part and was dressed for the age. African American, six feet tall, dark blue jeans hanging off his ass, grey FUBU sweatshirt and a pair of bright red untied Pumas. He could see a twinkle from the fake diamond in his left ear.

The kid dropped the gun and, unprompted, put his hands over his head and spread his legs. That told Tom he'd either been arrested before or had witnessed the act. Either way, he knew the drill.

Keeping the six-shooter on target and walking around to face him, he saw innocence in the intruder's eyes that reminded him more of Joe Leksa than a bandit. In fact, he didn't look like a criminal at all. He looked like a normal twenty-something-year-old kid, despite the circumstances under which they met.

It at least explained the kid's amateurish approach. The sensors by the mailbox at the end of the driveway had gone off immediately, indicating the kid didn't know they were there. From the moment the activation alarm sounded, the front-yard cameras gave Tom a clear view of the kid crawling in the grass. This made it clear he didn't know what he was doing. But why was he there in the first place?

Tom kicked the Colt pistol into the living room and stepped back. His revolver now the only weapon in the equation, he kept it pointed in the kid's general vicinity for appearance but had no intention of pulling the trigger.

"Who are you and why are you here?"

No response, just a nervous face.

"Start talking, boy. I'm a patient man, but there's something about folks breaking into my home that brings out the violence in me."

"Name's Jamal."

"Jamal, I'm Tom. Now that we're introduced, what the hell are you doing here?"

"Your … your ice."

"My what?"

"Diamonds. I'm here for the diamonds in your kitchen."

Tom paused … for a few seconds too many.

He should've connected the dots sooner. He should've been prepared that Jamal was no threat. That his real problem wasn't a kid who had no business in Maple Park, but simply a distraction from that real problem. He should've checked all the camera angles right away. But he didn't. He was pissed at himself, but not for long.

It was too late and he knew it.

He heard a quick pop from behind and immediately felt a surge of pain throughout his arm. He hadn't felt that sensation in over thirty years and the heat seemed even greater. His arm felt on fire and blood started flowing from it, confirming his costly oversight. Despite taking the bullet in the left arm, his right hand instinctively dropped the revolver.

A man dressed in all black with goggles around his neck approached him. The six-foot-tall, average build man *looked* like a killer. His scruffy face was focused and determined, and he didn't take his eyes off Tom. Tom could see muddy water dripping from the man's sweatshirt and brown footprints from his boots. *The pond*, he thought. The man had secretly swum through the pond in the backyard while he was watching young Jamal approach in the front. He'd been decoyed. Played like a fool.

The man held the only Type 73 machine gun he'd ever seen in person and looked quite comfortable doing so. A closer look revealed the man was about fifty, completely bald, shaven clean on top, and kept the gun incredibly steady the whole time despite dripping with muddy water. This was a professional.

This was Tom's real problem.

The man bent down to pick up Tom's revolver and looked at him, not Jamal, to whom he spoke. He kept the machine gun on Tom as Tom pressed into the pain in his left arm to stop the bleeding.

"Jamal, your services are appreciated," the man said in a rough yet quiet voice.

"Yo man, I —"

Without prompt, he fired five shots from Tom's revolver, each sounding louder than the last. It happened so fast that all Tom could do was watch as Jamal screamed, grasping the doorknob for life and quickly succumbing to death. The kid dropped to the floor after the second shot and stopped moving after the fourth. After the fifth shot, the man turned his attention back to Tom, pointing the Type 73 at his chest.

After a chilling smile, he moseyed towards Jamal as if on a stroll through the arboretum, kneeling down to the lifeless body. He looked up at Tom and offered an exaggerated wink, then pressed Tom's revolver into Jamal's left temple and fired the final round. Blood squirted from Jamal's head, splattering everywhere. The pool of red surrounding his body immediately doubled and the man smirked before speaking.

"I love six-shooters."

43

"You son of a bitch."

The bald man in black didn't respond. Rather, he casually stood up after blowing Jamal's head off and walked towards him.

"He was just a kid. You didn't have to kill him."

"Calm down, Tom. Jamal's the least of your worries now. He probably would've gotten himself killed anyway."

"I'm gonna bury your smug face in the dirt, you piece of sh —"

"No need for name-calling, Tom. Let's talk in the kitchen. You and I need to have the last conversation of your life."

"Screw you."

Again the man didn't respond, but instead pointed the Type 73 at Tom's right quadriceps and unceremoniously pulled the trigger. He immediately dropped to the ground unable to support his own weight, howling in pain. The man just watched, moving his index finger back-and-forth, pantomiming the "no-no" gesture.

"You're familiar with this weapon, I imagine. It's a Type 73 light machine gun, designed in North Korea for its armed forces. It's based on the Kalashnikov PK machine gun but it has its own twists. You don't see many of them here in the States, and it took a bit of effort to get one. Usually, weapons that hard to procure just aren't worth it. They're more talk than walk. But after using it, I'm a believer. Its unique design is actually quite pragmatic. Over six hundred rounds per minute, dual magazine and belt ammo feed options, removable muzzle sleeves. I could fire rifle grenades with this, Tom. But you know what I really like?"

"Screw you, you Communist bastard."

"Communist? You couldn't be further from the truth. I'm a businessman, and you're a fat check waiting to be cashed. But we'll get to that later. Like I was saying, what I really like about the Type 73 is that even though it's gas operated — with rotary bolt locking for automatic mode — it's also got this neat feature that lets you load non-disintegrating Kalashnikov PK steel bullets. That means I can shoot bullets into you that won't ever disintegrate one at a time. Now that's value."

"Good for you, you bald pot licker."

"Tom, I'd advise you to reconsider how willing to cooperate you are. I know you're tough. You're old school. You'd take a hundred of these steel pellets before you gave in for your own sake. I mean, look at this thing," the man said, holding the empty revolver before tossing it into the living room next to Jamal's Colt.

"You had an old fashioned six-shooter for heaven's sake. So I'm well aware there's no changing or influencing you. But young Joe Leksa … you don't want him to go through what you're willing to endure. I know he's here and I'll find him. When I do, the treatment he receives will depend on how cooperative you are now. So why don't you crawl over to the kitchen table so we can have that conversation."

His right leg and left arm in agony, lying facedown on his stomach, each movement forward brought more pain as Tom scaled the hallway towards the kitchen table. Leaving a massive trail of blood behind, he knew that to the bald killer making him crawl wasn't about forcing pain. It was about power. It was all about punctuating who had it and who didn't, who was in the position to dictate how things would go and who was only suited to follow.

After the twenty-foot struggle of a crawl, he finally reached the table. The man instructed him to pull himself up into the chair, which he did slowly and painfully. By the time he collapsed into the leather seat, he was exhausted, sucking wind and lungs burning. The pain in his arm and leg was excruciating and the trail of blood was even thicker than he'd imagined, indicating how much he'd lost.

He'd used the crawling time to try to figure a way out of this mess but came up empty. He'd been in deep holes before and had always managed to dig himself out, but something told him this was different. He wasn't going to give in, no matter what the man did. And the man wouldn't back down. Professionals don't do that. This was headed towards a stalemate, where ties go to the guy with the gun. At fifty-seven, he'd finally met his match.

44

Joe's instructions were very clear.

The dry practice runs and repeated orders from Tom the past few days were to get safe and let Tom take care of himself. He was to grab Jeffery, run upstairs to the guest bedroom, lock the door behind him and enter Tom's custom-built panic room through the hollow-core closet door. Once inside, he was to call the police and not come out for any reason whatsoever until Tom summoned him in person.

Its exterior was a steel core box with a door guarded by the biggest deadbolt Joe had ever seen. Long hinge and strike-plate screws you couldn't dent with an axe secured it, and even the bottom was a solid steel floor. There was no breaking into it.

The worst thing that could happen, Tom had said, was that with a lot more time than an intruder would likely have, someone could blast or cut out the floor beneath it. In which case the panic room still wouldn't be penetrated but would instead fall to the lower level as a giant solid box, likely killing whoever destroyed the floor and was presumably underneath it. Because of that implausible scenario, there was ultra-reinforced padding around all the inside walls, tons of pillows and a small, built-in section on the ground towards the back with chest, arm, and leg straps. If you got on your back and secured yourself, you'd be far more protected than on any airplane or rollercoaster.

Eight feet long, seven feet wide and six feet tall, it wasn't roomy by any means. But there was plenty of space for the padding and pillows, a laptop, a few tablet computers, some cell phones, chargers, a power generator, oxygen tank with two masks, a week's worth of non-perishable food for humans and dogs, bottled water, a First-Aid Kit and four different guns with several boxes of ammunition. It wasn't an apocalypse survival room but it offered a safe place to retreat and call for help. Hidden in a room with thirty-year-old furniture and archaic grandfather clock, it was another example of Tom's oxymoronic blend of old-fashioned living and cutting edge technology.

When Tom showed it to him, he couldn't imagine Tom ever using it for himself. Tom was the kind of guy who would strip off his shirt and stand in the foyer waiting for the intruders with a knife. But he was terrified, and the panic room would protect him. There was no getting in and he had everything he needed. He would no doubt be safe.

Except he was no longer *in* the panic room.

———

He tried. He took Jeffery into the panic room and secured the door behind them. He turned on the battery-powered Coleman lantern and dialed all four different cell phones but couldn't get service. He grabbed the tablets to log an emergency online but couldn't get a signal. He briefly exited the panic room to grab a landline portable receiver but there was no dial tone. Every outbound signal from the house was gone.

The only connection that wasn't severed was the one that by definition couldn't reach the outside: the closed circuit transmission from the house's security cameras to one of the tablets. Six cameras fed to it so you could describe the intruders to the cops.

He'd sat in the dark, creepy room, the small lantern providing barely enough light for visibility and not nearly enough for comfort. He'd watched, live, a guy about his age get shot to death. The gunshots' thundering blasts penetrated through the steel walls and jolted him each of the six times. There was a slight delay in the internal feed, so he heard the shots first and then watched them on the screen seconds later. The anticipation caused by hearing the gun before seeing it fired made it even more terrifying.

He knew that for however long he lived, these would be *his* nightmares. Once Mr. Siebert told him there were images from days in the Marines that had become nightmares he'd never forget. And although Joe understood what that meant on the surface then, it now made perfect sense.

When the man in all black fired the last shot into the already-dead kid's head, he saw chunks of brain splatter on the ground and had to cover his mouth. His eyes filled with tears that soon made their way down his cheeks. He wanted to crawl into the cutout, strap himself in tight and cover every inch of his body with the padding.

He wanted to tuck himself away forever and talk to Mrs. Anna through God.

But then he watched Tom get shot. Twice. He saw a man he'd always thought indestructible crawl inch-by-inch down the hallway, blood everywhere. He saw the evil glare from the man in black and it dawned on him … it was *him* the man was after. If it wasn't, Tom would already be dead.

He knew Tom would die protecting him. He considered that scenario, as well as Tom's orders to stay in the panic room, his desire to live and what that scenario meant.

And decided he couldn't live with it.

45

Joe tiptoed down the stairs so slowly his calves started burning, grateful the wooden steps weren't creaky. Tears of fear both dried on his face and starting to drip fresh, he held the .357 Magnum with jittery hands.

He didn't know much about guns and aside from mandatory trips to the firing range with Mr. Siebert had never fired them. He knew the basics — the safety mechanism, loading ammunition and never putting his finger in front of the barrel — but that was it.

He didn't know this particular gun nor had he ever fired it, best he could recall. Tom had rattled off a bunch of stuff — saying things like double action and calibers and two-tones — but all he remembered was it was a "good gun," Smith & Wesson made it in America and he got eight shots before he had to reload.

It only weighed about three pounds but after holding it with extended arms for thirty seconds on the slow walk down the stairs, it sure felt heavier. He lowered the gun and bent his elbows once to relax his forearms, but by the time he reached the bottom both arms were ablaze and the gun felt like a bowling ball.

The stairs led to a small laundry room on the northwest corner of the house connected to the living room, caddy-corner from the kitchen. He was glad he didn't have to see the body in the foyer up close, but even at a distance it was ghastly. He tried to keep his eyes away from the lifeless, half-missing head and outstretched arm, but they naturally gravitated towards both. Voices from the kitchen willed him to keep going.

"I'll be honest with you, Tom," the voice said. It sounded rough and hoarse, like the man was a chain smoker.

"This is new territory for me. Usually my job is to simply eliminate threats. I don't talk to them and I don't need anything from them. But in this case, I get both. As you know, this won't end well for you. But it can be relatively painless and you can die knowing the boy won't suffer. Or, your death can be painful beyond words and you'll die knowing the boy will experience the same. It's your choice."

Joe's heart sank when he heard that, inching through the living room before finally reaching the dining·room divider. He lingered behind the wall cutout, hugging the wall tight. He checked the angle from behind it before asking Ms. Anna for help.

No turning back, he ordered himself.

"How are those gunshots treating you, Tom? Those steel pellets feeling saucy? I soaked them in a nice little chemical compound before I loaded my Type 73. Accentuates the burning a bit. Just a little something extra to let you know I mean business. A chemical boost, if you will."

Tom said something but Joe couldn't hear what it was.

"Always the jokester, eh? Well, fun's over."

Joe heard a quick pop, much quieter than when the man shot the kid in the foyer. Tom's agonizing scream, however, was anything but quiet. Joe had to lower the gun to cover his mouth.

"Where's the kid, Tom? I don't have all day and neither do you. I've cut the phone lines and blocked the wireless signals. He's got nowhere to go and no one to call. If Siebert's smart, the kid will be fine. But I'm leaving this house with him and it's up to you how much pain he'll endure first."

"Shove your commie gun up your commie ass."

The words were strong and sarcastic but also tired and slurred. Tom was fading.

Fast.

———

"So you've chosen pain. It's time to take this to the next level."

Tom couldn't imagine what the next level was. After taking three steel bullets evidently coated in something to make them smoldering, his left arm and each leg felt a driving, incessant burn, as if his skin had already seared off and his muscles were ablaze. More time only brought more pain and less mobility. Whatever that chemical was, it'd made those gunshot wounds more agonizing than any other he'd sustained. It felt like he'd be crippled soon the agony was so intense.

He had no way to verify the man had cut the phone lines and blocked the wireless signals. The modem was upstairs and he didn't have his cell, so he could only pray the man was bluffing to get him to talk.

But it didn't sound like a bluff.

The scorching heat had overloaded his senses but he thought he heard a beep. Faint at first, but then louder and louder. Perhaps he was hallucinating or being deluded by the aghast feeling of fire on flesh, but he could swear he heard it again.

It was confirmed when his interrogator starting looking around and eventually got up, holding the Type 73. The bald man, face smeared with dirt, stared at the other end of the kitchen as the recurring sounds grew louder. He started to walk towards the source of the noise while Tom, unable to move without pain, turned his head to watch. He thought of trying to make a run for it but his throbbing legs dismissed the idea as foolish.

When the man reached the doorway into the dining room, he turned right and exited Tom's line of vision. Seconds later, Tom heard five loud, unambiguous pops followed by a heavy, rugged scream. That catapulted him out of his agony … and the kitchen chair.

He'd heard that sound before and there was no mistaking it. It was a .357 Magnum revolver, M627 V-Comp. When he reached the doorway, he saw his interrogator on the ground, unmoving, the Type 73 a few feet away in a growing pool of blood. On his back, the man clutched his soggy stomach with both hands, legs lifted off the ground, head tipped back towards his arched spine. His mouth was open but nothing came out, like a fish on land gasping for oxygen. A stream of red made its way from his stomach and chest towards the edge of the room, flooding a tablet PC along the way, its alarm app open and timer still beeping.

Ten feet away, half-concealed by the doorway wall into the living room, was a pair of twenty-three-year-old eyes and a shaking right hand. Joe's chest was convulsing and tears streaked his face. Tom could hear his teeth chattering as he stepped away from the wall slowly, holding the .357 in front of him as he approached the man on the ground.

"Joe, stop!" he yelled with as much energy as he could muster.

The tablet PC still beeping, Joe didn't. Eyes on his prey, the sniper-convert's face was infuriated, not sad. He didn't appear too virgin for the violence he'd witnessed. He looked like he was on a mission, just like Grasshopper, despite the adoptive relation.

When he reached the dying killer, he knelt down and stared at him.

Oh no, Tom thought when Joe pressed the .357 into the man's temple.

One bullet left, ready for use.

"Joe, drop the gun," he repeated, resting a hand on the kid's shoulder.

"No."

"He's still alive, Joe. You didn't kill him."

"Not yet."

"Joe! The gun!" he screamed with vigor and volume he didn't know he still had.

It worked. Joe looked at him, eyes filled with tears.

"Joe, the gun."

Joe reluctantly handed it over.

"Joe ... look at him. Right now, look in his eyes."

He did.

"Now look back at me."

He did.

"You did *not* kill this man. Remember that, son."

Tom reached into his bloody right pant leg and withdrew Betsy. Gripping her tight, he looked at his interrogator and saw no fear. Then he pushed aside the desires to revengefully torture the man and extract information. Joe was paramount. He needed to see this. He needed to see that he wasn't the one who ended a life.

All nine inches of Betsy's shiny blade slid into the man's throat with incredible ease. His attacker squirmed and pushed his hands into Tom's gunshot wounds, inflicting pain from the pressure, but Tom just pressed harder. The struggle lasted five seconds before the man's body went limp and his eyes closed.

He dizzily looked at Joe, covered in blood, tired and lightheaded now that the adrenaline was gone.

"Thanks a lot, Sport."

Joe extended his arms to embrace but didn't get the chance.

Tom's eyes shut all on their own and he fell into darkness.

46

"You're *positive*?" he inquired from the other side of the booth.

"Yes, Mr. Knoble. I spoke with his assistant, Barbara, yesterday," Genie, his increasingly dependable secretary replied.

"She confirmed the time?" he asked just as she was about to take a bite of syrup-coated pancakes. The timing was intentional. The egg white omelet in front of him just wasn't the same, and he lusted for the golden brown deliciousness and whipped butter on Genie's plate. Even with her figure, the girl ate liked a starved hippo.

"Yes, Mr. Knoble."

There was just no way to be sure. And because of that, an ulcer was coming on. The request in the white envelope two days earlier wasn't as daunting or difficult as he'd guessed. But in a way that just added to the pressure. Now there was no excuse to fail, and every day *Ben* proved to be someone he didn't want to let down.

Yesterday — the day after he gave Ben ten business cards — five brand new clients walked into the office. All wealthy, all legitimate, all referred. None specified who did the referring, but none had to.

He'd also received a call from Barry Lee Richard's wife's lawyer. Interestingly enough, the insurance company received a copy of a court order declaring Barry Lee legally deceased. The death benefit payment process had already begun and his widow would have her money in days. Just like that, a seven-year process turned into a week.

The letter in the envelope was very clear. Who, what, when, where and how ... just not why. Straying from its precise instructions in any way felt dangerous and like it or not, he reminded himself, the task wasn't assigned to him. All he could do was trust Genie. It didn't matter that he didn't know why.

Ever since that first meeting with Ben, he'd realized she was more capable than he'd originally thought. He'd turned over all the administrative duties and she'd handled the extra work with pizzazz and efficiency. She also coordinated his schedule, greeted clients and took care of all the paperwork and billing. And she did it all while attending night school — got a ninety-six on her first test.

He watched her take a gulp of fresh squeezed orange juice and looked down disappointingly at his glass of tap water.

"Thanks for your help, Genie, and for meeting me so early. I got held up with the new clients yesterday and had to touch base before eight this morning."

"No problem, Mr. Knoble. You focus on the clients. I like to get up early on the weekends."

In just two weeks, she'd turned into a daughter-like figure — no longer a potential score or convenient eye candy, but instead an invaluable member of his staff and a friend. He couldn't be happier about the transformation, but he was even more proud of her. Once she finished school, she'd be more than qualified to leave his measly firm for greener pastures. And he'd help her do it right. But it was refreshing to know now — while he had her — that he'd miss her when that time came.

"Hold on for a second," he stopped her pre-bite.

"What?"

"Those pancakes need more maple syrup," he said, picking up the warmed dispenser.

"Huh?'

"Do your teeth hurt after you take a bite?"

"Um, no … " Genie replied, a questioning smile across her face.

"Then allow me."

47

Ben shaved eleven minutes off the fifty-minute drive by going ninety the whole way, finally arriving at Sally Hubley's house just past five-thirty.

Joe had called an hour earlier, telling him all about the break-in, dead bodies in the foyer and dining room, how those bodies got there and what happened to Tom Fedorak. He sat in wordless agony at first, hearing the story told from his son's perspective and knowing there was nothing he could do to change its outcome. Over the next few minutes, his emotions changed. He first thanked God that Joe was safe, perfectly aware of how close he came to losing both a son and a wife.

But what happened to Tom and the fact the break-in occurred at all — on Tom's watch, no less — had evoked a new sentiment. The evening could never be undone and its events would change Joe in ways not even he could predict. A large piece of a good kid's innocence was stripped away never to be returned.

That *really* pissed him off.

He spoke with Dr. Mills, the attending physician on call at Kindred Hospital in Sycamore, where Joe was being treated for minor physical injuries and psychological trauma. That conversation helped him regain some of the balance he'd lost, and Dr. Mills assured him that Joe would be okay in the long run. He wasn't suffering from posttraumatic stress disorder, which was the best news he could hope for. But the poor kid did experience a horrendous and unforeseen event, the doctor noted, and the shock that comes with that doesn't just go away. Point in fact Joe was still recovering after three hours of close medical attention. When Ben asked what he could do, Dr. Mills said it was best to keep Joe at the hospital and monitor his progress. He thanked the doc, told him he'd be there soon and asked him to call his cell phone with any updates.

Joe in competent hands, Ben hopped in the Taurus and jetted to Sally's. He placed one call on the way to a friend who worked in forensics but spent the rest of the thirty-mile drive cursing himself for taking no for an answer from Sally the first time.

After what happened at Tom's place, he wasn't giving her the option now. She would have to face the world and stay alive as opposed to remain in her bubble and risk getting killed. He couldn't think of any risk she posed to Dominick Riddle, but why take the chance?

He left the engine running and sprinted up the paver sidewalk. Sunrise still two hours away, he dodged a few fallen branches and ascended the three front door steps with one stride. The brisk temperature had developed thick dew on the fallen oak tree leaves and his shoes left wet footprints on the porch.

When she didn't answer, he grabbed the hide-a-key from under the large FAITH stone below the white siding. Letting himself in, he reviewed the game plan. Wake her up, give her five minutes to pack, and get moving. Where? He wasn't sure. The kids were with Nick and Lisa and she could call them later. For now, he needed to get her to safety.

"Sally!" he yelled, running past the living room and plaque with scripture on it. Sprinting up the stairs to the third floor, he knocked on the master bedroom door before entering. The bed was still made and no one was in it. He proceeded to check each of the other rooms and saw much the same, leading him back downstairs.

"Sally, it's Ben!" he yelled, thinking she might be hiding in response to his unannounced visit. He darted into the kitchen, adjacent to the family room, which faced the backyard and was next to a small powder room that smelled like flowers.

When he made the corner, he froze.

There, sitting in a wooden rocker next to a gold reading light still powered on, was Sally Hubley.

Her arms were crossed, forming an "X" that pressed a large King James Bible into her chest. Her elbows rested on a red afghan draped down to the floor and tucked under her feet, fully covering her legs and waist. Her neck arched backwards, pointing her head towards the ceiling. Her signature long, red hair hung behind the rocking chair halfway to the ground. And dried streams of blood that had originated from the single bullet hole in the center of her forehead streaked down her face.

He withdrew his gun and approached slowly, unwilling to accept what was in front of him. Ashamed of himself, he looked at her innocent face and frail body, trying his best to honor her by thinking about things she'd want him to: her strong faith, her passion as a mom, the look of knowing in her eyes when she found out Peter had done nothing wrong, the day she told him Anna was in Heaven, and that she was excited about seeing her there one day.

But none of it worked. Even with all the good Sally had done, his focus wasn't on anything remotely decent. Taking note of her closed eyes, crossed arms and restful, undisturbed sitting position under the blanket, he could only think about one thing:

She'd stared at her killer, waiting for the trigger to be pulled.

48

"You do realize it's Saturday?" SAC Redmond answered the phone.

"I wouldn't be calling if it wasn't urgent, sir."

"What's on your mind, kid?"

"The Hubley case."

"What about it?"

"I think you might be right."

"Scratch the *might be* and I'm with you."

"I'm serious, sir."

"So am I, Agent Benton."

He was snappy, borderline angry. She couldn't tell if that was just because of the day or because of something more substantial.

"I just came from Sally Hubley's house."

"Any idea who would do such a thing?"

"A hunch."

"Like I said, it's Saturday. I'm not in the mood to play guessing games. Speak your mind."

"Ben Siebert knew Sally Hubley had been murdered even before I called him."

"How do you know that?"

"He told me."

"That's quite an interesting — and unauthorized, I might add — relationship you have with him."

"How could he know about her murder?" she ignored Redmond's comment.

"Why don't you ask him?"

"I plan to."

"You think he was involved?"

"I'm not sure. It doesn't fit and I can't see a reason. They were friends; he didn't have a motive."

"That you're aware of."

"You think he had a hand in it?"

"It's your case, Benton. I really don't know. It's just been my experience that the best killers rarely seem like the type at first."

She let that sit for a moment.

"It really surprised me that he didn't call. He always seems to know things, but he usually calls."

"I've told you from the start, kid. Siebert's a wild card. Sure, he seems to have good intelligence. But you never know from whom and can rarely check his facts. He's informed but not trustworthy, competent but not reliable."

Interesting take, she thought.

"I warned you about getting in too deep with him."

"I know. And like I said, you're right."

"That's not what you said."

"Okay, scratch the *might be*. You were right."

"Has he threatened you?"

"No."

"Has he ever made you feel unsafe?"

"No."

"Has he done anything illegal that you can prove?"

"No."

"So why do you think he was involved with Peter Hubley's murder?"

"Sir?"

"Don't sir me. I work for a living."

"Excuse me?"

"You didn't call me to talk about your victim's wife's death. *You* obviously think Siebert had a hand in Hubley's murder, and I'd like you to stop beating around the bush and tell me why."

She couldn't tell if he was just in a hurry or really pissed, but it felt like both.

"There's something … off. He runs here and runs there and he always comes back with these critical facts that we — the FBI — weren't able to get first."

"And we've got more sources than he does."

"Exactly, so it doesn't make sense. Something doesn't add up when he's getting better intelligence than we are."

"What's that tell you?"

"I'm not sure it tells me anything. But it makes me think he's getting it from people who have the answers we really need. It just seems too … convenient for it to be completely legitimate."

"So why are you talking to me?"

"I was wondering if you had any luck with the wire transfers?" she asked, getting a clearer sense of her boss's attitude by the minute. "I was hoping for a connection."

"Like I told you before, it's a dead end. Whoever transferred that money knows his way around the system and could probably run circles around our trace programs."

"Have I upset you in some way, sir?"

"You've done more than upset me, Agent Benton. I'm getting sick and tired of being undermined."

"What?" she replied, trying to mind her tone.

"From day one, you've been calling the shots on this investigation. And from day one, you've been defying my instructions," Redmond's voice rose, turning belligerent.

"In what way?"

"I told you to stick to Hubley, to do the groundwork and find what we were missing. You didn't. Then, I told you stay away from Siebert, to keep it official FBI personnel only and arrest him if he didn't comply. You were openly insubordinate. Finally, I resigned myself to the fact you wanted to work with him, but very reasonably requested, *as your boss*, that you provide me regular updates on what he's been doing and telling you. And I now know you haven't been doing that either."

"Sir, I've been trying to —"

"I didn't ride your ass about it, either. Not for any of it. When you stole confidential information from the evidence locker, I cut you a break. When you interrogated a CEO and community hero without cause and the next day he took his own life, I didn't call you on it."

His words silenced her. The reminder of the computer evidence and the revelation that Redmond not only knew about her visit to InvestSecure, but also implicated her in his suicide, made her heart drop.

"Of course I knew about that, Benton," he yelled, reading her silence. "But even so, I didn't interfere with your investigation. Looking back, maybe I should have. But this case was your baby."

Was?

"You said you wanted this case and promised me you could handle it, so I gave it to you. It's my fault, I suppose. Against my better judgment I trusted you with something that was clearly over your head and your incompetence has shown."

"Incompetence?"

"I know from experience that being a Special Agent requires a certain amount of leeway. It means having the freedom to do things your own way, even when you screw up. I know you can't always follow the playbook. You have to develop and use your own style to get the job done, and it's not my job to micromanage every move you make. But now you're coming to me, telling me you *think* Siebert might be dangerous, like it's some sort of major discovery! I've been telling you the whole damn time, Benton. That's incompetent as hell."

She couldn't believe what she was hearing. Here she was, being likened to the opposite of what she'd stood for her entire life, and her *boss* was doing the likening.

It felt like everything had abruptly turned against her, a complete one-eighty from who she actually was, painting the picture of an insubordinate, incompetent failure. She felt panic coming on and wasn't sure how to control it.

"Siebert asked to meet tonight. I was calling to keep you posted," she replied, fighting the tears that were coming soon regardless.

"Why does he want to meet?"

"He didn't say. He just said his friend had been killed and we needed to talk."

"Tom Fedorak? The guy he was in the Marines with? He's dead?"

"Yes."

"Son of a bitch, Benton! What kind of investigation are you running here? When did *that* happen?"

"I'm not su —"

"Bodies are dropping like flies all around this guy and you think he *might* be dangerous?"

"I screwed up, sir."

"You think!"

"I —"

"Agent Benton, you've lost control of this case and are as of now no longer its lead investigator. Effective immediately, I'm taking over."

"But sir —"

"No more buts. People are dying, Benton. We've got three more bodies than when you started and we're no closer to knowing who killed Peter Hubley. This has been a disaster by every possible measure."

She could picture the bulbous vein in Redmond's forehead. She could visualize him tightly stroking his graying mustache and rubbing his bald head in frustration. This was it for her, the end of the line and the end of her career.

"Agent Benton, tonight will be your final activity with the Hubley case. On Monday you'll be reassigned to a low-level case and put on six-month probationary status for insubordination."

"But sir, I —"

"Contact Siebert and find out when and where he wants to meet. Agree to do so and don't tell him you've been relieved as lead investigator. Call me with the exact location and plan to meet me beforehand. You are to never see nor speak with Ben Siebert after tonight. If I ever find out you do — *and I will find out* — you will be fired immediately and then arrested for impeding an official investigation. Do I make myself clear?"

She couldn't even get "yes sir" out.

"You brought this on yourself, Agent Benton."

49

David Keene was no goodie goodie.

At twenty-five years old, he'd had his fair share of screw-ups, oversights and poor decisions, and he'd learned more than a few lessons the hard way. He'd broken some promises — and some hearts — and had a handful of nights he wished he could do over. However, in an industry where the line between right and wrong was getting thinner every day, he'd proven he had not only the ability to walk it but also the desire.

He began his career three years earlier at *The Chicago Tribune* single, naïve, and cocky. Now, he was just single. Back then, in his own bachelor pad for the first time, he felt ready to conquer the professional world. When he landed his first full-time gig as a junior reporter for Chicago's second-largest newspaper, it felt like a perfect match. Not just because he majored in Journalism at Columbia College or because he wrote a biweekly column for the school paper, but because of his passion for periodicals. Despite the challenges the industry faced — electronic media ready to make it obsolete — he couldn't imagine going a single day without reading at least one newspaper. So what better way to enter the real world than by working for one? He arrived on Day One eager, hungry, and poised to learn the ropes from the best in the business, excited and determined to put his years of schooling into practice.

But the real world — as it turned out — was an entirely different kind of education that required him to check that excitement at the door.

Numbers were all that mattered to the man who'd trained him since his first day. Morals, ethics, methodology, timing, sensitivity, perspective, delivery, and to a certain extent overall accuracy were treated secondarily, if not outright ignored. They were considered only if convenient. The primary, overarching objective was much simpler and much rawer, David learned during orientation.

Make money.

And to do that, be *fast*.

Get the scoop however and from whomever you could, write what people want to read, and sell newspapers. Find the dirt before anyone else does and get the story out before the competition can. Force people to read your article by being first and they won't have a choice but to fall in love with both it and you. The rest, his mentor said, would take care of itself.

So David spent the next three years watching his mentor and manager invoke practices that gave his new profession a bad name. Sources were always protected through anonymity, pseudonyms or other means. But that was only because exposing them would encumber future stories. Repeat, reliable sources were paramount, and you didn't want to lose them. Eyewitnesses' requests regarding what was printed and what was omitted were also respected, but only in cases where a signed agreement included guidelines punishable by fines if not followed. Even that didn't always prevent it from happening — he'd seen his boss ignore said requests twice — but it did mean there had better be a fantastic reason to do so.

Yet in spite of it all, the still-somewhat-wet-behind-the-ears David Keene remained true to himself and his readership. He sought the truth, focused on the facts and didn't let dollar signs cloud his judgment. It was a phenomenally different approach from his supervisor's and, you could argue, a far more humanistic one.

All it meant to David, however, was a shit ton more work for him to do.

He'd learned that being honest in a profession where dishonest opportunities lurk all around meant a lot of things. Countless late nights, crappy assignments, reading so much your eyes burned, even getting mocked by your boss for writing legitimate stories instead of juicy gossip. It meant freezing your ass off outside in Chicago winters to get a beat on the story instead of just paying someone off to give you the scoop. It meant dedicating your days to playing catch up to coworkers who took advantage of those dishonest opportunities. He couldn't do it forever, and after three years at a hundred miles an hour, he was nearing the breaking point. But David Keene didn't complain or give in.

He was chosen for his nobility.

Saturday night, late October, eight-thirty, bars hopping, clubs rocking, DJs just getting warmed up. David Keene, alone at his desk, the reading light from his studio apartment one-bulb down but illuminative enough. The neo-gothic Tribune Tower's ninth floor otherwise dark, two monitors and a laptop were open on the junior reporter's desk and papers were sprawled across the floor. The cleaning lady skipped his workstation for the third night in a row. Every other cubical and office was empty, why clean the kid's?

He wore his reading glasses so much the nose pad formed permanent indentations. The words on the screen, revised six times, still didn't read right. Four twenty-ounce Diet Coke bottles were scattered about and the wastebasket overflowed with the same. It'd been three days since it was emptied, after all.

He'd fallen asleep at his desk countless times before and usually wound up just spending the night, but this evening would be different. He told Julie he'd be there at nine o'clock sharp. It'd been a thirteen-and-a-half hour day already and he could use a night out with his girlfriend of two years. He'd just hit SAVE — opting to postpone the seventh round of edits until tomorrow — when his phone began to ring.

Caller ID said UNKNOWN, as it all too often did.

"David Keene."

"Listen to me very carefully, David," a deep, clear, male voice answered.

"Who is this?"

"At twelve-thirty tonight, a package of significant interest will be dropped at your office's front door. Standard brown box, a few square feet. Unaddressed, but meant for you. Retrieve it and follow its instructions."

"*Who is this?*"

"You should be more concerned with the package, David."

"What's in it?"

"You'll see at twelve-thirty."

"I'm not going to be here at twelve-thirty. In fact, I'm on my way out."

"You're not leaving, David. The Wrigleyville bars can wait. You're going to be at your desk at twelve-thirty and you're going to get that package. Julie will understand."

"Wait, what? What did you say?"

"Tonight is a pillar night, David. You've been busting your ass for three years without a break. You're about burned out and don't see much hope, you've even thought of quitting. I love your articles. So plain, so direct, so factual. Too bad they don't sell."

"Listen, I'm not —"

"Tonight, everything changes."

"What are you talking about?"

"Twelve-thirty. Be there. Be sober. And be ready."

When he realized the line was dead, David punched *69 and got the disconnected number recording.

50

Self-defeat accompanied Nikki every step of the way to her final meeting with Ben Siebert. There was nowhere to hide and she was too tired to run. She had nobody to blame but herself for feeling like a bottom feeder in an empty pool.

It wasn't the fact that her career was essentially over. Nor was it being called a disappointment by her boss, being threatened with arrest or knowing she hadn't contributed a thing to solving the case. It was Sally Hubley.

It was that she'd let that poor widow down, that she'd failed to get her answers before her life was taken. Sally's long red hair and makeup-free face would join the little boy from Jamaica and remain forever imprinted in her mind, yet another reminder of her failures. That was the thought in her mind when she exited Bu at Ben's meeting point.

It was an abandoned two-story building off Rockwell Street in the Ukrainian Village that used to be a gourmet grocer and deli. Comprised of faded red brick from its foundation on up, its second-story patio and balcony was probably quite beautiful at one time. Now, its outdated orange-and-white striped awning and rusted white metal gate just looked look rundown and filthy. The only window on the main level was boarded up, covered with blue and yellow graffiti, a gang symbol of some sort, left there by the building's only regular visitors. Directly above the window was a large white sign with a red X in the middle. She wasn't sure what that meant.

To the building's immediate right and left were dark alleys with no streetlights and uneven, pothole-riddled concrete streets. The full moon exposed enough of the structure and neighborhood to tell her it hadn't been in commercial use for some time, and that this probably wasn't the best place for her to be alone.

When Redmond pulled up in his Lexus at just before eleven-thirty, the Special Agent in Charge wasted little time. The late hour, strong lake-effect wind and dangerous area prompted quick action. Not to mention he was still pissed at her. They didn't greet one another, merely nodded, and then headed towards the white-trim door with a rotted wood sign above it noting the address. The lock and chains had been snapped off and the boards had been removed with what she'd guessed was an axe, a clear indication Ben was already inside. Redmond took the lead, gun in hand, and entered. She did the same but without a weapon.

Inside the musty, warehouse-feel building there was even less light than she'd imagined. The shadows seemed to have shadows. What little illumination did exist came from moonlight that snuck in between the cracks in the wood covering the windows and now board-free front door.

Her pupils dilating to adjust, she saw a large open space, maybe sixty feet by forty feet. All the countertops, display stands and shelves from the old grocer had been removed, turning the former gourmet deli into a giant empty rectangle.

The only thing she could see on the chipped, uneven hardwood floors were piles of debris. The room had a thick funk of moldy cheese, but a few green plastic lawn chairs along the sides of the walls indicated someone had inhabited the building regardless. The disgusting smell of thick mold is a small price to pay if you're trying to keep warm on a blistery Chicago night.

Towards the back of the room was a staircase that led to the second-story patio. As her eyes followed its circular ascent, a gust of wind penetrated the open front door and she realized how cold it was. It was only October and she shivered in her winter coat. The poor insulation and porous wooden boards would be no match for February.

"Over here," she heard Ben say.

———

Both she and Redmond turned towards the voice and saw Ben twenty feet away, bent at the knees, holding a metal Zippo lighter. Dressed in all dark clothes with black shoes, he held the lighter's flame to the wick of a kerosene lantern. Seconds later, a puff of smoke emerged and Ben applied the lantern's glass chimney to reveal a vibrant yellow-orange flame. It quickly served its purpose, brightening up the entire room in seconds. She heard rats squeak behind her in response but kept her attention on Ben, who set the lantern on the ground and stood up, arms crossed.

"Ben Siebert … " Redmond announced with a dubious pride, lowering his weapon and staring at Ben, who remained still.

"After all this time … we finally meet," Redmond continued, inching towards Ben in a slow traipse.

After all this time? What was that supposed to mean?

"I've got to level with you, Benjamin."

Ben just stared at Redmond, not answering.

"I expected so much more," Redmond said, shrugging his shoulders and throwing his hands out in Ben's direction to display exaggerated disappointment. The SAC shook his head and made tsk sounds, as if to say "no, no" to a disobedient child. The tone in her boss's voice was one she couldn't quite decipher. It was dark, nasty almost, like finger pointing with a vile twist. But its I-told-you-so condescension seemed out of place considering the circumstances.

"After everything I've heard about you, after all I've read. Your missions in the Marines, your little justice vigilante side hobby and all your decorated medals … seeing you now, they leave me wanting more. You look so average, so run-of-the-mill; just another inflated-ego jarhead whose bark is bigger than his bite. Anna would be so disappointed."

What was Redmond talking about? And what was he doing? She hadn't told him anything that would make him say that, nor had she discussed Ben's late wife. What *reading* and *hearing about* was he referring to? And why was he trying to egg Ben on?

"She was innocent," Ben whispered.

"What's that?" Redmond yelled, moving closer to Ben, the vein in his forehead starting to make its appearance. "What did you say to me, jarhead?"

If Ben moved a muscle below his neck, she didn't see it. He did, however, finally show some emotion. She'd wanted him to for so long and couldn't figure out why he hadn't, but when he finally did she was shocked beyond her own comprehension.

"Sally Hubley was innocent, you son of a bitch."

What?

Redmond stared back, a smile starting to form.

What the … ?

"Sir, what's he talking ab —"

"Shut up, Benton!" Redmond snapped, his hideous, nasty snicker gone and the gun now lifted towards her head.

Oh my God …

"Throw your gun across the room or I'll put you both down like animals."

Her heart beating uncontrollably, she couldn't think. She'd been abandoned. *Again.* By the guy she'd spent the last six-and-a-half months trying to impress. She looked at Ben, who didn't look back. Redmond yelled again and she did all she could think to do: the wrong thing. Removing her weapon from its holster, she tossed it against the wall near the old green lawn chairs.

"Stupid girl," Redmond sneered, whipping the gun back on Ben. "I knew it was a good idea to put you on the Hubley case, Benton. You did perfectly. Exactly as I expected, bitch. The only mistake in this entire investigation is standing right there. If it weren't for Siebert, I probably would've promoted your stupid ass by now."

Redmond's words brought together shame, anger and pain in her heart and mind. Combined with the shock and terror already there, part of her thought about charging straight at him full speed. Maybe she could save Ben's life and put an end to her own miserable excuse for one at the same time.

"Just shut up for a minute, Benton. You might learn something," Redmond howled, releasing another villainous laugh with even greater volume. "Siebert here wants to play professor."

Redmond held a loaded revolver ten feet from Ben's head, but Ben didn't back down an inch.

"She had nothing to do with any of this. She was just trying to move on after you took her husband from her. You didn't have to kill her, you fat shit."

His voice was somehow calm and controlled, but it was his eyes that made the impression. They'd gotten … darker … focused. The blue pupils she'd once thought dreamy now instilled a chilling fear that couldn't be matched.

Not even as Redmond cocked the gun.

"*I* didn't have to kill her? You think *I* killed Sally Hubley? You think *I* killed Peter Hubley or your pal Tom Fedorak? Or had anything to do with any of this? You think this is *my* show? C'mon, son. Don't be such an idiot on the last day of your life."

"You could've stopped it."

"Do you have any idea who you're messing with? Can you even imagine how much you've screwed the pooch here? Go out with some pride. You think Hubley's where it stops? Fat chance, jarhead. You've set Dominick off and there's no calling him back. He'll go after the Gordons, Hubley's kids, everyone! No one is making it out of this thing alive, Siebert … not with Dominick running the show."

"You're just as bad as he is."

"You watch it right there, you jarhead motherf —"

"You sat behind that FBI desk pretending to be working the case, telling people you were trying to find Peter's killer. But the whole time all you were doing was feeding Riddle the FBI's intelligence. You're just Riddle's little bitch. Do you sit and fetch and roll over too, you pathetic slob?"

"Agent Benton, it's time to eliminate that sole mistake," Redmond yelled as he walked even closer to Ben, the gun outstretched. Ten feet wasn't close enough. Ben's head was about to be taken clean off at point-blank range.

Panicked, freaked out and confused, she couldn't believe what she was watching and hearing. Redmond … partners with Riddle the whole time. Her dizzy mind got dizzier and she could feel the room starting to spin. Ben just stood there, waiting for the end. What the hell was he doing? She couldn't take it.

"Adios, jarhead," Redmond announced.

"No!" she screamed.

But she was too late.

51

She heard a gunshot and slammed her eyes shut.

Then she heard another, and then another. And she slowly inched them open, just in time to see Redmond flail his arms back and drop the revolver, clutching a chest that was now entirely crimson. He gasped loudly for air, each attempt sounding more painful than the last as blood filled his lungs.

Her boss fell to the ground on his back, still gripping his chest, looking up at her with frantic, pleading eyes. Soon not even his gasps could he heard, and his head leaned all the way back before finally hitting the floor. She watched in shock as Redmond breathed his last breath.

Ben stood there; still motionless, not so much as a step away from where he was before, watching Redmond die with emotionless eyes.

"What?" she forced out. "But how did … " her voice trailed off.

Ben turned to face her, still without a sound.

Redmond's body was creating an already sizeable puddle of blood that seemed to grow larger every time she blinked. She dropped to her knees and gave way to tears that couldn't be stopped. Burying sobbing eyes in her stomach, she screamed but didn't speak. A few moments later, she heard the pitter patter of soft footsteps and saw yet another surprise.

Hobbling badly, a black gel foam arm sling around his left shoulder and two large braces wrapped around each of his thighs, Tom Fedorak approached her from the staircase. Back from the dead as far as she was concerned, he had a pair of what appeared to be night vision goggles hanging around his neck and moved at the gentle pace of one small step every few seconds. When he reached her, he dropped the sniper rifle and rested his hand on her head.

"Cheer up, Sweetheart. We've got work to do and I need you to pull my weight."

52

Ben left immediately after Tom emerged from the shadows.

Without so much as a good-bye, he bolted out the front door like he had a plane to catch, leaving her alone with the ghost of Tom Fedorak. Enduring pain with each step, Tom noted his trigger finger still worked and that wonder drugs — some legal, most not — helped with the pain. He summarized Ben's plan in five minutes, supposedly at Ben's request. Everything from the sniper station with the night vision goggles to the camera Ben brought to Ben's insistence that Tom not pull the trigger until Redmond confirmed his theory. The massive info dump helped her dizziness like fast food helped weight loss.

From what she was able to process, the next steps sounded farfetched. The plan certainly didn't give her the warm and fuzzies, but who was she to judge? She couldn't believe all the hints she'd missed that Redmond was a traitor. With each one she thought of, she felt like an even bigger failure.

"What's wrong, Sweetheart? You don't like the plan?" Tom asked from the filthy and broken green lawn chair.

"Nothing's wrong."

"Then why so glum? You're not the one who got shot three times by a crazy bald man with bullets dipped in ouch."

"I knew I had no business being lead investigator. I knew it from the start but I didn't want to believe it. I wanted to think I'd been chosen on merit."

"That makes you human."

"Redmond knew it, too."

"It could've happened to anyone, Sweetheart."

"His offer to give the case to someone else if it was *too much* was just to make me try to prove him wrong, to get me to do what he wanted. And I walked right into it."

"He was your boss. You did what you were told, what anyone would've done."

"That won't help me sleep. Ben was right. I just *have* to prove people wrong, even if they aren't. I've been that way since my parents died. And Redmond used it to make me his puppet. No ... his bitch."

"Wanting to impress your boss doesn't make you a bitch."

"He didn't even tell me why the FBI had the case in the first place. I knew something was wrong then but just let it go. He didn't tell me about the wire transfer until he had to cover himself. And he gave me just enough to keep me off his trail."

"Hindsight's twenty-twenty, Sweetheart."

"But the worst part ... you know what the worst part is?"

"What?"

"The worst part was Redmond keeping me on the case after I stole Hubley's computer from the evidence locker. How could I be so stupid? I knew that wasn't right."

"What wasn't right?"

"Redmond broke protocol after chewing me out for breaking protocol. It didn't add up and I knew it. I *stole* evidence. I should've been suspended, turned into internal affairs. But Redmond needed to keep it quiet, away from the federal office. He needed to see what I'd learn so he could protect Riddle. And he needed to remain the only authority in the investigation. So he brushed it off like he was doing me a favor.

"The sad part is not only did I misread it, but I was thankful. I thought he gave me a break. I told myself he *must* see potential in me because he didn't turn me in. He didn't even take me off the case, for Heaven's sake. He must have high hopes for me. How could I be so damn stupid?" she screamed, kicking a pile of debris against the wall.

Saying it out loud made her feel worse. Ashamed, she slid down the wall to the ground and buried her head in between her knees.

"You know something, Sweetheart," Tom said, getting up and walking over to stand next to her.

"What?"

"Sometimes you remind me of Grasshopper so much that I want put my own foot up my own ass."

"What?"

"Both of you ... you blame yourselves for things out of your control. You play Monday morning quarterback on yourself with the box score in hand. You force one bad decision to morph into another."

"It's my fault the —"

"Let me get this straight. Your boss — the Special Agent in Charge of the Chicago FBI field office — was a traitor who deceived you. Well boohoo, pretty girl. You think you're the only one he was lying to? What about the Director and the Executive Assistants of the nationwide branches? What about the deputies and Division heads? This guy manipulated the entire FBI food chain and you're pissed off because *you* didn't see it? Think about that."

"I don't need —"

"You can't carry that baggage. All that happens is you fall right on your ass. And I don't want that to happen, not when it's such a nice ass."

For the first time that day, she felt a desire to smile.

"Is Ben mad at me?"

"Grasshopper mad at you? Are you kidding me?"

"Does he think I should've —"

"Grasshopper's trusted you from the get-go. And he's a terrific judge of character. Why do you think he kept telling you not to check the FBI database for Riddle? Why did he give you a phone to call him? What do you think made him flip out when you went to InvestSecure? How's come he was so careful about controlling what you knew and what you didn't?"

"I, I —"

"It was for your benefit, Sweetheart. What you didn't know couldn't hurt you, but at the same time you had to know enough to be safe. Not an easy line to walk; and from where I sit, he did a pretty good job. Don't tell him I said that though. The last thing I need is a big-headed Grasshopper."

Her mind swam through the ocean currents of the past few weeks. The database and the phone ... she'd missed that too. Ben's insistence she let him check his own sources first. The web of confusion that irritated her so much before started to make sense. Ben was protecting her.

But Tom didn't let her ponder that for long.

"Sweetheart, you think I do everything perfectly? Well, wait. It's probably best we don't use me. I'm an impossible standard and the point is to build you up. You think *Grasshopper's* perfect?"

She gave into the desire this time and offered a half-smile.

"Point is, Sweetheart, I'm not gonna listen to any more of this self-degrading bullshit. That's exactly what this is, and I'd rather play golf and eat hot dogs. I've listened to it for four minutes too long already and we've got work to do."

—

Tom overstated how much work there was, and fifteen minutes later they were done. More to the point, *she* was done, taking direction from Tom.

"Quality, not quantity, Sweetheart," he assured her from his green lawn chair, the building's blueprint marked with yellow X's spread across his lap, eating his second hot dog wrapped in foil.

"What are these things again?" she asked, holding up one of the square devices about twice the size of a Rubik's Cube. Her first task was to retrieve all of the black devices from the sniper station. Each device had a cover with screws she didn't try to open and weighed at least thirty pounds despite its small footprint.

"It's kind of a cross between an IED and a hi-tech Squib."

"A what?"

"Think of it as a small bomb. There are trace amounts of explosive powder connected to a wireless detonator we can trigger remotely."

"I've never seen this before." She knew that didn't mean much. The weapons' class at Quantico was long obsolete and it didn't tickle her fancy to stay current on explosive devices.

"It's not exactly on the open market."

She knew the plan, so the fact she was placing explosives around the room wasn't a shock. But knowing the plan was one thing and executing it was another. She placed each one exactly where Tom said. He got his instructions from the blueprint and yellow X's. All twelve were along the first floor perimeter and each was synched to the detonator sitting next to Tom's third hot dog.

According to Tom, there would be no large explosion. No windows would blast out and the roof wouldn't explode "like the Ecto-Containment Unit at Ghostbusters headquarters." Rather, a few soft ignitions would precede maximum structural damage.

She wasn't convinced. A bomb was a bomb.

"I don't want innocent bystanders getting killed on my conscience."

"Rockwell Street is dead, Sweetheart. If Chi-West, the Ukrainian gang from the sixties was around, maybe. But it's ghost town now. Wide alleys on both sides of the building, there won't be a soul within forty feet. That's why Grasshopper chose it."

"Seems pretty close for twelve bombs."

"We'll be fine."

"How do you know?"

"Grasshopper's a bright boy. He might do that investing crap now, but he's a Structural Engineering wiz. Got a copy of the building's construction documents, all the structural members and design loads and free-body diagrams and everything."

"So?" she said, recalling Ben's major at Princeton.

"He marked on the blueprint exactly where to put the charges. You saw the white sign with the red X above the window outside?"

"Yeah," she answered, recalling seeing it but not knowing what it was.

"It serves as a warning to the Chicago Fire Department and other potential first responders. There are almost two thousand of them throughout the city. Chicago got the idea from New York after a roof collapsed on two firemen. To first responders, it means the building is structurally unsound, so they better be careful. To us, it means it won't take much force to bring it down. You just need to know where to apply it."

"How can you be sure no one will get hurt?"

"We have Ben's word. That's good enough for me. How 'bout you?"

Hard hats on, they exited the building through the same door she'd entered forty-five minutes earlier. Life sure had changed since then. She went in knowing she was finished with the Hubley case and came out certain she'd see it through or die trying. She went in exposed with a dangerous boss and came out protected by a trustworthy killer.

Tom walked like he needed crutches and told her to leave her car, handing her a set of keys to a K900 parked across the street. The full moon made her feel exposed and she sprinted to the Kia like on a prison break. She didn't see anyone but that felt less than reassuring.

The air had turned cold enough that she could see her breath. When she picked Tom up, he smiled and held the four-inch cylindrical detonator.

"Rock and roll, Sweetheart," he said, casually depressing the pushbutton lever.

A series of pops ensued, like gunshots only softer. Flashes of bright light appeared through the open front door and the building started to shake. Seconds later, that shaking turned to rumbling and the ground moved like a small earthquake. The bottom of the vibrating building then imploded, collapsing inward towards its center, resulting in a massive smoke cloud that funneled straight up. It lasted less than twenty seconds and to her amazement, caused no other damage. Even the sidewalks adjacent to the building were unaffected and relatively free of debris.

Seconds later, she heard the sirens.

53

The brown box was delivered to The Tribune Tower at precisely twelve-thirty and its contents were exactly as promised. David Keene carefully followed the instructions before making the best decision of his young career. After his Chief Editor reamed him for the late-night wake-up call and stubbornly refused to stop the presses to get the story in Sunday's print edition, he decided he was done bending over for *The Chicago Tribune*.

Newspapers employ people who comb the web seeking stories of interest and Keene's blog post was certainly of interest. Even at the late hour, within thirty minutes *Chicago Sun-Times*, *The Daily Herald* and a handful of regional outfits had published similar articles in their online editions. They'd also stopped their presses to get it in the morning's print edition and had no choice but to identify the blog post's author.

The implosion itself was what made it front-page news, but it was Keene's contribution that Ben needed. By the time Ben read it, the story was rapidly growing and three former competitors had already contacted Keene about new employment opportunities. The junior reporter had just hopped on the fast track.

The first line was perfect:

According to a source who spoke on the condition of anonymity, Special Agent in Charge Marcus Redmond of the FBI's Chicago Field Office, FBI Special Agent Nicole "Nikki" Benton and an unidentified man are all feared dead due to the collapse of the now-abandoned former Mercer Grocery & Deli building on Rockwell Street in the Ukrainian Village at approximately 12:15 this morning.

It went on to say nothing had been confirmed, but both Redmond and Benton were believed to be inside the building at the time of its collapse and their cars were still parked outside. It was accompanied by a date-stamped overhead video of Redmond and Benton walking in thirty minutes prior to its "comeuppance for being a gang hangout." There were also several still shots and close-ups of Redmond and Benton next to their FBI profile photos for comparison. Both the magnification and resolution were impressive, telling Ben the expensive camera was worth it.

Respecting the rules of journalism, David noted that no positive identifications had been made and that in all likelihood wouldn't anytime soon due to the massive cleanup required. *Attempts to contact Redmond and Benton were unsuccessful, but that alone doesn't confirm what at present is an allegation, not a fact,* the article said.

But it didn't matter.

The pictures were remarkably convincing and the video spoke for itself.

The unidentified man, also on the video, had entered the building a few minutes earlier wearing a mask and dressed in black. No identification had been made or even alleged and it was unclear what they were doing there. Because of this, the blog post and copycat articles that followed focused on the known FBI employees. Ben checked online and saw that as expected, as the hours went by with authorities unable to reach Redmond and Benton, even more hype had been created. Even FBI Executive Director Charles Thompson, Redmond's boss, had issued a statement.

Despite being smaller overall, *The Chicago Tribune* had nearly twice the Sunday circulation of *Chicago Sun-Times*, but it was clear who the last-day-of-the-week winner was this time. The junior reporter David Keene wrote a fantastic story that his own employer now had to watch other newspaper outfits profit from. The claim was clear and upfront. The uncertainty communicated in an ethical, easy-to-read fashion. The source remained anonymous. Questions regarding where the video came from were being postponed due to the straightforwardness of the story. The simple yet effective conclusion stated the search for Redmond and Benton would continue, and the building would likely be re-constructed as part of Chicago's overhaul program.

It wasn't the world Ben cared about, but the more it spread the more likely the one man would see it. In a few days, questions about the source of the video would refute the post's allegation. If they didn't, an anonymous tip would. By the time the debris was cleared,

David Keene would have a new job and officials would expect to find only one body. But for the next forty-eight hours, Dominick Riddle would read the papers and conclude one thing:

Both he and Nikki were dead.

54

The first appointment Senator Kevin Richardson had Monday was a seven-thirty with William T. Knoble, a local attorney who'd requested twenty minutes to discuss a joint-fundraiser for children's brain cancer. Although meetings with private, non-donor citizens weren't commonplace, the subject of the meeting warranted his attention. It might be the only worthwhile thirty minutes of his week.

"Senator, they're here," his assistant Barb said cheerfully, excited because he was actually doing something as opposed to moping around like usual.

They?

"Send them in," he answered from behind his century-old wooden desk. For over a year he'd wanted to take an axe to it and burn the pieces.

Much to his surprise, four people walked in. The leader was dressed like a lawyer — full charcoal suit, polished shoes, maroon handkerchief in the breast pocket, oily salt-and-pepper hair combed straight back atop a grossly undersized head. Richardson barely noticed the other two men behind him — one in khakis and a white polo, the other in a red flannel jacket with jeans — but he did note the woman in a Cubs sweatshirt who looked vaguely familiar.

"Bill Knoble. Thanks for your time," said the leader, extending his hand.

Barb shot him a look and he nodded approval for her to shut the door.

"My pleasure, Mr. Knoble. So ... tell me about your fundraiser?"

"No," the man behind Knoble in khakis and a polo interjected. "Let's talk about Dominick Riddle."

———

"I'm sorry?" the immediately nervous Senator Richardson asked Ben. Nikki noted that Richardson was quite awful at concealing

244

discomfort. She watched him closely as he pulled his hands in and out of his pockets and could swear his lips trembled.

Ben stepped in front of Bill Knoble and eyed Richardson, eight feet away.

"After Peter Hubley was brutally murdered for trying to do the right thing and four innocent people died afterwards, including his wife and a twenty-three-year-old kid, your being sorry doesn't mean jack shit."

Ben continued to inch closer; Richardson leaned back in fear.

"With the whole world looking in the wrong places for Hubley's killer and a corrupt FBI Special Agent in Charge who's now dead himself, what matters is why you're in cahoots with Dominick Riddle. Why are you letting him further the development and sale of malware that could put millions of lives at stake?"

"Maybe I should take off —"

"Sit down, Bill," Ben snapped. Knoble collapsed into a visitor's chair and ran a hand through his hair, clearly unaware of the purpose of this meeting or why he was there. She knew how he felt.

"Senator, I asked you a question."

If Richardson was scared before, he was downright petrified now. He fell back into his chair and stared, mortified, at Ben. His look said he knew he was talking to someone smarter than he so he'd better be careful about what he said next.

"How do you know all this?"

Nikki couldn't believe her ears — it was a form of admission. Ben was right:

The senator was in on it …

"Senator, do you know who she is?" Ben asked, gesturing in her direction.

Why are you bringing me into this?

"No."

"This is Special Agent Nikki Benton of the FBI."

Richardson turned his head towards her, squinting his eyes.

"As you can imagine, we're on a tight schedule. I need answers now."

Richardson took a few moments to consider that a woman reported dead yesterday was now standing in his office today, then cleared his throat.

"At first, I found ways to justify it to myself."

"The work you did for Riddle?"

"Yes. The money we made I gave to charity. Everything. I set up an account with support groups and poured every cent into the community. Told myself as long as no one got hurt and the money went to a good place, I wasn't doing anything wrong."

"*People got hurt*, Senator."

"Not at first. At first the money came from crooked international governments and kickbacks on billion-dollar investment deals. We weren't robbing from the poor and we sure weren't hurting anyone. We were manipulating broken systems to take fractions of a percentage of *illegitimate* profit from dirty bureaucrats and corrupt tycoons who spent it on twenty-million-dollar yachts."

"So it's okay to steal as long as it's from the rich?"

"I didn't say it was okay. I said I found ways to justify it to myself."

"How'd you meet Riddle?"

"About two years after I got elected, I drafted a piece of legislation I knew wouldn't pass no matter what I did. Too much corruption in this state. I chose to serve to try to fix that and here I am now. How ironic. Anyway, after beating my head against the wall for months trying to pass it the right way, Riddle showed up at my health club and offered to pull some strings to get it through."

"You'd never met him before?"

"Sounds crazy, right? I almost laughed him out of the gym right there, but he was *so* convincing. I'll give the prick that. He could sell sawdust to a lumber mill. Said he'd been watching me, that he was impressed by my drive and he wanted to help. I asked him how and he said don't worry about it, just that one day he might need a favor. I know it sounds stupid now. But back then I was young and ambitious. I *was* stupid. I'd heard favors were a part of politics, and the legislation really was going to help people. Plus, I didn't think he was legit. So I figured, what do I have to lose?"

"So you called his bluff, he got it done, and you owed him. Was it worth it? What was the legislation?"

"That stays with me until I die," he replied with a surprisingly defiant voice.

"That might be sooner than you think, Senator."

"You've got to do what you've got to do. But that bill is the only thing I've done the past eight years I'm proud of and I'm not about to risk it being repealed now. Its beneficiaries need it too much."

Richardson exuded passion Nikki hadn't seen since his campaign, his confidence incontrovertible. She wasn't sure if it was a good thing, but she believed him.

"Bodie told me Riddle threatened his family. Did he do the same to yours?"

"You can't imagine what that man has done."

"But why you? He needed Bodie to launder money and shelter transactions through InvestSecure. But Bodie was a private citizen that people didn't know. What did Riddle need from a public servant always in the spotlight?"

"Don't you see? That's the brilliance of his League of Crooks, as I've come to call us. With Bodie, he got financial assistance and connections in the Finance industry just as dirty only not as grandiose. With Redmond, he had national protection and the inside scoop on the world's best investigatory outfit. And with me, he got a well-connected lapdog that could push his agenda on Capitol Hill."

"Like what?" Ben said.

"You'd be surprised what unlimited bribe money and a dishonorable senator can get you. Plus, who knows how many others he owns? For example, he controls the local police and mayor to help him smuggle people and things into the country through O'Hare. Its worse than you think, and he has all the protection he needs."

"The perfect trifecta: power, money and influence."

"Not to mention information, the most valuable commodity there is. He's got dirt on everyone and knows how to use it."

"Like he did on you and Bodie."

"You know the things you're *sure* are private? That can't *possibly* be known? They're in his hip pocket. Those and advanced knowledge of government actions and political movements. You name it, he's got it. Dominick Riddle is always a step ahead and I'm a big part of the reason why. I'm the biggest hypocrite I know and I hate myself for it. I've thought about doing what Bodie did so many times I've lost count."

Nikki studied Richardson's eyes. They didn't fill with tears or even look all that sad. But they were empty. Empty and exhausted.

"Senator," Ben interrupted the silence, "Bodie told me he didn't turn Riddle in because he feared for his family. He couldn't put his wife and children at risk, even for the greater good. And I understand that dilemma. I know what it means to lose a loved one and I can't imagine ever doing something that might cause it."

"With Riddle it's not a case of *might*, it's a sure thing. Even if you killed him, he'd have people ready to find and massacre all your loved ones. He'd do things to your children that would make the devil cringe."

"I heard the Bullet Ant story … "

"How does a man knowingly sacrifice his family, especially if it's to catch someone who will probably get away anyway?"

Nikki watched Ben nod, all of the sudden sympathetic.

He knew something she didn't.

"What kind of man does that make you, a hero or a villain? Are you doing the right thing, or are you abandoning the people who need you most? Show me a man who says he'd do that and I'll show you a liar."

"You did, Senator."

"No, I didn't."

"You knew it had to stop, and you knew you had to be the one to stop it."

Richardson looked towards the floor.

"It was you, wasn't it Senator? You're the one who sent the letter about the wire transfers to the Cayman accounts. You sent the bank statements. It was you who tipped off the Sao Paulo Police and knew they'd contact Interpol. We've always assumed it was Bodie, but it was you. Wasn't it, Senator?"

Nikki's eyes ballooned as the senator looked up at Ben.

55

"Your son Reece … he's innocent, isn't he?"

His final question exposed like a radiation canister busted with a hammer, Ben watched Senator Richardson field the danger, pause and abruptly lose control, giving way to tears. That almost confirmed Ben's theory, combined with Bodie's hints in the church. But he had to be certain. There was no other way — he had to make Richardson say it.

"He didn't cause that accident. He didn't crash into that woman and her three kids a year ago. He wasn't four times the legal limit and he didn't wreck that car. Riddle framed him. He made it look like your only son was a fall-down drunk, reckless behind the wheel. But Reece didn't even drive the car, did he?"

Nikki gasped, covering her mouth. Tom stared at the senator with a sorrowful expression. Richardson continued to sob as Ben pushed him harder because he had to.

"That's why you used your influence to get him leniency, why you alienated everyone … from your wife to MADD to all of your constituents. You couldn't let your boy to go to jail or have his life ruined because of you."

"Yes," Richardson forced out.

"Why did Riddle do that?"

"A month before, I … I told him I wanted out. That people could get hurt and that the malware was wrong. I said I didn't sign up for that and couldn't be part of it anymore. He warned me … he said I'd better not mess with his perfect system. But I … I … "

"You did anyway."

Richardson choked the words out between voice cracks and gasps for air, clarifying the missing link while wiping tears and sniffing hard. He looked at the ceiling and then the ground, repeating the sequence over and over, not once looking at Ben.

"Riddle warned me … he told me in front of Bodie and Redmond. He said I'd be sorry if I ever disobeyed him. That he'd send me a message I'd never forget. But I figured he'd come after me. Never in a million years did I think … *My son* … it was my fault."

"It wasn't your fault."

"Tell that to my boy, who's got four innocent deaths on his permanent record. Or my family, who used to be together. Or to the father who lost his wife and kids in one night. Riddle *warned* me. But I just had to push it."

"Why didn't you fight back afterwards?" Ben asked, knowing the answer.

"Because Riddle said if I or Reece ever tried to claim he was innocent, he'd come after Abigail next," Richardson said, referring to his daughter.

What choice did the man have?

"Then, that smug son of a bitch put that rumor out there that I'd been sleeping around. And somehow everyone believed it. I went from a trusted public servant to a jackass hypocrite infidel in three days. Even Tiffany believed the lies; I guess I can't blame her for leaving me. *Cowardly Father Bails Out Son, Then Cheats on Wife* was one of those God-forsaken headlines. Kids at school tormented Reece so much he had to transfer. Abigail wanted nothing to do with me …

"But that's not even the worst part. The worst part is every *single* time I see that father on TV … or when the woman's mother is interviewed … It *destroys* me. I want to tell them so badly that Reece didn't do that to them, that I didn't take away their justice. I want to hug them and cry with them and trade places with their wife and daughter.

"I watched my son get framed and then made him sit there and take it because I was scared for my daughter. My family hates me. People stand outside my office, screaming for me to quit. They don't know how badly I want to. But if I do … "

Ben recalled his own assumptions when the accident occurred a year ago, and he wanted to tell Richardson *something*. Something like, "you can't beat yourself up for this." But he couldn't. He couldn't say something he didn't believe. It wasn't Richardson's fault … but it was. It was now clear to him that the senator's earlier questions about what a man should do if his family was on the line weren't rhetorical. They were him second-guessing his own decisions from a year ago. They were the indestructible pipeline to a never-ending supply of unbearable guilt and despair. Richardson would never recover from what Riddle had done to him.

In so many ways, it was worse than death.

56

Louis Pasteur said it best: "chance favors the prepared mind."

Even so, Dominick Riddle couldn't believe his fortune. Never before had so many unexpected twists even existed, yet alone morphed into such a perfect ending. Bodie offed himself, Sally Hubley and Eric Meyer were eliminated, Terrance Smith got what he deserved, Siebert's kid and right-hand man Fedorak wouldn't be talking to anyone, and Siebert and Special Agent Benton had died alongside Redmond.

Once he dealt with Richardson, the slate would be completely clean. And having spoken to the sap twenty minutes ago, he knew that would be easy as pie. Then he'd start again. Winners don't retire. They encourage others to do the work and watch the cash stream in. He'd be onto the next venture in less than a year.

But not before pressing EXECUTE on his phone.

Adir Mousa and the third-world terrorist organization had proven to be quite the partner. The $700 million had gone through clean and was now waiting for him abroad. More was coming, upon his command. The money was legitimate and the transfer secure. All for a few years of work he didn't even do.

Matthew J. Baker remained an uncertainty, but now for different reasons. After Riddle decided to spare his life, Redmond called to inform him that Benton confirmed Fedorak was dead. It was good and expected news given Baker's record, but Baker himself hadn't checked in. Perhaps Baker was smarter than he assumed and figured he was next on the list. It was a tenuous theory, but he wasn't concerned.

Yes, he said to himself, *it's time*. The twenty-three-acre estate was ready and his private jet was waiting. The Bullet Ant pressed EXECUTE and watched the account grow another $700 Million. Prettier than the most gorgeous sunset, his eyes glistened when the screen read TRANSACTION COMPLETE. That triggered the automatic e-mail with the malware's key-card to be sent to Mr.

Mousa. He left the phone in the garage and smiled before walking away.

They wouldn't know what hit them.

Slipping on Ray Bans and hopping in the green Lamborghini, he knew he'd miss the Lamborghinis the most. But he could buy more. With only eleven cars made each day and a cost of up to five million dollars apiece ... only the very best could afford them.

He'd buy ten.

57

Nikki had no idea what this was, but she'd long ago stopped trying to figure things out.

An hour earlier she'd just gotten out of a hot bath, having unsuccessfully tried to wash away the filth of the past few days. Men with guns then barged into her hotel room and whisked her away to a building she'd never seen in a part of the city she'd never been. Ten minutes later, in an interrogation room of sorts, large glass window and all, in walked Ben in shackles, escorted by two gentlemen in dark suits. Ben sat next to her in the tiny, creepy room with the two men in suits until finally the door opened again and a third man joined them. He had Middle-Eastern complexion, freshly buzzed black hair and a clean-shaven face. Standing six feet tall and wearing jeans with a sweater, he introduced himself as Salil Ahmad before sitting across from her at the six-person table.

"What's going on here?" Ben demanded.

"You'll find out."

Seconds later, someone Nikki *never* expected to see entered the room. The 5'6", fifty-something-year-old woman wearing pleated navy-blue slacks and a white dress shirt took a seat next to Salil Ahmed. Her straight black hair just below her neck, she ordered one of the men in suits to remove Ben's shackles. Without question the authoritative figure, she dismissively waved them away, leaving just the four of them.

Nikki kept her eyes squinted just to make sure she wasn't seeing things. But there was no mistaking the woman. She glanced at Ben in confused silence and Ben returned the look. Not even he foresaw this. It was Karen Hovey, InvestSecure's receptionist.

"Hello Ben and Nikki. It's time we had a formal introduction," she said, extending her right arm. "Susan Reynolds, CIA Senior Intelligence Officer."

———

"*What?*" Nikki blurted out involuntarily.

"I realize this is a bit of a shock, but it was our only option. I needed to remain as close to Bodie as I could and staying undercover, even from you, was the only way."

"And you needed to see if we were involved," Ben said.

"I didn't know for sure until I planted a bug in the conference room."

Ben thought about Bodie's complaint that his secretary was always barging in at the wrong times. He remembered her bringing refreshments when they met in the conference room, about her letting herself in without so much as a knock. *She's always doing that crap*, Bodie had said.

"But how are —" Nikki started to say.

"I'm going to give you the short version of a very long story. Then I need your help," Reynolds interjected, alternating glances between Nikki and him.

They both nodded as though there was another option.

"In early July we received an anonymous tip through the CIA website indicating that malware may be under development at InvestSecure. No conclusive evidence was provided, but the tip was clearly written by someone with an advanced understanding of programming and snippets of the code were furnished. That, combined with the fact that tips are never *really* anonymous, led us to Eric Meyer as the source. When we learned he'd been in contact with Peter Hubley and that Hubley had actually asked Meyer for help, I decided to join the InvestSecure team."

"Do you always send a senior officer undercover after a random tip?"

"This was anything but random, Mr. Siebert. The claim was that this malware could be inserted remotely to any standard issued military laptop or cell phone. It spoke the language of a programmer and provided examples of code that our experts deemed highly intelligent and functional. So no, we don't do that all the time. But if the risk justifies it, we don't hesitate either."

"And that's why you'd only been at InvestSecure for a few months."

"I started in mid-July with the objective of getting as close to Peter Hubley as I could. But he was very straight-arrowed and my research quickly confirmed he was clean, leading me to concentrate on Bodie."

"If you knew something was going on, why didn't you stop it then?" Nikki asked.

"First of all, it wasn't confirmed. Second of all —"

"You wanted the buyer," Ben said.

"We had the buyer. We wanted the mastermind. It was fairly obvious Bodie was involved, but we wanted the guru, the brains behind it all, the man blackmailing Bodie, Marcus Redmond and Kevin Richardson. We wanted Dominick Riddle."

"You had the buyer?"

"Meet Salil Ahmed," Reynolds replied, gesturing with her arm to the fourth person in the room. "As far as Riddle was concerned, Salil was Adir Mousa, a high-ranking member of an unofficial terrorist group paying top dollar for the malware."

Ben looked at the dark-skinned man whose face remained stoic, empathetically certain that Ahmed had seen things he wanted to forget but never would.

"You've actually met Dominick Riddle?"

"Unfortunately, no," Salil Ahmed replied. "He negotiated through a third party; a man with many names, most recently Matthew J. Baker. As it turns out, Baker was the same individual who tried to kill your son and Tom Fedorak."

"Where is Tom?" Nikki asked.

"He wasn't necessary for this conversation," Reynolds answered. "We thought it best for him to stay with Mr. Leksa."

Ben nodded a brief thanks.

"In any event," Salil Ahmed continued, "my job was to make contact with Riddle and win exclusivity on the malware deal by offering a hefty price."

"Why?" Nikki asked.

"To keep the malware out of the hands of real terrorists. And let me tell you — having reviewed it, it's everything it's advertised to be and more. If it fell into the wrong hands, it would cause immeasurable damage."

"But you knew all along you were going to get it?"

"Correct," Reynolds replied. "Riddle may have been talking with other interested parties before, but the malware wasn't complete and the bidding season was far from over. Once Salil got his attention, we knew the price we'd offered would be more than enough to obtain exclusivity."

"What was the price?" Nikki asked.

"We can't tell you that."

"How'd you get Riddle's attention?" Ben said.

"We definitely can't tell you that."

"So let me get this straight," Ben said, standing up to pace the room, eyeing Susan Reynolds, whose temperament remained completely different from Karen Hovey's.

"Bodie told me that Riddle instructed him to get Peter to look at the malware in April, about six months before Peter got shot. You said the anonymous tip came in July. So Peter looked at the malware for a few months and at some point, brought his buddy Eric Meyer into the loop. They decided together it was very serious, but every time Peter tried to say something to his boss, Bodie shot him down."

"Probably out of fear of Riddle."

"So whether Hubley knew Bodie was dirty or not, he and Meyer do the only thing private citizens would think to do."

"They submit an anonymous tip online and hope we'll take care of the rest."

"But then Peter gets killed in October, which certainly explains why Meyer didn't tell us any of this. Three months after he submits the tip, the guy who brought it to him gets murdered. He was scared shitless."

"To add to that, Senator Richardson sends the anonymous letter to the Sao Paulo Police, bringing the Hubley case back to the U.S. through Interpol," Reynolds replied.

"And it goes to you first, because of your ongoing investigation. But at that point you're already working at InvestSecure —"

"And we didn't know the Special Agent in Charge of the FBI was involved … "

"So you hand it off to the FBI."

"And from that point, there were two investigations going on in parallel."

"But you keep your cover at InvestSecure to stay close to Riddle."

"My undercover status is on a *strict* need-to-know basis, so there was no reason to inform the FBI field office. And since we had no reason to suspect Redmond, we assumed we'd get the intelligence his office gathered through FBI Washington."

"But Redmond doesn't submit anything because he's secretly protecting Riddle."

"Which is where you two come in."

"What do you mean by that?"

"Mr. Siebert, we need your help. I felt terrible when Eric Meyer's family died in that fire, which we've now confirmed was arson. If we'd pushed the panic button after Hubley got killed, we could've saved those lives."

"But you couldn't risk losing Riddle."

"Correct."

"I don't understand," Nikki said. "Couldn't you arrest him because he was negotiating with what he thought were terrorists? Why wait for the malware to be completed?

"We could have, but —"

"You didn't know where Riddle was," Ben interjected.

"I'm embarrassed to say that's correct. All negotiations were done through Matthew Baker, and Dominick Riddle isn't even a real name. Pulling the plug then would've captured Baker, but Riddle would've gotten away scot-free. Since we knew the malware was coming to us anyway, we sat tight to pinpoint Riddle."

"This is nuts!" Nikki yelled. "I don't understand how both the CIA *and* the FBI can't find this guy!"

"I understand Mr. Siebert wisely cautioned you not to check the FBI database for Riddle once he suspected your boss was corrupt. But I assure you that I had the Director check it and it came up just as empty as it would've had you checked. The only difference was that my way, it was done without Redmond's knowledge."

"You really never suspected Redmond?" Ben asked.

"That's one of my several regrets. He came to question Bodie and they went out to lunch shortly after Hubley's murder, and I knew that was outside FBI protocol. But I figured it was because he … " Reynolds glanced at Nikki.

"You figured it was because he wasn't sure I could handle the case."

"You have nothing to be ashamed of, Ms. Benton. To your point, it's embarrassing that we can't find Dominick Riddle. And it was pure luck that I had Director Thompson check the database without Redmond's knowledge. But candidly, there's a reason why some fugitives remain on Most Wanted lists for years if not forever. And in Riddle's case, Marcus Redmond was a big part of that reason. Special Agents in Charge have even more authority than meets the eye, and he used that authority to protect Riddle. You were doing your job, Ms. Benton. Director Thompson is now aware of this scandal and he's currently reviewing what changes need to be made."

"There's one thing that doesn't make sense," Ben said. "What made you think you'd be able to find Riddle once the malware was complete?"

"You're quite savvy, Mr. Siebert. The final piece of the malware was a key-card that unlocks the code's encryption. Think of it as a password to an unbreakable code. Without it, the malware was useless."

"And Riddle was holding it back until he got his money."

"It'd been arranged through Mr. Baker and Salil here that the key-card be e-mailed within five minutes of the final transaction. We knew it would come from Riddle directly — especially after Tom Fedorak killed Matthew Baker — so we triangulated his position between the account deposit and the source of his e-mail transmission."

"Did you make the final payment?"

"It was executed at 10:06 Eastern Standard Time."

"So you got Riddle's location?"

"Yes, the e-mail was transmitted from a cell phone on a private estate in rural North Carolina, registered to a dummy name."

"Well, what are you waiting for?" Nikki asked.

Reynolds paused, and Ben then realized why Reynolds had obtained them. And why they were hearing the classified and embarrassing CIA investigation's backstory.

"He set a trap, didn't he?"

Reynolds lowered her eyes and scratched her forehead, expressing deep regret.

"The cell phone signal was too strong for too long. I should've known Riddle wouldn't have kept himself exposed like that. But I was so excited to nail the bastard that I pushed it. We went in full steam ahead thirteen minutes after the password was sent. Fifteen CIA agents and a dozen SWAT team members were there."

"What happened?"

"Riddle left the house triggered to blow. Three different bombs, all tied to motion sensors with a backup timer ... " her voice trailed.

"We lost every single man, along with all the evidence that Dominick Riddle even existed. He escaped with full payment and left everyone to burn."

"But you know the account," Ben finally said. "You know where you sent the money. Can't you trace him through that?"

"The money has already been re-transferred to multiple accounts around the world, several of them Swiss-protected, all with worldwide access. The trace has been blocked and the very best analysts in the world are trying to track it down, but by the time they do there's no telling where Riddle might be."

Reynolds pounded her fist into the wooden table, vigorously shaking her head.

"We lost him. You're both here because I need to know every *single* piece of information you have. Anything that might help us find him, I need to hear it right now."

The shock of Riddle's escape left them both feeling empty and defeated. They spent almost an hour recapping everything — from Ben's conversation with Bodie in the church to Senator Richardson's son to his chat with Sidarta Perdigao in Brazil. Nikki shared her interactions with Redmond, her thoughts on the Hubley case and everything else she could conjure up. But after all that, there was nothing that could help track Riddle down. There were no more clues, no hidden answers.

Dominick Riddle had outsmarted everyone.

58

The eight-degree Celsius temperature — around forty-five Fahrenheit — didn't stop the young people in Campo Santa Margherita, Venice from enjoying the nightlife. The colorful bar scene — including Cafés Rosso, Blue, Noir and Orange — offered a wide variety of inexpensive cocktails, private courtyards with terrace heaters and energetic optimism, perpetuated by student-dominated crowds that swarmed the Dorsoduro district.

The long courtyard, with commercial and residential buildings as old as the fourteenth century on either side, was the Mecca of the Dorsoduro social scene. A far cry from the tourist attractions, Campo was designed for and enjoyed by the locals. During the week, there was a produce and flower market, plenty of quaint shops offering a wide variety of products, and the University of Venice close enough to watch students congregate and discuss their nightlife plans.

The man walked through the courtyard wearing a pair of worn blue jeans, a light-blue button down with the sleeves rolled up, and a hat he'd bought from a local shop. No one appeared to be eying or even noticing him as he strolled through the party scene, a small cooler in one hand and a drink in the other just for show.

It didn't take long to reach the seventeenth century palazzo and when he did, getting in was as simple as snapping the back door lock with a pair of pliers. No security system, no cameras, no protection.

The rent for the gaudy palazzo was outrageous: €5.000 per month, just under seven thousand bucks. It was certainly nice: two floors, seven rooms and three bedrooms, including a master suite. There were ten different windows spanning over 220 square meters, roughly 2,400 square feet. The fee included dedicated day servants and the inside spared no expense in décor. Was it worth that much? He wasn't convinced, but the man who'd started living there four weeks ago didn't care about money.

The loud music and crowds' reactions to classic soccer games being replayed on the café big screens carried through the thin-walled palazzo. Perfect white noise: not too loud to keep a person up, but loud and constant enough to drown out other sounds. Withdrawing the pistol, he slowly walked through the fully furnished living room en route to the stairs. As he turned the master bedroom doorknob, he heard raucous snoring coming from the king-sized bed. Tiptoeing towards it, he couldn't help but notice the pewter Bullet Ant paperweight resting on the nightstand.

He pointed the pistol at the snoring man and resisted the urge to pull the trigger.

"Get up, Dominick."

"Huh? *What?*" Riddle snapped out of a deep sleep, realizing where he was … and who was in front of him. Before Riddle could react, his arms were handcuffed to the bedpost, each elevated as the portly man in silk pajamas stared at his enemy.

"Well, well. Ben Siebert," Riddle said after a violent cough.

"Ryan Bodie made me promise to kill you if I found out how nasty you were."

"What a sissy. You're here because of him?"

There was no backing down in Riddle's voice. Both of them knew how this was going to end, but Riddle didn't want to give the satisfaction his fear would offer. Ben wasn't worried … he knew he'd get it when Riddle saw what was in the cooler.

"Nah," he replied, lowering the pistol and staring at the now-helpless Riddle. "To tell you the truth, I don't think I've even come close to finding out how nasty you are."

"Good point."

"No, I'm here because of Sally Hubley."

"What about that bitch?"

"She didn't want me to come after you. She didn't even know who you were, but that didn't matter. She was above revenge. She was a Christian, forgiving, loving. All she wanted was closure. She was too kind and too innocent to want anything else."

"Good for her."

"But I'm not. You took an innocent woman from her children and I'm here to render justice."

Ben wrapped the duct tape around Riddle's mouth to the back of his head three times, tightly sealing his lips. Riddle tried kicking but his legs couldn't reach. Satisfied, Ben stepped away and pressed the silenced pistol into Riddle's right thigh and waited a second or two before pulling the trigger. Riddle's howling scream was so well absorbed by the duct tape that it was barely audible over the music and cheers from the cafés, prompting Ben to repeat the act on Riddle's left thigh. The tape again muffled an equally satisfying scream.

He then walked over to the cooler resting innocently on the ground and picked it up to show Riddle. The combination of fear and pain in Riddle's eyes as blood streamed from his legs to the percale sheets neither distracted nor dwindled Ben's motivation. He only smiled. Opening the cooler, he retrieved the four oversized zip lock bags, one for each of Riddle's innocent victims. Each bustled with many tiny movements.

"I believe *Paraponera Clavata* is the binomial nomenclature, but as you know, they're better known as Bullet Ants," he whispered to a now-frantic Riddle. The ants were squirming so much he could barely keep a grip on the bag.

"Don't look so scared, Dominick. There's actually a Brazilian tribe in the Amazon — called Sateré-Mawé — that requires young men to endure hundreds of stings as part of its initiation process. See, they render the ants unconscious and then weave them into a leaf-made glove. The boys have to wear the glove for ten minutes once the ants wake up. If *they* can stand it, I'm sure a tough guy like you will do just fine."

Ben winked before continuing.

"Of course, the tribe applies a coat of charcoal to the skin for protection, and it limits the stings to the boys' hands. Not quite what I had in mind."

Slowly, he used gloved hands to unzip the first bag and turn it upside down on Riddle's right-leg gunshot wound. The wail that followed again only prompted him to do the same on Riddle's left-leg wound with bag number two. Riddle immediately began shaking as though enduring a hundred seizures. Ben used the third bag on his chest, careful to stay away from the ants but close enough to watch them scatter about under Riddle's pajamas and towards his nether regions. The pain would soon be so great that Riddle might just pass out, so Ben decided to quickly overturn the fourth bag on his head, watching the ants crawl down his neck and back, stinging along the way.

Riddle tried so hard to free himself that his wrists bled from the metal handcuffs. He continued to jolt and holler through the duct tape even as the ants crawled through his nasal cavity to his lungs. Just to make sure, with Riddle frantically begging for mercy, Ben fired the pistol into his stomach, instantly allowing the ants inside and triggering the stomach acids to go to work, ensuring Riddle's death would be slow and atrociously painful. He dropped the gun and shook his head before exiting the master suite.

Riddle was still moaning when he ordered his Coke at Café Rosso.

59

The most southeastern bench at Navy Pier was unassuming and uncomfortable to most folks. Metal, inflexible, and cold. But to Nikki it was a refuge, a sanctuary, a Godsend. She'd sat on it nearly every day she'd lived in Chicago before meeting Ben Siebert, overlooking the famous Ferris wheel, doing her KenKen puzzles, avoiding the reality that she regretted taking the job and missed Phoenix.

Things sure had changed since that day Ben held her at gunpoint in Bu. She'd just come from the Gordon household, where she'd visited often enough that Timothy Hubley had started calling her Aunt Nikki in a precious three-year-old voice. He invited her to his birthday party, and she'd be there. She still felt sad when she thought about him and Samuel growing up without Mom or Dad, but Nick and Lisa Gordon were great people and at least the kids had a good home. It didn't hurt that Ryan Bodie's trust included a five million dollar benefit to Sally Hubley, but it was the Gordons who brought her peace.

"Special Agent Nikki Benton," she heard his voice from behind, just as she thought through Timothy's present.

"Ben Siebert," she replied, gesturing him to take a seat. He did, and they both looked straight ahead at the mostly-empty park on the cold Chicago evening.

"I got a call from Susan Reynolds," she said.

"Oh? What's she up to?"

"It seems Interpol's Red Alert has worked its magic."

"How so?"

"Dominick Riddle was found dead in a Venice palazzo a little less than two weeks ago. Bullet ants and gunshot wounds, evidently. I would've told you sooner but didn't want to interrupt your … vacation."

"I guess his decisions caught up with him."

Reynolds sounded neither surprised nor upset that Riddle was dead, and Nikki wondered if Ben once worked with the CIA in some capacity. But she heard in his answer that she'd never find out, which was fine by her.

"Not only that, but with Senator Richardson's cooperation and the accounts Riddle used for the malware payment, the CIA has been able to track down quite a few folks from around the world and bring them to justice. They even found a few of the malware programmers."

"I heard something about that. Did Richardson get a deal for cooperating?"

"Yeah, a good break. He's out of office but wanted to be anyway. No jail time and a full pardon for his help. They're also going to issue a statement about what really happened with his son a year ago. The kid's going to get his name cleared after all. It doesn't erase what happened, but it's a start."

"You bet," Ben responded, clearly having known that as well.

"How's Joe?"

"He's doing great. Finals are tough, but he's working hard. He and Tom are as thick as thieves now. They hung out the whole time I was on vacation. I guess saving each other's lives can have that effect."

"I'm aware," she smiled widely.

"How do you like your new boss?"

"I can't believe Stevens did it … he actually left Phoenix to come to Chicago."

"*You* did."

"I guess so. I'm just glad he did. He's the only thing that kept me in the FBI."

"Good. It needs people like you."

"Ben?"

"Yes?"

"Remember when we first met, and you told me I didn't know you just from reading your file?"

"Uh-huh."

"You were right."

"Of course," he quickly responded, evoking a chuckle.

"But guess what … I think I know you now."

"Agreed, but there's always more to learn." He turned to look at her. His blue eyes — the same blue eyes that somehow turned dark when he got angry and could frighten just about anyone — danced in front of her filled with possibility. She didn't respond but returned the look, each of them captivated by the other's gaze. She was *this* close to leaning in for a kiss when out of nowhere:

"Dad, you're going to be late for your seven-thirty."

She turned around to see Joe Leksa in jeans and a black North Face jacket.

"Hi, Ms. Benton."

"Good to see you, Joe," she responded as Ben got up from her bench.

"Meeting?"

"Dinner meeting with Bill Knoble. We're going to review his law firm's scholarship offer to Jamal White's sister."

"Word on the street is you're partners with him now."

"Partner is a strong word. But I've invested some money in his firm. The guy's making a difference in less privileged communities."

"It helps when someone like you vouches for him."

"I'm just an investor. The change came from him. Care to join us? We're meeting at The Gage and I'm sure he wouldn't mind."

"I have fond memories there, but I'll pass. I've got a tortoise to tend to."

"Spot?"

"That smelly reptile grew on me. Even his stench is tolerable now."

"Maybe some other time, then."

"I'd like that."

"So would I."

Epilogue

The sand between his toes was warm and grainy and impeccably white.

Within thirty minutes of arriving, Terrance Smith decided that Whitehaven didn't have a thing on Western Australia's Cable Beach, and the past two months had only further reaffirmed that conclusion. The sand was pristine, the water so clear and still he could see his reflection in it, and the soothing Indian Ocean waves were the perfect recipe for eighty-five degree days and repeated nights of blissful sleep. Still relatively unknown to the world, the place wasn't packed full of tourists and families, and no surfers ruined the peace and quiet because they were all on the Pacific side.

Yet even with all that, it was the sunsets that got him. The bright red-orange ball in the sky turned the surrounding clouds into wisps of exquisite beauty that not even the most skilled photographers or poets could capture. He'd read about the sunsets, even seen a picture or two, but nothing compared to actually witnessing the majestic conclusion of each day. He took a sunset camel ride on his first night and thought that couldn't be topped, but then he visited Sunset Bar & Café and realized there's absolutely nothing better in the world than seeing a Cable Beach sunset with a cold drink in hand.

Nothing, that is, unless you add to it $28 million in the bank, your enemy thinking you're dead, and nothing but relaxation and sexy young local women to look forward to for the next forty years.

Thankful for being underestimated, he smiled when he replayed the events of October 23rd in his head. As sure as he sat on the beach today, he knew faking his own death was the only way then. And Dominick Riddle's bald hit man had served up his opportunity to do so on a platter. When he saw him plant the car bomb on the surveillance tape from the hidden camera in the garage, he knew he had his chance. A combination of smart timing between hitting the garage door opener and his remote start on the convertible, a good fake body in the front seat, a stupid hit man and quick escape out the back door through the woods to the parked Honda, and Terrance

Smith was assumed dead by the only man he needed to make such an assumption.

The Cadiz house, Camaro and $20 million he made sure Riddle found were a small price to pay. By design, Riddle assumed he was headed to Somerset Village in Bermuda that Saturday, the 24th. That made the 23rd the clear-cut day for the hit, and he was ready. But the $28 million in Australia and private jet flight that Friday morning … Riddle didn't have a clue about those.

Spin Artist, he chuckled to himself. *I'm so much more than that.*

He didn't read about Plan X or anything with France's President in the news, and for all he knew that meant Riddle had made out clean with his billions. Good for Riddle. He didn't care. He was more than happy to read about Redmond and Siebert and that hot FBI agent dying from the comfort of his favorite reclining beach chair. Riddle could conquer the world, so long as he stayed away from Cable Beach.

The Cuba Libres were going down even smoother today and as the sunset concluded, he realized his food was probably ready at Sunset Bar and Café. He didn't mind getting up for it — it would give him another reason to tease his gorgeous teenage waitress when he next saw her. In classic vacation attire — swimming suit and sandals, shirtless — he trudged through the sand and his inebriation to get dinner.

Sitting on the bar was his hot bucket of fresh prawns with a side of Aussie fries and his fourth Cuba Libre. He grabbed each and noticed a white envelope beneath the bucket, *Mr. Smith* written across the top. Half curious, half excited, he chuckled as he set the bucket down and tore into it, eager to see the young waitress's new message.

He read it, then reread it, stymied.

Terrance:

I know what you've done. You thought you got away, but you didn't escape me. I got Riddle and we both know I'm getting you. So run, you coward. Run like you've never run before. Because you just saw your last sunset.

Ben

CPSIA information can be obtained
at www.ICGtesting.com
Printed in the USA
LVHW021601011118
595633LV00004B/684/P

9 781945 181429